Secrets
and
Revenge

Secrets
and
Revenge

a novel

Noël F. Caraccio

Published by SparkPress, a BookSparks imprint,
A division of SparkPoint Studio, LLC
Phoenix, Arizona, USA, 85007
www.gosparkpress.com

Published 2023
Printed in the United States of America
Print ISBN: 978-1-68463-202-2
E-ISBN: 978-1-68463-203-9
Library of Congress Control Number: 2022921898

Interior Design by Tabitha Lahr

When Great Britain left the Persian Gulf in the early 1970s, Dubai and Abu Dhabi formed the United Arab Emirates with five other emirates. Dubai and Abu Dhabi hold the majority of control and policy making in the United Arab Emirates. In the late 1960s, there was a massive injection of money into the economy due to oil. Oil revenue accelerated Dubai's development by leaps and bounds.

Dubai has often been called the Hong Kong of the Middle East. It was a major trading center even before the discovery of oil. If Dubai's oil supply dried up, Dubai would still exist as a major center for trading.

The wealth in Dubai is on display everywhere, even to the point of having an indoor ski run in the middle of the desert. Steve knew he was a wealthy guy, but by comparison with the sheiks, he was a nobody. Steve really didn't care anymore about being accepted by the wealthiest in Dubai. In fact, Steve had disdain for them. They hadn't done anything to earn their money as he had. Steve was proud of what he had done with his life to afford a house like his and a lifestyle of the "rich and famous" as they were called. Well, mostly proud of what he had done.

Steve was born the son of a cop who had risen to the rank of detective in the New York City Police Department, one of the finest, if not the finest, police departments in the world. He always knew that he wanted money, lots of money, and he knew there would be nowhere near enough for him if he followed in his father's footsteps. As a great student and an even better go-getter, he went to Holy Cross College in Worcester, Massachusetts, on a full scholarship. He went to Fordham Law School and graduated number one in his class. He turned down the offer of Law Review, which would be a prestigious chance to write scholarly articles offered to the top 10 percent of the law school class and hopefully be a ticket to a job in one of the very large law firms. Steve's professors in law school tried to talk him into Law Review, saying that he was being shortsighted and passing

CHAPTER 1

Steve Goldrick leaned forward toward the glass from inside his office to watch his grandson swim the length of the pool. The boy was on the swim team, and Steve's pool was large enough to swim regulation laps for tournaments. Steve looked at the digital thermometer on his desk, which recorded the outside temperature. One hundred and twelve degrees, and this wasn't the worst of it. *Despite the opulence, the place really was a hellhole*, Steve thought to himself. *Maybe hell actually is cooler in the summer than here.* If this place didn't have oil, it would be nothing more than a vast wasteland, miles and miles of sand—another cruel cosmic joke. It should feel like paradise, but mostly it felt like the inside of a frying pan to Steve.

Steve, his wife Torrey, daughter, son-in-law, and grandson were permanently "exiled" to this hellhole, even though they had actually picked Dubai because of the absence of extradition laws to the United States. The sheer opulence of the country was mind boggling.

Dubai is located on the eastern the part of the Arabian Peninsula on the coast of the Persian Gulf. For many years it was considered a major transport hub for both people and cargo.

up a wonderful opportunity. Even though he essentially seemed to shoot himself in the foot by alienating his law professors, he managed to land a clerkship with a judge in the very prestigious court in the Southern District of New York. His career was on a meteoric rise after that. He was—no, had been, being the operative words—the managing partner in a huge law firm in New York City and earned megabucks.

As Steve reflected on his career, he let his mind wander to the day he had been approached by the senior partner to help him in an "enterprise" that only Mr. Braddock and now Steve would be in on. Mr. Braddock was offering him an opportunity to be taken into his inner circle, something to be treasured. The only problem with the "enterprise" was that it was illegal, and all the monies collected went directly into the pocket of Mr. Braddock without the knowledge of any of his law partners. The amounts of money that were going into Mr. Braddock's pocket were staggering. It was all so easy—and lucrative. As time went on, Steve's cut grew larger and Mr. Braddock eased out, but the deal was Braddock was to receive payment until the day he died. And he did. At one point in his career, Steve could remember laughing and thinking that Braddock probably had made provision for himself to be kept alive on a respirator just so that he could receive his payments. Steve remembered reading once that Walt Disney had been "frozen" so that he could come back when there was a cure for what killed him. He figured Braddock was probably cryogenically preserved somewhere so that he could come back for more money at a later time.

Steve was waiting for the clock to strike five o'clock so that he could make the call at the time he said he would. He reached down into the bottom left-hand drawer of his desk for the burner phone. It didn't matter which one he pulled out; he had about eight or ten stashed away in there. He pulled a small piece of paper from the breast pocket of his shirt and dialed the number on the paper. He did the calculation in his head. *If it's 5:00 p.m.*

here, it's 10:00 a.m. on the East Coast of the United States. "The guy" probably was in New York already, but it didn't matter, as long as he got there by Monday.

Steve dialed the number, and "the guy" picked up on the second ring. He had a voice that sounded a little like he needed perpetually to clear his throat. In its own way, the voice was distinctive enough that Steve was sure he was talking to the same person each time. He couldn't peg how old "the guy" was, and he was mildly interested in what he looked like. He guessed that "the guy" was nondescript so that he could blend in and not be noticed. That probably ruled out being either very tall or very short, and Steve couldn't detect a foreign accent. Neither could he detect any regional accent, like a Southern drawl or a Boston accent. He sounded average and probably looked average, but Steve knew from past experience and from the price he was paying to "the guy" that he was anything but average.

Steve had asked him a number of questions about how he intended to handle the pickup of the package. "The guy" had the answers and had also volunteered a few details. It seemed to Steve that "the guy" knew exactly what he was going to do and had been to the house and the neighborhood to check things out in advance. The conversations were brief and all business, but Steve believed that "the guy" was thorough.

"Are you in New York yet?"

"Yeah, I'm staying about ten miles away from the house."

"Where are you staying?"

"Doesn't matter. As long as I pick up the package on Monday, that's the point. Did you wire the down payment?"

"It should be in your account this afternoon. Check your account."

"Of course, I will. What happens if the bank screws up and the money isn't there? How do I let you know that?"

"My bank says that the money has come out of my account. There shouldn't be a problem."

"Big deal. The bank says there shouldn't be a problem. Easy for them to *say*. I'm asking you what happens if there *is* a problem," he growled. "Everything is set for Monday. All the people are in place and ready for Monday."

Steve heard the emphasis on the words "says" and "is." He stifled the urge to give "the guy" a brusque answer, but he needed him. Steve was certainly not going to give him a phone number to reach him. They knew each other only by voice and by payments. "I'll call you tomorrow, but it will have to be much earlier in case I need to talk to my bank before they close. I'll call you at 7:00 a.m. your time."

"Okay," was the only response from the other end of the phone.

"One more thing," Steve said. "There's an extra five grand in it for you if I learn that you didn't kill the mother. I want her alive and able to remember what happened. Every detail. Got it?"

"I can do that. It's your money, man."

"Good, then I'll call you tomorrow morning to check on the down payment."

"Okay."

Steve heard the phone go dead. "The guy" was not much of a conversationalist. It didn't matter. The wheels were in motion.

CHAPTER 2

At 6:30 a.m., Rick extracted himself from the rocking chair with a chubby baby propped against the baby blanket leaning against his shoulder. How could one little person need so much attention and make so much noise? Rick had taken over on baby patrol about three thirty in the morning to relieve Maizie so she could get a few hours sleep. He needed to get into the shower and get dressed for work. Fortunately, he didn't have to be in court today because he didn't think he would be sharp enough to represent anyone on this little sleep.

Through his sleep-deprived haze, Rick painfully remembered that his son, Adam, had had these crying jags as a baby. That was a long time ago. The dull ache of losing Adam and his first wife, Jennifer, was still there, but the sharp stabbing pain had finally subsided. It hurt deep in his heart if he thought about it. Rick was secretly glad that this baby was a girl. He wasn't so sure what his feelings would have been if this baby had been a boy. It might very well have sliced open the scar in his heart that he hoped was continuing to heal. Maizie had liked the name Grace for this little bundle. Rick liked it, too, but perhaps for different reasons than Maizie's. Rick saw his whole life with Maizie as one large abundance of grace that had been showered on him after his ordeal. There were some things he just didn't tell Maizie about the lingering pain he felt about his deceased wife Jennifer and son Adam.

He didn't want to burden Maizie, nor did he want her to feel bad about their deaths in any way. If Jennifer and Adam had still been alive, Rick would certainly not have met Maizie. There were also other secrets that he had kept from Maizie. These were secrets he was not proud of, and he didn't think he would ever tell her about them. Rick sighed and realized that there were some burdens in life you had to carry alone. He had hoped that at some time in their marriage he would be able to tell her, but as time went by, he could never seem to broach the subject with her. He knew he loved Maizie unconditionally, and he felt that she loved him in the same way. He couldn't imagine any scenario in which telling her about his secret would work out well for either of them.

Once in a while, he would see a young boy who reminded him of Adam, and he would think of how old Adam would be today. It seemed like a lifetime ago, and maybe it was. Jennifer and Adam had been killed in a car crash when the car they were riding in was hit head on. For a very long time, Rick blamed himself for not being there when the accident occurred. He had been called back to work at the law firm in New York City and had to cut his vacation short. Jennifer and Adam got in the car a few days later to return from vacation but never made it home. Rick dwelt on it for a long time after their deaths, and it haunted him almost nightly in his dreams. No, not dreams—nightmares, which left him jolted awake in a pool of his own "what ifs."

One night when the pain of his loss was so intense, Rick decided he couldn't bear it one more agonizing day. He climbed up on a bridge, sure that he was going to jump and end it all, to put an end to the pain that made him feel that the weight on him was so great that he could no longer breathe. He was so close to jumping when this woman and her dog appeared on the bridge just before dawn. Her name was Abby, and she refused to let him jump. Abby was a tall blonde woman. She was athletic, but it was by the sheer force of her personality that she kept him from jumping, when he was so close, so close.

The most remarkable thing was that Abby herself climbed up on the bridge and risked her own life to try to save him—him, a total stranger. Fate wasn't done with them either. Abby lost her footing on her way up to Rick on the bridge, and Rick had to climb down on the bridge to pull her to safety. The rescuer became the victim. Fate apparently had yet another surprise for him. Abby made it a point to stay in touch with him after the night on the bridge, and her daughter was Maizie. And the rest, as they say is history.

Grace was beginning to stir in Rick's arms as he moved around the room, and she was getting cranky—yet again. The pediatrician said Grace had good old-fashioned colic. She had been such a good baby for the first two months, but now it was becoming a nightly ritual of crying for Grace and, Rick thought ironically, crying for him and Maizie since Grace was inconsolable and so were they. Rick suggested that perhaps they bring the nanny back overnight, so Maizie and Rick could get some sleep. Maizie seemed somewhat reluctant, but the crying and the lack of sleep were beginning to bring Maizie around to his side. Rick was sort of afraid to say to Maizie that she at least could get some sleep during the day when Grace napped, but that he was having a hard time in the office. Not only did Grace need a nap during the day but so did Rick.

CHAPTER 3

Fannie wasn't sure she was pleased about how this discussion was going. "Discussion" was an absurdly funny word to describe what was happening, since discussion implied that two or more people were having some sort of discourse on a particular subject or subjects. Fannie was doing none of the above. She could hardly say there were two people having a discourse on a particular subject, and as far as she could tell, no words as she had come to know them were being said out loud.

Fannie didn't think she was saying anything out loud, as she did when she spoke to her family, yet she thought she heard her own voice. She also seemed to be able to comprehend what was being said to her.

"I'm not sure I understand what it is you want me to do. It seems that I've already done this once before."

Fannie "heard" the response in her head.

Fannie continued the discussion. "You, more than anyone else, know that I am so grateful to you for giving me a second chance with my daughter Abby. I'm sure there are millions of people who would kill for the chance to go back to the physical world after death, and have an opportunity to make amends. I know, killing is one of your ten least favorite things, as you said in the Ten Commandments." Fannie managed what she perceived was probably the equivalent of a wry smile. At least she hadn't lost her sense of humor.

Apparently, the Divine Being had a sense of humor as well because Fannie's little joke was noted and appreciated.

"There certainly were some wonderful moments that I got to see firsthand—well, sort of firsthand. I mean I was there, even if I wasn't there. The whole thing of being able to make things right with Abby after all those years and all the mistakes I made with her, I know very few people ever get that opportunity.

"I was so proud of Abby when she risked her life to go up on that bridge and save Rick. Most people would have stood there frozen in indecision, but not my Abby. She was fearless as a kid, and she was fearless as an adult. She is such a wonderful and determined person that she'd risk her life for a complete stranger. She's always had that connection to people. I'd like to think she got that from me."

Fannie felt some sensation that on earth she probably would have recognized as being a little choked up with emotion.

"I guess it was all in your divine plan that Abby and Rick would become such good friends and then Rick would fall for Maizie. But then there were the awful things, like that poor Dannie Bevan being murdered in her own house.

"You know, I've always wondered why it is that you don't prevent those things from happening. I mean, Dannie is just one small example, but you have the power to prevent wars, murders, famine, and tsunamis. Why don't you use it? I hope I'm not being too presumptuous, but I gotta tell you, I have always thought you could do better than let all those people get wiped out."

The words tumbled out of Fannie's mouth or consciousness, or whatever it was, and she realized she had just challenged the Divine Being on the ways of the universe. Well, she certainly couldn't be struck dead because she was already dead. Was she going to be annihilated or vaporized or wiped out as if she never existed? Here she was defying some grand Divine Plan.

Apparently, the answer was simple because the response came to Fannie in less than a nanosecond and she wasn't annihilated. Humanity had to work these things out for themselves. It was a little thing called free will.

"If I go back to the other side, will I be with my family again? . . . Okay, so part of the time, but what will I do with the other part of the time? . . . Watch and observe what? How will I know what I'm supposed to see? How will I know what I'm supposed to do?

"Are there bad things going to happen to my family and that's why they need me? Can't you be any more specific? Hasn't my family had enough bad things happen to them? Look what happened to my grandson Jason in that car crash when he was run off the road. What about Rick's first wife Jennifer and his son, Adam? We're not perfect, but we've had an awful lot, and we dealt with it as best we could. How about giving us a pass?"

CHAPTER 4

Rick was half muttering to himself and half talking out loud to the universe or fate, as he drove to the office, as to how unfair the world was when you needed something important done. It had taken quite a bit of persuading to get Maizie to agree to let Vladdina come back and live in until Grace got over her colic and settled down to a few consecutive hours of sleep each night.

Vladdina was in her early thirties, a stunning woman with almost jet-black hair and blue eyes the color of the Caribbean Sea. She had come highly recommended from an agency, and her prior references were excellent as a nanny.

Rick thought about bribing Maizie with a big and expensive piece of jewelry, which often worked. Then he thought about enlisting Maizie's mother, Abby, to help talk to her. What cinched the deal was almost something from the theater of the absurd. One night Rick was waiting in the kitchen to start eating dinner and Maizie was just finishing up with a phone call in the den. In the few short minutes that Maizie was on the phone, Rick had fallen asleep at the table, hit the spoon with his elbow, and the spoon fell into the tomato soup. Rick had soup dripping down his cheek when Maizie came back into the kitchen. He was lucky he hadn't drowned in the soup bowl. Maizie couldn't contain her laughter, but did so just long enough to grab her cell phone and take a picture of him for all posterity. When she finally did wake him up, it dawned on her how tired and sleep deprived they both were, but that it really was worse on Rick, who had to think and function as an attorney all day. No wonder they were both quite cranky.

Now that Maizie was finally convinced that Vladdina should come back as a live in, Vladdina called in sick and said she had bronchitis. She didn't sound all that hoarse on the phone, but Rick knew Maizie wasn't going to let her anywhere near Grace. He muttered to himself that Maizie was so paranoid about Grace that Vladdina would probably have to get a note from the surgeon general himself before Maizie would let Vladdina back in the house. He cursed at whatever black cloud or little microbe had made Vladdina sick when they really needed her, and toyed with the idea of calling Abby himself and asking her to come stay over at the house for a few nights until Vladdina was well enough to return.

◻◻◻◻◻◻◻◻◻◻◻◻◻◻◻◻◻◻◻◻◻◻◻

It was about two thirty that same afternoon that Maizie heard the doorbell. She was expecting a package from Amazon, but the package was arriving more quickly than she expected. She looked through the window and saw a man in a UPS uniform holding a package. As she opened the door to take the package, he hit her in the face with the hard box and knocked her backwards and down onto the floor. Maizie was stunned for a moment with the sharp pain in her face. She was also stunned with fear, which gripped her instantly as her brain came to terms with the fact that this was a home invasion. The man gave her a menacing look and snarled, "Don't move and don't scream if you want to live."

Maizie's breaths were coming in thin gulps, and she could feel a rush of adrenaline. She was looking up at him from the floor but didn't know what to do. What seemed like a million thoughts raced through her brain, but she seemed powerless to move. It was as if the fear were cutting off her ability to have her brain give a command to her body and have her body follow it.

A strangled voice that she didn't recognize as being hers said, "What do you want? My purse is in the kitchen, and you can take the money and my credit cards."

"Shut up, bitch, or I'll kill you. No one wants to hear anything from you." He knew he was saying that to keep her quiet, but he also remembered very distinctly that there was another five grand in it for him if he didn't kill her.

He pulled a gun to show her not to try anything. Most times it was enough to intimidate people, but every so often there was a crazy one who thought they could take him in a fight. Not that they could, but it was a royal pain in the ass to have to fight them, and then he had aches and pains for days or maybe a broken nose or a lost tooth. Not worth it.

"Lie on your stomach and put your hands behind your back." Maizie hesitated, and he screamed at her, "Do it!"

She rolled over and he tied her wrists behind her back with some sort of plastic tie that cut into her wrists. "I told you already, you move or scream, you die." He was so close to her that she could feel his breath on her neck. He felt it, too, because he pushed her hair away from the back of her neck and licked her behind the ear. Maizie froze. He definitely felt her tense up, so he did it again. He flipped her over onto her back. He was on his knees straddling her and he reached down and grabbed her breast and squeezed and kneaded it.

"Stop, please, stop," she pleaded.

"You love this, don't you bitch?" he growled. "What else should I do that you'll love?" Maizie started to whimper. With that he started to caress her. She started to scream, and he forced her head down into the floor. "Shut up!" he raged at her. She was now screeching and bucking to try to get him off her. He was just too strong for her, and now he was leaning on her with all his weight. He was enjoying himself, caressing her and terrorizing her all at the same time. She was now hysterically crying. Just as quickly as he was there, he was gone.

He kicked her in the ribs with his work boot and left the room. Maizie could hear his footsteps recede on the hardwood floor, but she was crying too hard to hear anything else. As the pain in her ribs receded a little, she tried to think of what to do. Maybe if she lay there and stayed quiet, he'd take what he wanted from the house and leave.

Then another thought sent her into full blown panic, as she heard him ascend the stairs. She could hear his heavy footfall. Grace was upstairs! Grace was quiet for now. Would he hurt her? *Oh God, no!* But what could she do tied up on the floor? She had screamed, and no one heard her. If she screamed again, would she antagonize him? Maybe he really would kill her and then maybe kill Grace? By now Maizie was in such a panic that she could feel her heart racing and she was panting. However, no matter how hard she tried, she couldn't make her brain come up with any rational plan to do anything.

In the few seconds or few minutes that she was on the floor—she couldn't tell how long it had been—he returned. She froze with fear. She was afraid to look up at him, but she did. She saw Grace in his arms. He put Grace down on the hard floor, far enough away that Maizie could see her but not reach her. She then heard something that made it feel as if her heart was going to stop. She heard a whimper from Grace. "Oh, God, no!" She then began to talk to Grace to comfort her. It was the best she could do for now.

He had walked into the kitchen, and Maizie heard him dump the contents of her purse onto the kitchen floor. Her senses were heightened, and it was as if everything were being amplified through a microphone. Maybe he was only after the money and credit cards, she prayed. She didn't care what he took, as long as he left the house.

He came back into the room and kicked her again in the ribs to turn her over onto her back. Maizie felt the sharp pain and thought she heard something crack. As bad as that pain was, it was nothing compared to the fear for her child.

"Shut the fuck up. Don't make me kill you. I took a few things from upstairs and the kitchen to make it worth my while, in addition to taking the kid. Say goodbye, Mom, cause you're never seeing this kid again."

Maizie started to scream. "Get out of my house. Take what you want, but leave me and my baby alone. Leave her alone!"

He stared at her as he stood over her. He then bent down, grabbed her by the hair and smashed her head into the hardwood floor. All went dark.

Maizie began to come around sometime later, but her vision was blurry, and she had a massive headache. As she tried to move, she felt the ties digging into her wrists. That jolted her back to what had happened. She tried to free herself from the ties, but they wouldn't budge. She had to get free, she had to get free, was the mantra. She had to save Grace, she had to save Grace. Despite the blurry vision and the headache, she remembered that her cell phone had been in her purse. She pushed herself across the floor in painstakingly small amounts, but she was determined to do this. *Do this for Grace.* After a few minutes, she was sweating with exhaustion from the effort and she was getting nauseous from the headache, but she kept on. At one point, she turned her head and vomited on the floor, but then she realized that she had vomited on the kitchen floor. She started to cry again from pain and from relief that she had made it to the kitchen.

Now she had to find the phone. Where was it? She managed to turn herself over onto her stomach, so that she could see what was ahead of her on the floor. She didn't see it. She inched closer to the detritus from her purse on the floor. She still didn't see it. Oh God, suppose, he took her phone and she had come all this way for nothing? Panic set in again, and she pushed aside her car keys, her lip balm, lipstick, and tissues with her face. Then she saw it! It was there on the floor. But how was she going to dial the phone with her hands tied behind her back? Panic set in again. *Think, Maizie, think.*

Then she remembered that she had voice recognition on the phone. If she could just get to the right page on her phone. Maizie was getting dizzy again, but she was determined. She was going to do this for Grace. As she touched the phone, the screen brightened. It was on. That at least made it a little easier. She took a deep breath and prayed, "Dear God, help me. Help me help Grace. I don't know how I'm going to do this, but please help me. Please."

Maizie touched the phone she held behind her back. She tried swiping the screen a few times, without success. She tried to get up off the floor thinking that perhaps she could use the landline, but as she got up, the nausea engulfed her. Her vision started to blur, and she grabbed the back of the chair to steady herself and the cell phone dropped. Her head felt as if it was going to explode, and she slowly slid back down to the floor.

She grabbed the cell phone again. She now tried to move her arms from behind her back more to her side to be able to see the screen on the cell phone. This time she could see the screen. She was crying again, but she was desperate to succeed. With her hands at an angle behind her, she was able to see the voice recognition screen. With as much strength as she could muster, she said, "Dial 911."

It worked, and Maizie heard ringing. "911, what's your emergency?"

Maizie did her best to hold it together and said, "I'm Maizie Singleton. There's been a home invasion at my house. I need you to come quickly. My address is 24 Forest Avenue in Rye Brook. I'm tied up on the floor, and he took my child." With that, Maizie started to sob uncontrollably. The 911 operator said to her, "I'm sending the police right now. I will stay on the line with you, honey, until the police arrive. They'll be there in just a few minutes. Don't worry, we're going to help you."

CHAPTER 5

Maizie heard sirens in the distance. They couldn't get there fast enough for her. She heard banging on the door and the police calling her name. She yelled as loud as she could that she was tied up. In a few seconds she heard a loud crash and the door to the kitchen was knocked off its hinges. Two police officers with guns drawn burst into the kitchen. They saw her on the floor and said, "You okay? Are you alone in the house?" Maizie shook her head yes and one of the officers knelt down to untie the plastic ties and simultaneously pulled her sweatpants up to cover her. Maizie was hysterically crying.

"Ma'am, my name is Officer Ramsey. You're safe; no one is going to hurt you. EMS will be here in a minute, and they'll check you out. It's okay, it's okay," he repeated in a soft voice.

Maizie calmed down a little at the sound of his voice. She tried to talk and explain, but all that came out was, "Grace! He took Grace!" she screeched. "He took my baby."

"Can you describe him? What did he look like?" With that, Officer Ramsey looked at his partner who came back into the kitchen and said, "House is empty. The crib is empty."

There was the sound of more sirens, which were quite close. In a few seconds, two women EMS workers came into the kitchen through what remained of the door and the door frame. The taller of the two said to Maizie as she was walking toward her and the cop was taking a few steps back to make room, "My name is Chloe. What's your name? You've got quite a bruise on your cheek and the beginnings of a shiner. Where else are you hurt?"

Maizie was beginning to go into shock even as Chloe was taking her pulse and blood pressure.

Suddenly she started screaming again that he took Grace.

Chloe said to Maizie, "We'll do everything to find her. Stay with me and focus. What else hurts?"

Maizie said, "He kicked me in the ribs a couple of times. I think something's broken, because I can't even take a deep breath."

Chloe's partner was setting up an IV for Maizie when Officer Ramsey touched her on the shoulder and said in a low voice, "I don't know if she was raped."

The second EMS worker, Susan, said to Maizie, "Were you raped, Maizie?"

Maizie shook her head no, and the tears flowed more freely again.

As the two EMS workers lifted and slid Maizie onto the gurney, Officer Ramsey held up his hand to them. "Give me a minute," he said. "Ma'am, we want to get an Amber Alert out as quickly as we can. How old is Grace and what was she wearing? Do you have a picture of her?" Maizie started to sob again, and the officer said to her in a more authoritative voice. "It's important. Focus and give us some answers so we can find Grace."

Maizie nodded and said through the tears, "There are picture of her right over there that we took two days ago." She pointed in the direction of the kitchen table. "She's three months old and she was wearing a pink onesie with kittens on the front. I need you to call my husband. I want to speak to him," she wailed.

"We'll call him for you and tell him to meet you up at Greenwich Hospital."

"No, no, you can't call him! I have to call him myself." Now Maizie was hysterical again. "He had this happen once before when they told him to go to the hospital, and they were dead! I have to call him!" she screamed.

Chloe looked at the police officer and said, "Give us a minute and let me call him and she can speak to him. What's the number, Maizie? I'll call him on my cell." Chloe dialed the number and Rick's secretary, Lauren, answered the phone.

"Mr. Singleton's office, may I help you?"

"Lauren, it's Maizie. They took her, they took Grace!"

"My God, Maizie, what happened? What are you talking about?"

Since Maizie couldn't answer through the tears, Chloe took the phone and explained to a dumbstruck Lauren what had happened, that they were taking Maizie to Greenwich Hospital, and that the police were putting out an Amber Alert. She wanted to talk to Maizie's husband. Lauren finally was able to respond and said Rick was in court, but she would find him and get him to the hospital ASAP.

CHAPTER 6

Lauren hung up the phone with a bang and pounded on her keyboard as quickly as she could type to bring up the list of phone contacts for the Supreme Court in Westchester County. She found the phone number for Judge Stengler's chambers and dialed it.

"C'mon, c'mon, answer the phone," she prayed. Sometimes they answered and sometimes they let the voice mail come on and it could be hours before anyone got back to you. Lauren definitely didn't have hours or even minutes to waste. On the fourth ring, a live woman's voice came on and said, "Judge Stengler's chambers."

Lauren took a deep breath and in one run-on sentence explained that Rick was appearing before the judge and what had happened. She had enough presence of mind to tell the secretary in chambers that she didn't think Rick was going to be able to make it to the hospital without killing himself in a car crash. She said they would be there in a very few minutes to take him to the hospital, but she asked that the judge keep Rick there until Lauren got to court to collect him.

The courtroom was on a different floor from the judge's chambers, so Jean dialed the judge's court clerk. "Judge Stengler's part," Martin Thornwood answered.

Jean asked Marty whether the judge was in the courtroom and who was appearing before him. "Don't let anyone out of the courtroom. I'll be right down."

"Jean, what are you talking about?" Before Marty got the last word out, he heard the line go dead. What the hell was the matter with her?

In less than two minutes, Jean appeared on the floor where the courtroom was located and gave Marty the low-down on what had happened. "Rick Singleton's office is on the way to get him, and we have to keep him here until they arrive. You have to go into the courtroom and tell the judge."

Marty nodded and scribbled a note on the top page on the pad on his desk. Marty grabbed his suit jacket, putting it on as he walked into the courtroom. The judge glanced at him with a somewhat annoyed expression on his face since one of the attorneys was in the middle of examining a witness and the judge was listening intently. Marty held the piece of paper up in the air to get the judge's attention and walked briskly toward the bench where the judge was sitting. He handed the note to the judge, who held up his hand to stop the attorney from continuing. The judge read the note and frowned.

"Counsel, I apologize for the interruption, but we need to take a fifteen-minute recess so I can attend to an emergency. I will be back on the bench shortly." The judge took the three steps down off the bench and strode out of the courtroom. He turned to Marty and said, "What the hell happened to Rick Singleton's wife? That poor son of a bitch must have the worst luck in the world."

Jean had remained in Marty's office until Marty and the judge came back. She told the judge what she knew and said that Rick's wife was alive but hurt.

The judge rubbed his chin as he thought things through, and said, "Jean, go back upstairs, and when Rick's secretary arrives, bring her down here and I will bring both attorneys here and tell them what happened and let them leave."

As soon as Lauren hung up with the judge's chambers, she literally ran out of her office and down the hall into Chris McKay's office. She breezed right past Chris's secretary, Lisa, who looked up from her desk to see a blur of Lauren go past her. Lauren burst into Chris's office, and he was on the phone. He gave her a "What the hell is going on?" look, but before he could say anything, Lauren blurted out, "It's Maizie, and Rick is in court. We have to go get him." Chris could tell from the look on Lauren's face that something bad had happened.

Chris put his hand over the phone and then said to the client, "I need to call you back. There's an emergency," and he hung up. "Lauren, what the hell happened?" Chris McKay had been partners in the law firm with Dannie Bevan, who had been murdered in her home. Dannie's murder had never been solved.

Chris and Dannie had been friends and then a little more than that since law school. Even though they broke up shortly after graduation, Dannie and Chris stayed in touch professionally throughout their careers. Chris was thrilled when Dannie told him she was leaving Braddock, Lindsay, Goldrick and Schoeneman, a huge law firm in New York City, and wanted to start a partnership with him.

Chris took a few of the best associates from his firm, and Dannie did the same from the firm in the city. Rick Singleton had been one of the attorneys Dannie took with her to the new firm. Chris knew the tragedy that Rick had been through with the sudden death of his wife and young son; the guy had had enough misery in his life. If something terrible had happened to Maizie, his new wife, and their infant, it showed how precarious and fickle life was. Chris felt a shudder go through him.

Lauren said, "I need you to drive me to court. I already spoke to the judge's chambers and they are going to keep Rick there until we arrive. They're in the middle of a hearing. I'll drive him up to the hospital, or he'll probably kill himself trying to get there. I thought you could deal with the judge and the client while I whisk Rick away. Somebody has to stay on track, because I know Rick is going to flip out when he hears anything has happened to Maizie or Grace. She was hysterical when I spoke to her, but at least he can talk to her. She's hurt, but it's nothing life threatening. I don't know any of the details, other than it was a home invasion, and they took the baby."

Chris winced as he heard the details. "It's so weird that they broke into the house and took the baby. Has there been any ransom call?"

Lauren gasped as Chris said the word "ransom."

Chris got them to the courthouse quickly, and they parked in the underground parking lot and literally ran across the plaza to the courthouse. The judge had called down to the sheriff's deputies manning the security checkpoint in the lobby, and when Chris presented his Secure Pass, which allowed attorneys into the courthouse without going through security, the deputy looked at his name on the card and asked if he was by himself. Chris pointed to Lauren and the deputy waved her through without screening her or the contents of her purse.

They raced to the elevators and went immediately to the fourteenth floor where the judge's chambers were located. As they pushed the intercom and identified themselves, the judge's secretary answered and said she would be right out. Jean ushered them down two floors and swiped her pass to open the door to the back area where the court personnel worked. As they walked down the corridor, Jean finally stopped and knocked on the door. The judge was sitting at a desk talking to Marty, his clerk, about schedules. Jean introduced Chris and Lauren to the judge and Marty Thornwood.

Judge Stengler said to Marty, "Please go into the courtroom and tell counsel I would like to see them back here. Make sure they understand it's counsel only and not the parties."

Marty returned a few moments later with Rick and his opposing counsel in tow. The opposing counsel came into the room first with Rick behind him. He looked surprised to see two strangers in the room with the judge. As Rick came in, he caught sight of Lauren first and in a split second later saw Chris. It took Rick less than a nanosecond to realize something was wrong—very wrong.

Rick felt all the color drain from his face. Lauren blurted out what had happened in what appeared to be one long breath.

Chris said, "Lauren will drive you to the hospital, and I'll stay here and work things out with His Honor and counsel. I'll get your things out of the courtroom . . ." Before Chris could say ". . . and talk to the client," Rick was already running out of the office with Lauren following closely behind.

Before Chris could say anything else, the judge said, "The matter is adjourned without a date." That sentence and a pointed look at Rick's opposing counsel sent the message that the judge didn't want to hear anything about a new date. "Mr. McKay, will you please inform the court what transpires with Mr. Singleton's family in the next few days. Tell him the court understands the seriousness of the situation and wishes him and his family the best."

CHAPTER 7

Lauren literally wrenched the fob for Rick's car out of his hand. "I'm driving," Lauren said forcefully. "You'll kill us both if you drive."

Rick thought about it for a second and said, "Yeah, just get there fast!"

As the car raced through the streets of White Plains, to get to the highway, she ran a few lights as they turned red.

Rick turned toward Lauren and said, "So you were the one who spoke to Maizie, right? Is she badly hurt? How many men were in the house? How did they get in? Did Maizie get a look at their faces? Does Maizie have any idea why they took Grace? Did they hurt Grace?"

After he blurted out that staccato series of questions and before Lauren could answer, Rick started pounding his fist into the dashboard of the car. Lauren took a quick sideways glance at him, and said, "Rick, you need to get a grip on yourself. Maizie is going to need you, and Grace is going to need you. Let me tell you what I know from Maizie."

With that, Lauren proceeded to tell him every detail she could remember from her brief phone call with Maizie and the EMT. Rick stopped pounding the dashboard while Lauren recounted the story.

Lauren had enough presence of mind to say to Rick, "Do you want to call Jason? It would be good if he came to the hospital. Might be good to have your brother there. I think you should call Abby too."

At this point Rick had his head in his hands. He looked up at Lauren with tears glistening in his eyes, and said, "Yeah, I should. This whole thing is like a frigging nightmare, but I know I'm awake." With that, Rick reached into his suit jacket and pulled out his phone. He stared at it for a few seconds, without making any motion to slide the screen open.

Lauren cast another sidelong glance at him. She was driving so fast that she didn't dare take her eyes off the road for long. "Rick," she prompted him, "Rick."

He looked at her with a somewhat dazed expression on his face, but apparently calling his name with an authoritative tone in her voice got his attention and snapped him back. He tapped the contacts section on his phone, scrolled down to Jason's name, tapped it, and put the phone to his ear. The phone rang a few times and Jason's voicemail came on.

"Jas, it's me. Call me as quickly as you can. Something happened to Maizie."

Rick tapped the phone off, and Lauren thought to herself that Rick's voice sounded flat and devoid of emotion. She took a quick sideways glance at him and noticed that he was pale and sweating. Lauren didn't know if he was going into shock or what to make of the lack of emotion in his voice when clearly he was beyond upset. The best place for him was the hospital to be with Maizie and in case he passed out. She pressed the accelerator even harder.

"Rick, are you okay?"

"Yeah," was the one-word answer.

"I think you should call Abby too. Do you want me to call

her for you?" No answer. "Rick, do you want me to call Abby for you?" This time with more insistence in her voice.

"What? Yeah, go ahead."

Rick was unfortunately lost in an endless loop of very bad memories. The first was the Sunday afternoon when the police had pulled up in his driveway to tell him that Jennifer and Adam had been in an accident. They were already dead in the car crash, and Rick had blamed himself for not being with them when they died. Now he was on his way again to Greenwich Hospital where his close friend and colleague, Dannie Bevan, had been taken after the home invasion to her house in Rye several years ago. Dannie didn't make it either. Rick blamed himself for Dannie's death, but this was a burden he had to bear alone. No one could ever know what he and Dannie had done.

To make matters worse, while they were in the intensive care unit waiting room with Dannie in surgery, Rick got a call from his sister-in-law, Beth, that his brother, Jason, had been in an accident and he was being taken by ambulance to the same hospital. It had been touch-and-go for a long time with Jason, and there were many times when it appeared that Jason was not going to make it either. Jason had finally pulled through, but it was after many long months in the hospital and even more setbacks. However, Jason was doing much better after a number of operations.

This loop of misery was playing and replaying in his head. Good things had started and turned his life around with Maizie. And then Grace had come along. Now Rick felt he had been pulled back into a maelstrom of bad karma.

Lauren said to Rick, "Dial Abby's number for me and I'll talk to her. We should tell her what happened. She's going to want to come to the hospital."

Rick responded somewhat like an automaton. He tapped his phone again, put it on speaker, and held the phone out closer to Lauren. The phone rang several times and then Abby answered.

"Hi, Rick, what's up?"

"Abby, it's Lauren, Rick's assistant. Rick and I are on the way to Greenwich Hospital. There was a home invasion, and Maizie is okay but shaken up. She's hurt, but nothing life threatening."

Abby gasped noticeably into the phone. "Oh, my God! Is she going to be okay? You're sure?"

"Yes, she was beaten up, but she was well enough to call the office looking for Rick. I spoke to her, since Rick was in court."

"Oh, shit, how can this have happened?" The alarm in Abby's voice seemed to jolt Rick back to reality.

He finally responded, "Abby, we hardly know anything. We're almost at the hospital. This is my worst nightmare. Who the hell would do such a thing?" Rick's voice trailed off as he tried to get his emotions back under control.

Abby said, "I'm in Westport. I finished with a client, and I was just walking to the car. I'll be down as soon as I can."

Abby ran to the parking lot, and the tires screeched as she hit the street. She wasn't far from I-95, but at this hour it could easily be bumper to bumper traffic and not moving at all. She opted for the Merritt Parkway, which was a less direct route to the hospital, but hopefully she would make better time. It didn't take her long to get to the parkway, and she prayed traffic would move. For the first part of the trip, she was moving at about 75 miles per hour, which was extremely fast for this road, with a lot of twists and turns. Then it happened. Traffic came to a crawl, and Abby cursed. She needed to get to the hospital. She desperately needed to get to the hospital.

Finally, Abby couldn't stand it anymore. She pulled on to the shoulder and continued to drive, perhaps not at seventy-five, but as close to it as she dared. She kept blowing her horn, to make sure the other drivers knew she was coming up fast on their right. She got a lot of dirty looks from the other drivers, but she thought blowing the horn as she tore down the shoulder would let them know something was wrong and she was not purely crazy. It was working for a few miles, until she heard a siren and then saw the flashing light in her rearview mirror. Abby's heart sank as she saw this, but then the proverbial light bulb went on in her head.

The state trooper pulled her over and, as he approached her car, Abby did something that almost got her killed. She jumped out of the car. She startled the trooper, who yelled at her to get back in the car. Abby darted between the trunk of her car and the front of the trooper's car. Before he could say anything else, she started screaming, "My daughter was attacked. My daughter is at Greenwich Hospital now. I need you to take me there now. Please help me!"

Abby looked as distraught as she felt. Apparently, the trooper saw it too. The trooper said, "Get back in the car. I have to call dispatch."

The state trooper's car pulled into the ramp toward the ER at Greenwich Hospital with the siren blaring. Abby made it to the hospital in record time, waved a thank-you to the trooper, and ran through the sliding glass doors to the ER.

CHAPTER 8

Abby ran up to the desk in the emergency room, gave the secretary Maizie's name, told her she was Maizie's mother, and asked to see her. The secretary at the desk said Maizie was in Exam Room 5 and opened the doors remotely to the exam rooms. Abby took a deep breath and went in, afraid what she was going to see and afraid of how bad Maizie might look. As she walked into the exam room, Rick was pacing back and forth like a caged animal, but the bed was empty and Maizie was not there. Rick turned and saw Abby, and there was some relief on his face as if the reinforcements had arrived.

"When I got here," he said, "they had just taken her to X-ray. I missed her. She must be so scared. I want to be with her. I'm out of my mind with worry."

Abby answered, "I know, but Maizie can be tougher than you think. It's better that they take care of her. We'll be here waiting for her when she comes back. What happened? How much do you know?"

"Well, you know pretty much what I know about Maizie, but we don't know anything about the baby."

"What do you mean, the baby? Has something happened to Grace?" Now it felt as if the fear enveloped her like a blanket.

"Didn't Lauren tell you when she called?" It was as if Rick had no memory of being in the same car with Lauren when she had spoken to Abby.

Abby shook her head no.

Rick took a deep breath, and in a torrent of words told her what little he knew. Rick said he had called the police and was waiting for them. "I'm going out of my mind just waiting here doing nothing. Maizie and Grace are the two most important things in my life. I can't even imagine anything, anything at all, happening to either one of them."

Abby really had no idea of what to say to try to comfort him, because there was a hurricane of emotions going on inside of her as well. She merely walked over to Rick and gave him a hug. "We'll get through this, Rick. We'll do it together."

Abby thought of the first time she met Rick up on the bridge and that he wanted to commit suicide after Jennifer and Adam's deaths. She couldn't imagine Rick having to go through anything that horrible again.

As she let go of Rick, he looked at her and said with sadness in his voice that was almost palpable, "Looks like you're here to save me a second time."

Abby gave him a small, loving smile. She sat down in the chair by the bed and let out a big sigh. Rick continued to pace.

After a few minutes Abby got up and said to Rick, "I'm going to the ladies' room. I'll be right back."

Abby walked back into the emergency room waiting room and went into the ladies' room. She felt the tears stinging her eyes. *Damn it, Abby, get a hold of yourself. You can't fall apart now. They need you.* At that very moment, she thought of her deceased husband, Jerry. Now the floodgates opened. He had been gone for so long, but she still missed him very much. For once, Abby wanted someone to take care of her. She didn't always want to be the strong one. After a few minutes, she got herself back under control and stopped crying. She took deep breaths to try to calm herself.

Then another thought came very clearly into her mind—her own mother, Fannie. Although Fannie had been dead for quite some time, she had come back from the other side to tell Abby about a secret she'd had kept from her for almost forty years—a secret she had taken with her to her grave. But the secret was about to come to light. Fannie somehow was able to come back and communicate very clearly to Abby, almost as if Fannie were speaking to Abby as if Fannie were still alive. Abby could not only hear Fannie, but she could also see her as well. It had changed Abby's life profoundly then and to this day.

Abby decided that this was a situation in which she ought to try to contact her mother and see if she could help them in some way to find Grace. Fortunately, no one else wanted to use the ladies room and no one was knocking at the door.

"Mom, it's me. I don't know what you are aware of from the other side, but Maizie was attacked and beaten up and they kidnapped Grace—that sweet little thing. I'm hoping she's too young to be afraid, but we certainly are. Can you help us? We really need you to help us find her and find out who did this. Mom, are you there? We really, really need help."

No answer.

Abby tried again. "Mom, I know how much you love us. I need you, but Maizie and Grace need you even more. I know that if you can help us, you will. Can you answer me, Mom?"

No answer of any kind.

Abby said it a third time. "I've put it out there to you, Mom. I know you'll do whatever you can. Please." Abby didn't know what else to do. She hoped her mother had heard her. She believed that if Fannie heard her, she would do something—whatever something was.

Abby decided she should go back to the exam room and

stay with Rick. Hopefully, Maizie would be back from X-ray and Abby could help comfort her. Maizie was the one with the most information.

oooooooooooooooooooooooo

Jason was picking his way through traffic as fast as he could toward the bridge, but it was getting toward rush hour and traffic was getting much heavier. He had called Rick twice to tell him he was on the way, but it was like slogging through molasses. Maizie wasn't back in the exam room either time he had called, but at least the second time he called, Rick said that Abby had arrived. Jason felt a little tension go out of him now that Abby was there. Abby had that effect on people. She was kind, yet she was strong, and she certainly could have a calming influence on people. And she was his biological mother.

Jason hadn't known that until a few years ago. At the time Abby had revealed that to him, Jason was extremely upset that Abby hadn't kept that fact to herself that he had been adopted as a baby. He thought she was being selfish in telling him because that was what she wanted, not what he wanted. But it had turned out to be the proverbial blessing in disguise for all of them in a very short time. Today that was looking like the understatement of the year.

Jason uttered a few choice curse words as he looked at his speedometer. He was now going a whopping 30 miles per hour on the Thruway. "C'mon, c'mon, give me a break. We need to move, damn it. Now!"

All of a sudden Jason distinctly heard his name and almost jumped out of his seat belt. The radio was playing Bruce Springsteen's "Born in the USA," and the windows of the car were closed. There was no one else in the car with him.

"Jason, it's Grandma Fannie."

"Grandma, are you talking to me from the GPS?" Jason's tone was clearly perplexed, if not downright shocked.

Despite herself, and the seriousness of the situation, Fannie wanted to laugh. Were human beings always so literal and concrete? She tried to remember what she was like when she was alive, but the feeling eluded her.

"No, Jason, I'm not talking to you from the GPS." The sarcastic side of Fannie still seemed to be intact after all these years on the other side. Would he understand her better if she started the sentence with the words, "Recalculating, recalculating"?

His eyes were darting all around the car, yet he saw nothing. Fannie tried to be patient with Jason and keep the tone in her voice kind and sympathetic.

The more she thought about it, she might actually be freaking Jason out. It had been quite a while since she had been present, and the last time she had been present, she was mostly communicating with Abby.

"Jason, I know I haven't been present to you for a while. I think the last time you saw me was several years ago, when the whole family was at the Jersey Shore and I came to say goodbye to Abby. I waved to you from the beach, and you waved back. That was such a wonderful moment between us. I will never forget it." She let out a soft chuckle. "I was actually going to say I will never forget it as long as I live. That's stupid, since it happened after I was already dead.

"Anyway, I heard from Abby a few minutes ago that you all need my help to find Grace. I distinctly heard everything that Abby said, but I tried to answer her and she couldn't hear me. Then all of a sudden, I find myself on the New York State Thruway in Rockland County in your car. Or sort of in your car," Fannie corrected herself. "From your reaction, I presume you can hear me."

"Oh my God, Grandma, I can hear you. How can that be? I only ever heard your voice that one night after I was in the car crash and I was in the ER on my way up to surgery."

"Jason, believe me, I never quite get the rules, if that's what you want to call them. I know that I was meant to come back last time to tell Abby the secret I kept from her was about you and to make amends for what I did. That made sense to me, although I never understood how I actually communicated with her. I remember telling her it was a big picture sort of thing, and that was true. But the actual mechanics, if that's what I should call them, were always a mystery to me.

"It's even more baffling to me that I'm talking to you in your car, when you didn't try to contact me, and Abby did. You're my grandson, and I love you. I have always loved you from the moment I first saw you as a newborn in the hospital. But why I am talking to you in particular and not Abby is beyond me. I have no idea of what happened to Maizie and where that little cutie Grace is. So first, you and I have to figure out why I'm here with you of all the people in the family. Then we have to find Grace."

Jason, who was always so talkative, couldn't think of one word to say.

CHAPTER 9

A member of the transport team wheeled Maizie back into the exam room where Abby and Rick were anxiously waiting. She started to cry when she saw Rick and Abby. They both jumped up from their chairs and from being locked in their own thoughts, none of them good. Maizie looked extremely pale and from the look of her puffy eyelids and red eyes, she had been crying.

An emergency room nurse followed the gurney into the exam room and looked at the three of them, one looking more upset than the next. She said in as cheery a voice as she could muster, "We're waiting for Radiology to read the X-rays and then we'll know better whether you're going to be admitted or not. The doctor will be in to talk to you as soon as we have some answers. Would you like some tea or ginger ale and some Jell-O?"

Through the haze of tears, Maizie said she would like some ginger ale. The nurse smiled at Maizie and said, "I'll be right back with the soda. Just try to calm down a little. It's good you're back here now with your husband and mom. This is a good duo to help you." With that she turned, winked knowingly at Rick and left.

Maizie reached out both hands, one to each of them, and started crying harder. She had a splint on her left forearm. Both Rick and Abby moved forward to hug her. After some time and more tears on everyone's part, Abby let go of Maizie and looked at her over Rick's shoulder as he continued to hold her. Maizie continued to cry. Abby pulled up a chair and sat down right by the bed. After another few moments of holding her, Rick did the same. Maizie leaned forward and took both of their hands again.

Finally, Rick said to her very softly, "Maiz, where do you think you're hurt?"

Maizie said through the tears that continued to roll down her cheeks, "He kicked me in the ribs a couple of times while I was on the floor. I think I heard a rib crack, and it hurts when I take a deep breath." She held up her arm with the splint on it. "My arm really hurts, too, but I don't know what happened. He banged my head into the floor, and I had a bad headache when I woke up."

Rick winced as he listened to her.

"But it's Grace. It's Grace." Now she started to sob.

"Maizie, what happened? Can you remember anything?" Abby asked.

Maizie nodded, even as she sobbed. Her voice was raspy and her sentences were choppy, but she told them pretty much what happened.

Rick asked, "There was only one guy? Someone told me two."

Maizie shook her head no.

"Did you recognize the guy or was he wearing a mask?"

Maizie answered Rick that he wasn't wearing a mask but said she had never seen him before.

"Did you tell all this to the police?" This time it was Abby.

"Honestly, Mom, I tried to tell them everything, but I'm afraid it came out so jumbled because I was terrified."

"I'm sure you told them plenty, and they know how to question victims to get the most info from them." At the mention of the word "victim," Abby shuddered to think that her daughter, her baby, had been a victim.

Rick said, "They told us that they were putting out an Amber Alert as soon as they left the house. I'm waiting for the police to come and meet us here. We were also waiting for you to get back here to the ER from radiology, but maybe now I should call them and see where they are."

Right after Rick finished talking, his cell phone rang. All three of them jumped. Rick answered and said, "Hi, Jas. Yeah, I'll come out and get you from the waiting room."

Abby volunteered and said, "You stay with Maizie. I'll go get him."

As Abby walked through the double doors leading out of the ER to the waiting room, she saw Jason leaning up against one of the stanchions and talking on the cell phone. She was looking at him in profile, and as she did, she couldn't help but look for family traits. She saw those traits because they were definitely there. He had darker hair than Maizie, but the two of them looked enough alike since they were half brother and sister. Abby still felt a pang of loss of how much of his life she had missed once she gave him up for adoption. At the same time, she still also marveled at the events that brought her mother, Fannie, back from the other side, to reunite Jason with her.

Jason turned and caught her eye just as he punched the phone with his finger to end the call. He came over to hug her, and said, "My God, how's Maizie? How bad is she? I was just on the phone with Beth, and I told her I'd call her back as soon as I knew something. Rick sounded pretty bad on the phone, and I wasn't getting much out of him."

Abby told him as much as they knew and that Maizie wasn't as bad physically as they thought she might be. Abby said, "She is understandably extremely upset and crying, but she has been able to tell us what happened. She's pretty clear about what went on, but she gets hysterical at the mention of Grace's name. Rick was told that the police put out an Amber Alert, and we're waiting for them to come here to talk to her again. We're not sure yet if she's going to be admitted to the hospital. I said I'd come out to get you so that they'd have some time alone."

Jason listened intently to everything Abby had to say, occasionally interrupting with a question. Finally, when Abby was done, he took her by the elbow and walked her away from everyone in the waiting room and out into the hallway. He looked around conspiratorially to see if anyone was standing near them. Abby had no idea what Jason was doing, but she let her herself be led by him.

Jason started to speak, swallowed hard, and started again. "Abby, I know this is very weird after not hearing from her for a few years, but on my way over here, Grandma Fannie spoke to me in the car. She said that you had spoken to her about Maizie and Grace and she heard you, but for some reason, she couldn't answer you. She started talking to me! What the hell do I do?"

Abby shook her head softly, smiled a little and said quietly, "Jason, you have to listen to her and answer. I felt, no, I knew, she would help us. Now we know how."

For the second time in about an hour, Jason who never seemed to be at a loss for words, had nothing to say in response.

CHAPTER 10

Steve Goldrick surveyed the array of burner phones in his desk drawer. He picked out one and dialed the number on the piece of paper in his hand. "The guy" answered on the third ring. "Hello," he growled.

"Well, what happened? Did it go as planned?" Steve asked.

"Yeah, everything went fine. According to the plan. I get the extra money. I didn't do nothing to the woman. Tell me where to send it. I'll send you the picture of her. She's still alive. Scared the shit out of her. Like you wanted. Where's the money?"

Steve listened to the staccato cadence of words from "the guy." No flourishes, no extra words. It reminded Steve of Sergeant Joe Friday, from the 1950s TV show, *Dragnet*. Joe Friday's famous line was, "Just the facts, ma'am, just the facts." "Send me the picture and you'll have the money in your account this afternoon. This way I only have to make one transfer into your bank account."

"The guy" gave Steve the bank account number, and Steve repeated it back to him. Steve wanted to make sure that "the guy" got the money and got it on time. That was how you did business. Besides, you never know when you might want to use his services again in the future.

Steve said to him, "Where's the kid now? Is she okay?"

"Gave her to the woman. Just like you told me. She's got some crazy Russian name. You gotta talk to her now. I'm done."

"Yeah, her name is Fatima. I'll be in touch with her myself. Send me the picture on my phone. Okay. Good job. Bye."

Steve waited a few minutes and then looked at the picture of Maizie tied up on the floor. Steve was thinking about what a professional "the guy" was, even though he was expensive. He got the job done, with a minimum of problem to Steve. He really didn't need any direction from Steve, and he didn't need to have his hand held. Steve shook his head. Too bad "the guy" basically only operated on these kinds of matters.

Steve knew that he had to reach out to Fatima, but he felt that she would take care of Grace and nothing bad would happen to her. He had actually been surprised that Fatima was so willing to take Grace after she had been abducted. On the other hand, this just confirmed what Steve knew most of his life. Money talks. Most people would do almost anything if offered enough money.

<hr />

Back in Greenwich Hospital, the doctor had been in to see Maizie. She had three broken ribs, and her wrist was fractured. They had performed the concussion protocol, and she did have a concussion, so they had decided to keep her overnight in the hospital. She had been moved out of the emergency room upstairs to a room in the hospital.

Rick had called the detective who had was now in charge of the case. He met Rick in the lobby of the hospital as the nurses were getting Maizie settled in her room. Abby had stayed with Maizie. Then the detective wanted to speak to Maizie. Rick wasn't so sure he was going to be happy dealing with a small-town detective on a kidnapping. After all, how many kidnappings had the guy ever worked on in a little place like Rye Brook?

Rick was pleasantly surprised by Detective Williams. He had on a dark grey suit with a muted tie and could have passed as a businessman or a professor. Nothing about him was flashy, but it certainly wasn't obvious from his clothing or his mannerisms that he was a cop. Rick hadn't done very much criminal work as a young attorney, but in the little he had, when he had appeared in court, he could tell by the clothes and haircuts which were the cops, which were the defense lawyers, and which were the DAs.

Detective Williams was more than willing to listen to Rick and answer his questions. One of the things that Rick liked about what he said was that there was a joint task force set up with the district attorney's office so that the local police departments could use the expertise already in place for kidnapping cases and didn't have to reinvent the wheel. That gave Rick a little comfort that this wasn't the first case being handled by Rye Brook. Rick certainly didn't want his family to be the guinea pig.

"Mr. Singleton, your wife told the responding officers that she had never seen the kidnapper before. Is that correct?"

"Yes, she said she had never seen him before. She said that he took some money from her wallet, but it appeared the main thing he wanted was Grace."

"I understand that you're an attorney. Do you do any criminal work? Has anyone made any threats against you or your family? Any disgruntled clients suing you or threatening to sue you?"

Rick said no.

"What about someone on the other side of a case who took a particular dislike to you? Someone you beat in court or you're collecting money from for a client?"

Again, Rick said no.

"Do you do any matrimonial work? Sometimes those cases can get pretty nasty. What about an ex-husband who feels he got a raw deal because of you?"

Rick was beginning to feel a tightness in his chest. He had answered no to all the questions Detective Williams had asked, but there was one thing from his past.

"Detective, do you know that one of the partners in my firm was killed in her home in Rye a few years ago? They never found the killer. It was a home invasion, and nothing was taken. Her credit cards were right there in her purse in plain sight. She was alone in the house. Nothing was disturbed in the house. I don't know that this has anything to do with me, but perhaps you should speak to the Rye Police."

Rick knew that he was taking a big risk telling the detective this, but he felt that it was important enough to bring up. Anyone who had even been peripherally involved in such a horrendous crime would have brought it up to the police. Rick knew if he didn't bring it up and the Rye Brook police found out about it later that it would look very suspicious.

Rick was virtually certain that he knew who had killed Dannie Bevan because the killer had practically told Rick that he had done it for revenge. Dannie and Rick had blackmailed Dannie's former partner, Steve Goldrick, about the black-market adoptions he had been doing for years and raking in hundreds of thousands of dollars. However, in a cruel twist of fate, Rick had also found out from Steve Goldrick in the same flash drive message that he was Rick's grandfather. Steve had told Rick that he was going to give Rick a free pass precisely because Rick was his grandson. Rick was praying that Steve meant it when he said that he had given Rick a free pass. However, the tightness in his chest was telling him otherwise.

The detective said he would certainly check with the Rye Police.

"What's going on with the Amber Alert?"

The detective said that the Amber Alert was already sent out, that law enforcement all over the country knew about it, and that the Amber Alert was posted on signs on all major highways. "The problem is we don't know the make or model of the car your daughter may be in."

Rick asked how effective the Amber Alert was in getting children back. He couldn't hide the pain in his voice and the anguish in his eyes.

The detective said tips came in almost as soon as the Amber Alert was posted.

"Do we have any tips yet?" Rick asked.

"Not yet," was the answer. "But my officers have been instructed to text me as soon as anything comes in. I know it feels like an eternity to you, but it's only been a couple of hours since Grace was taken. We don't know yet if the kidnapper is on the move or if he is holed up someplace. That's why we should get you back to the house and have your calls monitored in case there is a demand for ransom.

"Please take me up to see your wife now, but then we really should have you at the house. We don't yet know what, if any, motive there is in taking Grace. I have technicians at the house checking for fingerprints, too. This could be a pro, and perhaps we'll catch a break and his fingerprints will be in a database because of a prior conviction. I know you're torn about being with your wife now, but is there someone who could stay with her, while I take you back to the house? We don't want to miss a call."

Rick said, "My mother-in-law is in the room with Maizie now while I came downstairs to meet you. I'm sure she'll be willing to stay with her."

Rick led the way to Maizie's room on the second floor and tried to keep the proverbial poker face. He hoped the detective would not see that his hands were trembling and he was starting to sweat. Rick hoped the detective would chalk it up to being upset about the whole situation.

CHAPTER 11

The following morning, Rick came downstairs just as daylight was breaking. He was very pale, which was apparent under the stubble on his face, and had dark circles under his eyes. His eyes looked sunken. Rick had been in the family room with a police officer until about four in the morning when a replacement officer came to take the first officer's place. Even though Rick had gone upstairs to his bedroom at four, he hadn't turned off the lights in the room and had merely stared at whatever was on TV without comprehending anything that had gone on in the show.

The officer was sitting in the family room reading something on his iPad. There was some sort of electronic equipment sitting on the table right in front of him. Rick guessed that the officer was in his early to mid forties with a full head of curly dark hair and rimless glasses. Rick greeted him and asked if he would like some coffee.

The answer was yes, so Rick went into the kitchen and started making the coffee. After a few seconds, the officer ambled into the kitchen and leaned against the wall. "Did you get any sleep?" There was truly a sympathetic tone in his voice.

"Not one bit. It's like my mind is on an endless loop of anxiety. This is a goddamn nightmare."

"I know. The waiting is the hardest part for any parent."

Rick noticed that the officer had his suit jacket off and his gun was in a shoulder holster. Rick had seen guns on police officers many times before in his career, but he had never seen a gun in his own home. "Do you do this a lot? The waiting?"

"Yes, I do. I was always into tech stuff, and I wanted to be a cop. It was a great marriage of the two interests."

"You just do kidnappings?"

"I do that and lots of different kinds of surveillance. I like the variety."

"You married? You have kids?"

"Yes, I have two boys, so I can empathize with what you're going through. I'd be a lunatic if one of my kids was kidnapped. I've been through this before with other families, so I know how this is agony for the parents."

Rick nodded and then said, "How long does it typically take before they call?"

"That's the problem. I wish I could tell you that there's some pattern. Often there isn't. From what I've read in the report and from what Detective Williams told me, it seems that you were somehow targeted. We don't know the reason yet."

Rick handed him the coffee. "I'm sorry I never even asked you your name."

"No problem. You have other things on your mind. My name is Adam Brentano."

Rick's head jerked up. "Your name is Adam?" The tone in Rick's voice was somewhere between incredulity and fear.

The officer eyed Rick, clearly surprised by Rick's reaction. He waited for Rick to say something else.

Rick swallowed hard and said, "It's just that my son was named Adam. He and my first wife were killed in a car crash. It's kind of a weird coincidence that the person who is sent here to help me get my daughter back has the same name as my deceased son."

Adam let out a small whistle. "Wow, that's a coincidence."

Fannie smiled and said, "Well, Rick, I'm glad you're not too exhausted or too stressed out to miss that sign I sent you."

CHAPTER 12

Steve chose yet another burner phone from his desk drawer. It reminded him of being a little kid and reciting the chant to pick something from a group. "Eenie, meany, minee, mo, catch a chicken by the toe. If he hollers let him go, eenie meany, minee, mo." Steve could see himself as a little boy, choosing in this very "scientific" way. *Those were simpler times*, Steve mused. He thought about all the twists and turns his life had taken since then.

Steve pulled himself out of his reverie and got back to the business at hand. He pulled a dark blue phone from the desk drawer. He had to use these burner phones; you couldn't be too careful.

He dialed the number on a pad on his desk, and a young woman's somewhat breathless voice answered on the second ring.

"Fatima, how are you doing and how's the baby?"

"Everything's fine," came the answer. She sounded scared to Steve.

"Is the apartment okay?"

"Yes, it is very nice," came the polite reply with a distinct accent.

"Do you need anything? You have enough supplies, formula and diapers?"

"Everything is fine," came the same answer as before.

"Is that the baby I hear?"

"Yes, she is awake and happy this morning. I just fed her."

"Don't forget that there's money in the account for you to use if you need something for the baby. That's in addition to the money that's for you."

"Yes, I know, thank you."

"Has Vladdina been in touch with you yet?"

"No, not yet."

"She will be shortly. Think of this as an all-expenses-paid vacation. In a short while, you'll have enough money to go on an extended vacation. If you don't need anything else, then I'll hang up now. I'll be back in touch soon, and Vladdina will have some information for you."

"Yes, thank you."

When they hung up, Steve thought that if Fatima and "the guy" were ever in the same room together, there might be a maximum of thirty words said between them for an entire afternoon. Fatima's English was not as good as her sister's, Vladdina. It didn't matter. Everything sounded like it was under control. Yep, under Steve's control. Just the way he liked it.

∘∘∘∘∘∘∘∘∘∘∘∘∘∘∘∘∘∘∘∘∘∘∘∘∘

Back in Rye Brook at Rick and Maizie's house, the wire in Adam's ear went off and a voice said, "We have a woman who just pulled into the driveway and is getting out of the car." Adam bolted off the couch and stood behind the curtains to peer out into the driveway. "Mr. Singleton, there's a young woman with dark hair who parked her Toyota in your driveway and is walking toward the door. Do you know her?"

Rick had seen Adam bolt off the couch, and he was startled at Adam's catlike quickness and fluid motion. "Yes, it's Vladdina, the nanny. She was out sick for a few days. With all that went on, I totally forgot to call her."

They both heard the key turn the lock in the door, and Vladdina walked in. She saw Rick first and then the man with the gun in his shoulder holster. Vladdina had been coached, so while she was expecting that there might be police in the house, she acted startled and surprised. She stopped in her tracks and looked at Rick again. "What is going on, Mr. Singleton? Is everything okay?"

Rick walked over to her and said "Vladdina, with all that has gone on, I should have called you, but I forgot. This is Detective Adam Brentano. There was a home invasion, and Grace has been kidnapped."

Vladdina gasped. Rick went on to explain what had happened and that Maizie was still in the hospital as a precaution and for observation but was expected to be released today. Vladdina liked Maizie and Rick, and she was glad to hear that Maizie hadn't been badly hurt. In fact, Vladdina was hoping that Maizie hadn't been hurt at all. As the whole scenario had been described to her, this was not going to be a messy situation and would be over soon and life would return to normal. Vladdina was not so naive that she totally believed that, but most of what she had been told sounded plausible enough. Besides, she needed the money, and this was a golden opportunity that she couldn't pass up. She was going to earn more money for this than she could ever have imagined, and she was going to be able to help her own family.

Vladdina was a good actress and asked all the right questions. Rick said he was going to call Maizie shortly to see when she was going to be released. "Since I have to stay here in case the kidnappers call, I may ask you to go pick her up from the hospital. Is that okay?"

"Oh, yes, I will do whatever you need. I cannot believe this terrible thing has happened."

Adam listened intently to the whole conversation and watched Vladdina and her reaction to everything Rick was telling her although he pretended to fiddle with the surveillance equipment.

The cop in him kicked in, and everyone was a suspect until they ruled the person out. Adam had a very good ear and picked up on Vladdina's accent, and he was pretty sure it was Russian.

An alarm bell went off in Adam's head, and he made a mental note that she had been out sick when Grace was kidnapped. This was the first he had heard of a nanny, and he wondered if his colleague Detective Williams knew there was a nanny from overseas. Adam decided that he would wait a few minutes and then text him to see if they had a full name to check against databases and to check with Immigration and Customs.

CHAPTER 13

The phone rang and Rick and Adam jumped. Rick looked at the caller ID and shook his head. It said Greenwich Hospital, which meant it was Maizie calling. Rick punched the button on the phone and said, "Hi, honey, how do you feel? How's the pain in the ribs?"

Maizie answered that she still had pain, but that they had given her something for the pain. "Don't worry about it. Did anyone call?" she asked with more than a little trepidation in her voice.

Rick said, "No, honey, no one's called. I told you I would let you know the minute I heard anything."

Maizie's voice quivered. "I am so terrified, Rick. I've been over this a thousand times in my head, and it doesn't make any sense to me. It seems we were targeted. Who would want to target us? It's not like we're millionaires. You're not Bill Gates with a trillion dollars. I really think it was all about taking Grace. He took some money from my wallet, but the more I think about it, the more it seems to me that his prime focus was Grace." Her voice trailed off, and she struggled not to burst out crying.

Despite the fact that Rick wanted to sound upbeat for Maizie, he could hear the weariness in his own voice, and it had been only one day. "Maiz, when you get home, I think you should go over this all again with the police. Maybe you'll remember something that will help them that you forgot earlier because you were so scared. We might be missing one little detail that could make all the difference."

The more Maizie talked, the more Rick was sure that Steve Goldrick had something, if not everything, to do with this. With Steve, Rick wasn't sure if this was about money or revenge or both. All Rick knew was that Steve was a dangerous person.

"Rick, I don't have my cell phone here, and they only turned the phones on now. Are the police still there?"

"Yes, they changed officers at about four this morning. The new officer's name is Adam. Don't know what to make of that coincidence."

Maizie acted as if she hadn't heard him on that subject and went off in a different direction. "The doctor said if I felt okay today and I had no symptoms that I can come home. He said he'll be in to see me this morning."

"Maiz, Vladdina is here, so she can come pick you up. I need to stay here in case we get a call."

"I have to call Mom this morning and let her know what's going on. Should I have her pick me up? I know she's not going to want to stay home while all this is going on. She's going to want to be with us. And I want her with us too."

"Whatever you want to do is fine. Whatever makes it easier for you."

The thought flashed through Maizie's mind that as much as she loved Rick, this was a situation where she wanted to be with her mother. She wanted to be comforted by her mother. She was trying to be strong for Rick, but with Abby, she could fall apart if she needed to. She got choked up as she realized that she wanted to be there for her daughter, her Grace.

"The doctor said he had called in a prescription to the pharmacy for pain killers for my ribs and wrist. Can you ask Vladdina to pick up the prescription for me? If Mom's not up and ready when the doctor comes in, then maybe I'll call back and have Vladdina come pick me up. I just want to come home." Maizie's voice trailed off. Then in an even softer voice, just above a whisper, she said, "I want Grace to come home. I want this to be over."

"I know, Maiz, I know."

Rick sat down heavily on the couch and exhaled. Adam had made himself scarce when Rick was on the phone with Maizie. He came back into the room with another mug of coffee. Adam had learned that since the families of kidnapping victims were in such tremendous pain, it was better if he waited for them to open up to him. If they wanted to talk, he talked, and if they wanted to sit in complete silence, he would do that too. The invention of the Kindle and then the iPad had been godsends for him to deal with long boring hours. He read voraciously, technical journals, biographies, and novels. Lots of all of them. He had a friend who was a US marshal. He described his job as long hours of boredom broken up by short bursts of adrenaline. It was in those short bursts of adrenaline when all the action and danger occurred, that all your training and instincts took over.

Rick told Adam what Maizie had said about the kidnapping. "Maybe you should talk to her when she gets home and see if anything jogs her memory—something that she forgot to tell Detective Williams. She seems a little more pulled together today. She really experienced the triple whammy of the terror of the home invasion, the injuries, and, and, you know, the kidnapping," Rick stammered.

"Rick, I'm here to help. I mean it. Those are not just pious platitudes. I wouldn't have lasted in this kind of work unless I cared about the people I'm here to help."

Rick smiled a weary smile at Adam. He liked this guy. Rick felt that a small amount of the heavy burden on him had been lifted.

CHAPTER 14

Two days had gone by, and there had been no contact from the kidnappers. Rick hated the interminable waiting and the never knowing when, or even if, they were going to get a call. He felt as if a wet blanket had been thrown over his whole being and that he was having trouble breathing through it. The anxiety was greater than the boredom, but together they were taking a tremendous toll on all of them.

Abby cooked meals, but no one really ate much of anything. She kept wrapping up leftovers to put in the refrigerator, and it seemed she was wrapping up almost as much as she had cooked. The various police officers sitting in the house seemed not to have lost their appetites. They were the only ones who ate anything substantial. The officers were all polite, and in other circumstances, Abby probably would have chatted more with them and learned about their wives and families. But Abby just did not have the emotional wherewithal to chat right now.

Abby could see that Rick liked Adam and the two of them even had a few chats that were not related to Grace. Abby was glad that even for a few minutes, Rick was distracted by his conversations with Adam. She heard them discussing law enforcement and a few criminal cases that Rick had handled early on in his career.

Adam had a very inquisitive mind, and so many things interested him. His abilities had been recognized by the various departments he had worked in, and he had moved up the ladder quickly. Adam told Rick that he had just finished his twenty years on the force, so he was thinking of retiring with his pension as a detective and moving on to another career off the police force. Abby heard Adam tell Rick that he had two kids in high school who were college bound, so there was almost never enough money for college tuitions since the boys would be in college at the same time. Adam said that he was too young and had too much energy to retire. It was just that he wanted something different to challenge him.

Abby even heard them discussing the Yankees and the Mets when Maizie wasn't in the room. Abby was glad that Rick had a few minutes of relief from the gloom which was almost palpable in the house.

On the third morning about ten thirty, Abby decided that she was going out for a run and then to teach her extreme bridge climbing class. Abby poked her head into the den and motioned to Rick that she was going to go out for a run. He shook his head yes. Abby nodded to the ever-present officer sitting in the living room and went out the front door. She had thought about asking Rick if he wanted to come with her, even if they kept it to a short run. She decided against it, in case they did get a call from the kidnappers. She thought Maizie would fall apart by herself if the call came in and Abby and Rick were both out of the house.

Maizie and Rick were sitting on the couch in the den, Maizie leaning on Rick's shoulder and draped in a comforter. It seemed that Maizie was dozing off. Rick was staring at the Kindle in his lap, but he hadn't turned a page in a long time. After a few minutes, he could tell that her breath was rhythmic and that she had fallen asleep. Since neither of them had had a full night's sleep, he was glad that she was getting some rest, even if it was short lived. Rick was somewhat surprised that even with the painkillers, she wasn't sleeping much at night. Neither of them were. They were both so on edge. Any incoming phone call jolted everyone in the house, including the police officers, who were at the ready. If Rick had hated telemarketers before this, he despised them now. Some idiot was always calling with a stupid "once in a lifetime" offer that he wouldn't have accepted in a million years under normal circumstances. Now he wanted to kill them for calling at all. Any noise in the house also made them jump.

Rick carefully extricated his shoulder from Maizie and then laid her head against the pillow. He made sure she was well covered with the comforter and quietly walked upstairs to the master bedroom and pulled his cell phone out of his pants pocket. He scrolled down the contacts list in his phone and found what he wanted. He looked at the number on his phone for a few minutes before he moved his finger to dial the number. He was really torn about whether to make this call. He wanted to make the call, but at the same time he was terrified to make it. He was in agony and that this call might help him climb through the morass that had become his life over the past few days. However, there was another part of him that knew he might very well be opening Pandora's box. Rick understood the analogy quite well to his own life. Once he opened the proverbial Pandora's box, he was pretty sure he would never be able to close it again.

Fannie had been looking out the window in the master bedroom when Rick walked in. She had seen Abby go out the door for her run. When Rick walked into the bedroom, Fannie turned to look at him. Rick could not see her, nor did he have any indication that Fannie was around. Fannie had never communicated directly with Rick in the previous times that she had come back from the other side. She had only communicated with Abby and in a very limited way with Rick's brother, Jason. Right now she could hear Abby, but Abby didn't know Fannie was around, nor could Abby hear Fannie. Fannie had no idea why this had changed.

Fannie saw how drawn and tired Rick looked. She wanted to help him. She wanted to help Maizie and, most of all, she wanted to help Grace be returned to her family—Fannie's family. It just had not yet been made apparent to her how that was going to happen.

Rick looked at his cell phone again and tapped the number in his contacts. Rick knew that this man had helped him before when he was at his lowest point. Rick believed he could help him again, or he would never have made the call.

The phone rang several times, and the voicemail came on. "Hello, Dr. Burke, this is Rick Singleton. My daughter, Grace, has been kidnapped and we're all in a really bad way. I need to talk to you as soon as possible."

Fannie wasn't sure how all the pieces fit together yet, but she knew she would probably find out soon.

CHAPTER 15

In what appeared to Fannie to be almost simultaneous with her having been in the master bedroom with Rick when he made the call to Dr. Burke, she found herself in a strange house, which was very large and very beautifully furnished. Fannie had absolutely no idea where she was. She "wandered," at least that was the term she would have used when she was still alive, from room to room. Nothing looked the least bit familiar to her, and no one was home. She found herself in an office and, if she had still been alive, would have uttered several obscenities. She recognized a few photographs she had seen before. She had seen these pictures in Steve Goldrick's private office in his law firm a number of years ago in New York City. There were a variety of pictures of Steve Goldrick with various famous people, politicians, and professional athletes—Steve with Mayor Giuliani right after 9/11, Steve with Derek Jeter, and Steve with Ed Koch, with the caption, "How'm I doing?"

All of a sudden, Fannie heard a very unfamiliar sound. It was the sound of the muezzin calling Muslims to prayer. Fannie couldn't see exactly where the voice was coming from, but she had seen mosques before with the muezzin's voice being piped over a loudspeaker. As Fannie looked out the window, she could make out a mosque with a minaret in the distance, which was where the voice was probably coming from. A thought flashed through Fannie's mind that she was in some country in the Middle East. Fannie didn't have a clue where she was. She had never been out of the United States while she was alive. Now she was in some Middle Eastern country, and she didn't know where, and to make matters worse, she was in Steve Goldrick's house. It was hard to imagine that a day could get much worse than this. Clearly, if she was here, wherever here was, then Steve Goldrick was most probably involved with Grace's kidnapping. That was a very bad thing. The only good thing Fannie could think of was that this was the first solid clue she or anyone else had about Grace's kidnapping.

She heard the garage door open and then a beeping sound in the house. Fannie presumed it was some sort of alarm being turned off. After a few minutes had elapsed, Fannie saw the door to the office open and she was staring at none other than Steve Goldrick. He looked somewhat greyer than she remembered him. He looked older, and there were definite crow's feet around his eyes which she didn't remember him having before.

Fannie wasn't sure what to do. She wasn't sure if Steve could see or hear her. She decided to stay still at first and see if he in any way acknowledged her presence. Steve seemed to be going about his business normally, so it didn't appear that he knew she was there. After a few minutes had elapsed, she decided to move around and see if he noticed her. Still nothing.

Steve turned on his laptop. Fannie went to stand directly behind him to read what was on the screen. He read a few emails that were of no consequence to Fannie. As he continued to scroll down, he opened an email that was a confirmation of a wire transfer of a very large sum of money. For some reason, this email seemed very out of place with the other emails, which appeared to be about mundane subjects. Especially due to the fact that Fannie had serious suspicions about Steve Goldrick's involvement with Grace's kidnapping, a recent wire transfer for a significant amount of money to a bank in the United States made Fannie even more convinced that Steve Goldrick was either directly or indirectly involved in it. Fannie had no idea where she was in the Middle East, but if she was in Steve Goldrick's office looking over his shoulder at his emails, there was certainly something that Fannie was meant to know. If it involved Grace, and Fannie could help, so much the better. Steve didn't know what Fannie had done to take Steve down before and shut down his black-market adoption ring. That was going to be nothing compared to what Fannie was going to do with him now since he had messed with her family—her family.

Fannie moved to the other end of the office and purposely and noisily moved a heavy cut glass vase across the wooden cabinet directly across the room from where Steve was sitting. The cut glass vase was directly in Steve's line of vision. Steve jerked his head up from where he was staring at the computer screen. There was no one else in the room, but he definitely heard something and thought he saw something move out of the corner of his eye. Fannie let a few more seconds elapse. Then she moved the bottle of iced tea that was sitting on the corner of Steve's desk. Steve didn't just see this bottle of iced tea move out of the corner of his eye. He saw it directly in front of his face. Steve jumped up from the desk, knocking the chair over in the process.

He yelled, "Who's there?" But even as he said that, he knew it was stupid. Steve said half to himself and half to the room in general, "There's no one here. Right. There's no one here." His mind told him no one was there, but Steve still clearly looked distressed. He ran his hand through his hair. He reached out and almost touched the bottle of iced tea that had moved, but then pulled his hand back as if he had touched a scalding object.

Fannie smiled a smile which could be described as nothing less than wickedly happy. "Gotcha again, Mr. Goldrick. We are not done with each other. I expect that I will be seeing a lot of you, and very soon."

CHAPTER 16

It had been a long time since Rick had been in Dr. Burke's office. They had met years ago when Dr. Burke first saw Rick the night Rick had tried to commit suicide after Jennifer and Adam's deaths.

That evening began the first of many sessions between Rick and Dr. Burke. Dr. Burke helped Rick cope with the guilt of Rick having been called back to work early and therefore missing the horrendous car accident when Jennifer and Adam were crushed and killed in the car. Rick had tremendous survivor's guilt from thinking that if he had been there he could have saved them. Then the survivor's guilt surfaced again when he met Maizie. At that point, Rick was having trouble coping with whether he was allowed to be happy when Jennifer and Adam were dead. Was it a betrayal of them for Rick to start a new life with Maizie? Did he deserve to be able to go on with his life while Jennifer and Adam were lying in their graves? Rick felt that he had been through a lot with Dr. Burke and that he probably wouldn't have made it without Dr. Burke's help and support.

Rick had a big dose of déjà vu when he walked into Dr. Burke's office again. A quick glance revealed that nothing much had changed since he was last there years ago. The office had been painted a brighter shade of blue, and there were more pictures of the Burke kids, who had gone from little kids when Rick was first in the office to now what looked to be high school kids.

Rick put out his hand to shake Dr. Burke's hand. Instead of shaking Rick's hand in return, Dr. Burke pulled Rick to him in a hug. Rick felt so much relief and gratitude toward Dr. Burke. Merely seeing him made Rick think that things would get better. He felt that maybe now he wouldn't have to carry the burden alone.

Dr. Burke spoke first. He looked at Rick and said, "I'm very glad you called me. It's good to see you again, but I'm sorry about the circumstances. I want all my patients to do well, but you always had a special place in my heart. It seemed that fate had stacked the deck against you, and I wanted to help even things up for you."

Rick smiled back at him and said, "I know. I could feel how much you were on my side and rooting for me. You helped me so much, and I will always be very grateful to you."

Dr. Burke motioned to Rick to sit down. "I was very pleased that you let me know you had married Maizie and thing were going well between you. I was even happier to hear about that little girl who came into your life. I loved the pictures of her. Thanks.

"Now tell me everything that has gone on in the past few days. Our phone call just gave me a superficial overview of the situation."

Dr. Burke could see how haggard Rick looked, and he could only imagine how brutally exhausting and horrible the past few days had been and how much of a toll it had already taken on Rick. He asked how Maizie was holding up throughout this ordeal.

"Right now she's totally focused on getting Grace back. She has broken ribs and a broken wrist from the attack. She has a concussion. Even though she's on painkillers, she hardly sleeps. I think she's holding up for Grace and probably for me. But I'm really worried what will happen to her. In the little she sleeps, she has nightmares, and I think they're about the attack. I think she's going to need to see someone to help her through this."

Dr. Burke answered, "I can recommend someone who can see her. I have a colleague who specializes in post traumatic stress disorder."

Rick nodded. "I just don't think she'll see anyone now. She doesn't even want to leave the house until everything is over."

"What about you? How are you coping?"

Rick shook his head. "Not very well. I'm terrified that this is not going to end well. We haven't heard anything from the kidnappers. The police don't know what to make of it. It seems that they somehow singled us out and Grace was the target. There was one man who was the kidnapper, and he took some cash out of Maizie's wallet but nothing else. No credit cards, no jewelry. Maizie gave the police a description of the guy, but she had never seen him before."

"What do you make of it? Is it someone you know? Someone disgruntled or crazy client? Lawyers often don't make a lot of friends by virtue of what they do."

"I don't think it's a client."

"So do you have any idea of what this is about? Can you take a guess? Sometimes a guess may not be as farfetched as you think."

Rick hesitated for a long time and looked down at his hands. Dr. Burke waited as Rick was wrestling with something very powerful.

"There may be something. But it goes back quite a few years ago. I'm not sure that this is even it, but it may be. Dr. Burke, you are the one person on this planet who I feel completely comfortable with, and I guess that's why I'm here. I've been lying to a lot of people in my life, but it's eating me alive. I don't want to lie to you, of all people, and I suppose I don't want to lie to myself anymore."

CHAPTER 17

Jason was driving on the Palisades Parkway in Rockland County. Over the past few days, he felt that he was in perpetual motion. He would get into the office as early as possible to try to accomplish as much as he possibly could in a few hours. He would then bolt out of the office and head to Westchester to Rick and Maizie's house. Late at night he would turn around and go back to his own house and his own family. He was dog tired, but he would get up and repeat the pattern the next day. There wasn't much to do at Rick and Maizie's house except wait. He wanted to do something positive to help Rick, but there really wasn't anything to do. It was making him crazy just sitting there, so he could imagine how absolutely gut wrenching it was for both Rick and Maizie.

Jason had heard that when he was in the intensive care unit, Rick, Maizie, and Abby had been there every single day for him. Jason couldn't remember that because he was in a coma for part of the time and then he was on serious painkillers. If they were able to withstand that pressure long term, especially when things looked bleak and sometimes even hopeless, Jason decided he had to suck it up for as long as it took to help them get to the end of this nightmare.

He caught himself thinking that it was like sitting at a wake. That was how morbid things were in their house. Then he realized that there was the very real possibility that they could be sitting at a wake in the near future, and his stomach wrenched.

As Jason was driving lost in his thoughts, all of a sudden he heard something and jumped. His nerves were already frayed. "Hello, Jason, it's Grandma Fannie. Somehow I think you are going to have to get used to hearing my voice, so I hope that it's not going to give you a nervous breakdown every time I speak to you." There was a hint of a smile in Fannie's tone of voice.

"You've gotta admit, Grandma, this is just a bit out of the ordinary," he answered, with more than a little sarcasm.

"True, but that doesn't mean it's not happening or it's not true."

When Jason hesitated and didn't say anything, Fannie continued. "Jason, there are so many things in this universe that we can't see, but exist nonetheless. We can't see love or devotion or generosity, but they are very real, and no one would deny their existence."

"Good point, but who's going to believe that you're talking to me from the other side?"

"Who do you need to convince? I don't see a jury anywhere within earshot. You know what you know. I'm here. Abby understands this too. She gets it. I told you before, but for some reason, I can hear Abby, but she can't hear me. Right now you and I are speaking to and hearing each other. I don't know why, nor do I know how long this is going to last. So for now, it's us, and we're going to make the most of this. I'm certainly not happy about the circumstances of Grace's kidnapping, but I am pleased to be able to help. I'm also very happy for the opportunity to get to know you better, Jason. After all, you are my grandson. I feel I've always known you, but from a distance. I feel as if I have missed a lot of your life. This part of it is a gift for me, even if I am not still technically in this world."

Jason was more than a little nonplussed. Even though she was dead, it was apparent to him that Fannie was a force to be reckoned with. She was on a roll, and there appeared to be no stopping her. He made a mental note to spend some time with Abby and find out more about Fannie when she was alive. He had heard Abby call Maizie "Hurricane Maizie." He had some idea of what that meant. Maybe that was where Maizie got it. Maybe it was in the genes. Then he realized that he had some of those genes too. *Very interesting.*

"So let me tell you what I have found out so far," Fannie said. "This is very odd, and I don't really understand what I saw."

"About what?"

"Well, that's just it. One minute I was standing in Maizie and Rick's house and it seemed at virtually the same minute I was in Steve Goldrick's house.

"You'll probably remember the name from being one of the senior partners in Rick's old law firm in New York City. He promised to help Rick come back to the firm after his suicide attempt, but then he stabbed Rick in the back. Then there was the huge scandal when the story broke in the news that he had been running a black-market adoption ring for years from the big New York City law firm, right under the noses of his unsuspecting partners. The rumors of how much money he pocketed from the adoptions runs into the millions. No one really knows if those are true numbers or if the numbers expand with the retelling of the story. Anyway, he disappeared into thin air, and no one really knows where he and his family are. Then it also came out that his secretary disappeared at the same time, and no one's been able to track her down either. Or if someone has tracked them down, it's not been made public."

"Yeah, I do remember now. I remember how upset Rick was when everything went down in the firm. Rick couldn't believe what the bastard did to him. Sorry, Grandma, didn't mean to say 'bastard' in front of you."

Fannie laughed a little over Jason's apology. "Oh my God, Jason, I'm your grandmother. I'm not a saint. You've heard of St. Francis? Well, I can assure you that wasn't me, although we both have a very strong love of animals in common. Even though he lived several hundred years earlier than I, I have had the pleasure of meeting him. We had such a good talk about animals."

Jason swallowed hard and said, "Grandma, are you talking about St. Francis of Assisi? That St. Francis?"

Fannie tried to make light of it when she saw Jason's reaction. "He really was a remarkable person when he was alive. Makes sense, doesn't it, since he's a saint now? Don't get the wrong impression about me. I was anything but a saint when I was alive. When we have more time, I'll tell you some stories about me. I was quite a hell-raiser when I was young—when I was older as well. Well, maybe almost until I died. It would be better if I tell you the stories, and not Abby. She sort of tends to exaggerate these things."

For the second time in a few minutes, Jason made yet another mental note to ask Abby about Fannie when she was still alive. Jason was beginning to think that Grandma had really been a hell-raiser when she was alive.

"So what about Steve Goldrick?"

"As I said, one minute I was standing in Maizie and Rick's house and then, almost simultaneously, I was standing in Steve Goldrick's house. All I know is that his house is in some Middle Eastern country, but I don't know where. As you would expect with all that money he stole, it is a gorgeous house. He looked a lot older, but it has been quite some time since I've seen him. It did strike me that he is that much closer to meeting his Maker. Somehow, I don't think that meeting is going to go all that well for him, but I have to keep reminding myself that it is not for me to judge. However, there is some part of me that thinks he'll be going to an even warmer place than he's in now, if you catch my drift."

Fannie smiled what could be described as nothing less than a smug smile. "Jason, always remember that there is something to karma."

Fannie mused about that thought for a few seconds and then continued. "If I was standing in Steve Goldrick's house in some foreign country, then the only thing I can think of is that he must be connected to Grace's kidnapping. It's entirely possible that he was the architect of the whole thing. He is an evil person.

"I think you should tell Rick and Abby. It's not much, but it's more than they have now. We have to figure out how he's connected first and then decide what we should do. You understand that because of my 'situation,' there are only a few people who are even going to understand that this information came from me. Right now, the only people whom we can involve until we know more are Rick, Maizie, and Abby. I know that Abby has been trying to get in touch with me, but as I told you, for some reason, she can't hear me and you can. I want Abby to know that I hear her and that I'm doing the best I can to help."

CHAPTER 18

Adam Brentano walked into Detective Williams's office and sat down while the detective was on the phone. After he hung up the phone, Detective Williams looked at Adam with a raised eyebrow. "Got anything on the baby?"

Adam shook his head no but picked right up where Detective Williams left off. "Did Mrs. Singleton tell you that they have a nanny from Russia?"

The detective opened a small notepad on his desk and flipped through a few pages. "I don't remember her saying anything about a nanny, but I wanted to make sure."

Adam nodded in assent. "Then you certainly can't have known that the nanny was out sick the day of the home invasion. The nanny's name is Vladdina something or other Russian last name. Seems like a nice enough woman on the face of things. But as we both know, things are very often not what they seem. I'm going to do a little digging to see what I can find out. I'll start with Immigration and see what they know."

"What does the family think of her?"

Adam said, "I think I should do my own research first and then move on to see what the parents' opinion is of her. The father, Rick, is holding up much better than his wife. She's still pretty shell-shocked by the home invasion and then you add the kidnapping, and she walks around like she's almost in a trance. I really feel for these people. We need to do something to move this thing forward. Right now it's like we're mired in molasses."

"How do they act toward this Vladdina?"

"They seem to genuinely like her. It seems mutual, but we're back to that damned word, 'seems.' I hope she's not involved in any way, but a red flag went up in my mind when I heard she was out sick that day. We're paid to be suspicious, so until we know if there is any back story on this Vladdina, I won't be satisfied. She is from Russia and I want to know if she has family here. The Singletons are sophisticated people, so I assume they got the nanny from an agency. He's an attorney, and I think he's a smart guy. Let's see how much background the agency has on Vladdina."

Adam continued, "The baby is only a couple of months old, so the nanny hasn't been with them that long either. I also want to try to check on her family back in Russia. You never know what that might turn up. We know that certain of our immigrants from Russia who have settled in Brooklyn are not exactly what you'd call 'model citizens.'"

"All right, Adam, I know you're pretty damn good on the computer, so let's see what you can find. If you need me to make any calls to our counterparts in other agencies to remind them that they need to be cooperative and forthcoming, I'm willing to do it. Some of these people are such asses. They forget that what goes around comes around, and one day they'll be asking us to do them a favor. Just keep me in the loop."

"Sure, no problem."

Adam got up and left the office. In his mind, he already formulated a list of sources to check. He was also starting to compile a list of questions for Rick and Maizie. After he had done the research, he was pretty sure that he was going to talk to Rick first. He felt that he and Rick had developed a rapport. Rick was a level-headed guy and not someone who was so taken with himself merely because he had "Esq." after his name. Under different circumstances, he and Rick could be friends. Adam felt for him.

CHAPTER 19

As Jason was about five minutes from Rick and Maizie's house, he called Rick on the cell. Rick answered on the second ring when he saw Jason's name come up on the phone. "Hey, Rick, it's me. I'll be at your house in a couple of minutes. I need to talk to you alone. Can you come outside the house and talk to me in the driveway or garage?"

"Yeah, sure, what's up?" Rick answered a little warily.

"Look, I'll be at your house in literally three minutes, so just come outside. It's important."

"Okay. See ya. I'm coming out."

Jason pulled into the driveway, and Rick was standing in the garage with the garage door open. Jason flung open the car door and walked with purpose toward Rick. He walked right into the garage and looked around to see if anyone was within earshot.

"Rick, I know this is gonna sound weird, but you know a couple of years ago when we were down at the shore and we were sitting on the deck and I saw Grandma Fannie talking to Abby on the beach? You couldn't see her, but I did. Remember, she even waved to me?" The words tumbled out of his mouth at breakneck speed.

Rick nodded yes but didn't say anything.

"Well, it's been a few years, and I haven't seen or heard from her again. I don't know if Abby has heard from her either."

Rick was beginning to get impatient with Jason's prelude. He was sleep deprived and stressed, and he had no patience for a stroll down memory lane. "What's the point, Jason?" Rick asked with more than a little annoyance in his voice.

Jason was surprised by the clear tone of annoyance in Rick's voice. Of the two of them, Rick was certainly the more patient one of them. Jason was often impatient and quick to jump to conclusions. He shrugged it off and plowed forward, because he knew the importance of what he was about to tell Rick.

"I've heard from Grandma Fannie." Rick was about to interrupt him, but Jason held up his hand. "Just shut up and listen. This is really important. I've heard from Grandma Fannie twice now. The first time she told me that Abby asked her to help. Grandma Fannie could hear her, but for some reason, she couldn't hear Grandma Fannie. But I could hear her. Neither of us quite knew what to make of it except that Abby had asked her to help us find Grace, and Grandma Fannie thought that she was somehow going to be able to help, but she didn't know how.

"I just heard from her again. We don't entirely know what to make of this, but Grandma Fannie found herself in some Middle Eastern country. She didn't know which one. But here's the incredible thing. Of all people, she was in Steve Goldrick's house. She saw him sitting in his office in his house! That son of a bitch must somehow be involved with Grace's kidnapping. No one was quite sure where he was when he fled the country, right?"

Rick felt as if he had been punched in the stomach. Was he ever going to be free from that bastard? That guy was like a curse in his life.

Jason was waiting for an answer to his question. Rick said, "I don't know where he went. I really didn't care enough to follow up. The law firm might have hired someone to try to find him, but even if they did, you can be sure he's in some place where they don't have extradition to the United States."

Jason nodded. "But why would Steve Goldrick be in any way involved with Grace's kidnapping? You never had any contact with him after you left the firm, did you?"

"Nope," Rick lied. He had never told Jason, or for that matter anyone, that he and Dannie Bevan had blackmailed Steve about the illegal black-market adoptions that Steve had done for years and raked in millions of dollars.

Rick was extremely suspicious about Dannie's murder. The police had never been able to solve her murder, but between the time she was attacked and the time she died in the hospital from her brain injuries, Rick was beside himself with worry. He couldn't give the police any leads because he couldn't tell them that he and Dannie had blackmailed Steve. Everyone attributed Rick's upset to the fact that he and Dannie were close friends. Dannie had thrown him the proverbial life preserver. She offered him a job and put him in a position of authority in the new law firm she was starting in White Plains. At the same time, Steve had been lying through his teeth, telling Rick that he would go to bat with the partners in the law firm in New York City to let Rick come back to work after he had tried to commit suicide.

When Steve Goldrick disappeared into what seemed like thin air, they thought they were home free. They were certain Steve had fled the United States and would never dare return for fear of being arrested and spending the rest of his natural life in prison, instead of in some tropical paradise living off his considerable fortune. They should have counted on Steve's greed and that he was also smart and devious.

The other secret that Rick carried with him every day was from the day of Dannie's funeral. As they were leaving the grave site, some man had "accidentally" bumped into Rick. Instead of picking Rick's pocket, this man had left something in Rick's coat pocket. It was a flash drive. Late that afternoon after the funeral, when Maizie had gone upstairs to take a nap, Rick played the flash drive. When the picture came on there was a man in the shadow with his voice disguised who laid out the scenario.

Apparently, Steve Goldrick had fathered a girl with a married friend, Rita, when she was separated from her husband for a short time. Rita never told her husband after she reconciled with him. Steve tried to get her to leave her husband for good, and she may have been the one person that Steve deeply loved in his whole life. He helped her monetarily with the child, and it turned out that that girl grew up and became Rick's mother.

The person on the flash drive also said that because Rick was Steve's grandson, Steve was going to give Rick a free pass and let him live. Rick had hoped against hope that this was going to be true, but the circumstances of Grace's kidnapping made him believe what he had always feared. Steve Goldrick would exact revenge in some way sooner or later. Steve might not kill him physically, but he might kill Rick emotionally by kidnapping Grace. Steve would technically keep his promise by not killing Rick as he had done with Dannie, but that was it.

All of this raced through Rick's mind at lightning speed. It seemed like a nanosecond to Rick, but it may have been several seconds. When Rick finally looked back at Jason, Jason was staring at him intently, waiting for Rick to say something, which was unusual. Jason always had something to say and had little ability to sit or stand still while others were lost in their own thoughts.

"Were you going to say something?" Jason asked.

Rick shook his head no and gestured to Jason to continue.

"I'm going to call Abby and tell her about Grandma Fannie talking to me and that Steve Goldrick is in some Middle Eastern country, but in any case, the son of a bitch is somehow involved with all of this and may have been the prime mover in the whole thing. Do you have any idea of what to tell Grandma Fannie about how to figure out what country she was in? She seemed to have no sense of where she had been."

Rick leaned over on the hood of the car and put both elbows on the hood and rested his head in his hands. He was trying to make some sense out of what was beginning to feel incomprehensible.

Jason read Rick's body language. It seemed that the absurdity of the situation was taking over Jason. It was something akin to laughing out loud at a funeral. Wholly inappropriate, but laughter can be borne out of nervousness all the same.

Jason said, "It's weird that we're trying to figure out how to tell my long dead grandmother to wander around in some Middle Eastern country and see where the hell she is." With that, Jason tried very hard, but completely unsuccessfully, to stifle a laugh. The next instant he was laughing out loud despite himself.

Rick looked up from where he was leaning on the hood of the car, first with a quizzical look on his face, and then as he realized that Jason couldn't contain his laughter, Rick grinned and then started to laugh too.

Jason said, "Can't you just imagine Grandma Fannie running around the streets in some Middle Eastern country yelling at some guys in long robes that they are in her way?" Because Rick nodded yes, he emboldened Jason to continue and to get more outrageous. "From what I know, Grandma Fannie liked to throw back a few. Can't you visualize it with her walking around with a beer in one hand and a cigarette in the other, and all the Arab guys moving out of her way as she stares them down?"

Rick was laughing so hard that his shoulders were shaking. "I wish I had known her. From what I hear, she got what she wanted when she wanted it." Rick raised his voice several octaves to sound like a woman. "You, sir, over there, exactly where is this? I know we're not in Pearl River, New York, but this place is like a toaster oven, and the beer is hot and disgusting. You can never get a proper drink outside the United States."

Rick and Jason were wiping their eyes they were laughing so hard. God, it felt good to laugh and even for a few minutes enjoy the absurdity of the imagined situation—and get away from reality.

CHAPTER 20

After getting themselves back under control, Jason and Rick went into the house. Abby was sitting working on her laptop. "Hi, Abby, how are you doing today?" Jason asked as he walked over and kissed her hello on the cheek.

Even though a few years had passed since Abby and Jason had been reconciled as mother and long-lost son, Abby still felt a tug of emotion whenever Jason kissed her. It had taken a while for Jason to come around, and at the beginning he had been cautious with her. Abby told Jason he was the son she gave up for adoption. It took time for Jason to be comfortable with that. However, after Jason's two daughters fell in love with Abby as their grandmother and Jason's wife Beth really liked Abby as well, a lot of Jason's initial resistance eroded, and he gave Abby a chance to be in his life.

Rick asked, "Abby, where's Maiz?"

"She's upstairs."

Rick said, "I'll get her. Jason's got some really interesting things to tell you and Maiz."

Abby looked from Rick to Jason, who had now busied himself with checking out what was in the refrigerator. In a few seconds Rick and Maizie appeared in the kitchen, Maizie with her hair pulled back into a ponytail and no makeup. Abby couldn't help but notice the dark circles under Maizie's eyes, and her heart ached for her.

Rick said, "Go ahead, Jas, tell Maizie and Abby what you told me."

Abby and Maizie both looked expectantly at Jason.

"Okay, so we all know that we haven't had any leads on Grace's whereabouts or the kidnappers." Jason took a deep breath as he struggled for the next thing to say. Abby and Maizie were both staring at him so intently that he thought they were going to jump in his mouth and drag the next words out. Even though Jason knew that what he was about to say was true, he still felt stupid saying it out loud. "Well, I've heard from Grandma Fannie. Twice."

Abby and Maizie both leaned forward noticeably in their chairs.

"Oh, for God's sake, Jason, just cut to the chase," Rick said with some annoyance in his voice again.

Jason gave Rick an "I'll turn you to stone" look but continued. "Anyway, Grandma Fannie knows that Abby has asked her for help. She can hear you, Abby, but for some reason, you can't hear her responses."

The thought that flashed through Abby's mind was that this was probably the first time in her life when she wasn't grateful for not hearing her mother's opinions and ideas since some of them were outrageous and often ended up getting Abby into a predicament.

"Grandma Fannie found herself in some Middle Eastern country and in the home of Steve Goldrick, of all people. The problem is that she doesn't know where she was, nor does she know why she was in Steve Goldrick's house. She assumes that he has something to do with Grace's kidnapping or even that he orchestrated it, but right now that seems to be a hunch. She hasn't seen any evidence that Grace is there in his house, but she doesn't know why else she would be in Steve's house if he wasn't somehow connected. Grandma Fannie acknowledged that Abby had asked for her help and that's why she thinks if she was there with Steve—he's a link to Grace in some way."

Jason looked from Abby to Maizie in much the same way that a kid who just finished playing a new piece he learned on the piano looks to his parents to clap at his accomplishment.

"All right, Mom, way to go!" Abby said. "I knew you would help us. I don't care how you do it, as long as you do it."

Maizie looked at Abby and said, "Mom, you have the most experience with this. You know that Nana can communicate with us. Is there some reason why she can't go see what country she's in?"

Abby looked at Maizie and said, "Honestly, Maizie, I never knew how or when she 'appeared' to me. She may have known, but she sort of just showed up, for lack of a better term, when she wanted to tell me something. Sometimes I wished she hadn't shown up when she did." Abby looked pointedly at Rick. Abby continued, "If you remember, it was Mom who told me to bring the water bottle up to you on the bridge. On my way up, I lost my footing and fell over the edge of the bridge. You had to come down while I was hanging on for dear life and pull me back to safety. That was another of Mom's brilliant ideas. She had lots of those brilliant ideas throughout my life, but that was the quint-essential bad idea. Mom does what she does, and I'm not sure that has changed even though she's been dead for a long time."

Jason looked somewhat bewildered. "So what should I tell her?"

Abby took another second and then answered. "Jason, why don't you just ask her if she can somehow get herself back to Steve's house. Then when she's there, maybe she can go out and see a landmark that would tell her, and us, where she is. This is a little bit like asking who's buried in Grant's Tomb." Abby finished and shrugged.

Jason asked, "Why do you think it would be that easy?"

Abby looked at Jason as if she were explaining something to a child. "Why do you think it's not that easy? We have no way of knowing which it is. Maybe she simply never thought to do that. Unless she tells us differently, she may be able to do this. She 'floats,' or whatever it is, all over the world. She talks to you in your car on the Thruway, and then she's in the Middle East. How do we know that she can't go outside the house and see what's there? I know this is freaking you out, Jason, but she's communicating with you. Let's try to think logically and see where this gets us."

Jason looked at Abby as if she had spoken to him in Chinese and he had no idea of what she was saying. "But . . ."

"But what?" Now Abby really sounded as if she was speaking to a recalcitrant child.

"Okay, I guess I'll ask her." Jason didn't sound all that convinced.

Maizie, who had been uncharacteristically quiet during this exchange, finally said something. "So go ahead, Jason."

"Go ahead, what?"

Now Rick chimed in. "God, Jason, how stupid are you? Try talking to her now and see if she answers you. Abby, is there any reason why Jason can't initiate the conversation?"

Abby said, "I think you can certainly try. Sometimes I'd speak to her and even 'see' her. Sometimes I'd initiate the conversation and she'd answer, and sometimes I'd hear back from her at another time."

Jason had the look of someone who was being pushed off a high diving board and didn't like it one bit. "Okay, Grandma, it's Jason." He hesitated and then went on. "I don't know if you're around or if you heard this whole conversation with Abby, Rick, Maizie, and me. Can you go back to Steve's house and look around to see the name of a hotel, school, or something that will let us know where he is?" Now Jason was warming to the task. "While you're at it, if you could get his address, that would be terrific. We also need some proof that Steve's involved with the kidnapping. We're assuming that's true, but right now we don't have any hard evidence. We'd need more than what we have now to go the police. Right, Rick?"

Rick nodded and said, "Yeah, we need something to tie him to the kidnapping that we can bring to law enforcement that would make them act."

Jason was like a kid who was getting ever more excited and into this. "Did you hear that Grandma? Did you hear Rick's answer?"

Abby put her hand up in front of her mouth not to laugh. First, he was freaking out that he was supposed to talk to Fannie, then he was reluctant, and now he was acting like an interpreter at the United Nations.

"So Grandma, what do you say? Did you hear my questions? Can you answer me?" came the staccato questions.

No answer.

Jason looked at Abby as if she were supposed to do something to make this happen. "What do you think, Abby? Is she going to answer me?"

Abby smiled at Jason's exuberance. "I really feel pretty confident that she will answer you—when the time is right. Don't forget, it's not like you're talking to her on the phone. She's coming back from the other side, which is a remarkable feat in and of itself."

CHAPTER 21

Rick was doing a little work for the office but nothing significant because he didn't have very much concentration considering the situation and that he still wasn't getting uninterrupted sleep. He'd read and responded to some emails, and he looked at a few short agreements. The other attorneys were being terrific and handling his court appearances and covering his real estate closings. He felt so good about the people he worked with since they were all pitching in to help. He wanted very much to believe that this was good karma returned to him for his helping the young associates in the firm and not taking credit for it. However, he had a hard time reconciling that with the fact that his wife and son had been killed in a senseless car crash and now he was being put through hell again with Grace. What kind of karma was that?

Then there was that voice sometimes close to his consciousness and sometimes tamped down that reminded him that Dannie Bevan had been killed probably as the result of their having blackmailed Steve Goldrick. So maybe the karma was proceeding as it was supposed to with him. He could never resolve this in his own mind, although it played out over and over.

He took in the mail and glanced casually at the magazines and the letters. The last letter in the group, right above the magazines, had no return address, but had a postmark not from the United States. In fact, it was in Arabic, and it made Rick freeze in his tracks. His mind raced and made the connection, and he hoped against hope he was wrong. He tried to walk deliberately to his office. As soon as he closed the door, he ripped open the envelope and he saw a small flash drive. If his heart was beating fast as he walked to his office, it was now racing. Rick knew he was going to find out in a matter of seconds what Steve wanted.

He made sure the door to his office was closed tightly, and he tried to breathe normally while he waited for the laptop to boot up. This was agony. The computer booted up in the normal amount of time, but in that few seconds, a jumble of thoughts sped through his mind. He was certain this was not going to be good, but now the low thud of fear in his brain became a roar. He closed his eyes for a second before he put the flash drive in the port, then exhaled a long breath and waited for something to show on the screen.

It was the same image of a man with his face in the shadows and the voice distorted as Rick had seen on the flash drive put in his pocket at the cemetery on the day of Dannie's funeral. Rick wanted to know, but he didn't want to know. This must be the same feeling a cancer patient had while waiting for the doctor to come in and give the patient the test results. You wanted to know, but you didn't want to know.

The distorted voice said, "Hello, Rick. No doubt you remember our last conversation some years ago. I kept my promise not to kill you, but you know that I'm an Old Testament kind of guy. An eye for an eye and a tooth for a tooth. You really messed up my life for no good reason, except your own greed.

"Your life wasn't the least bit impacted by what you did. No, I take that back. Your life actually got better. You bought your big house and, now that Dannie Bevan is dead, I understand that you moved up and became a partner in the law firm. Yeah, things worked out very well for you.

"I wasn't ready to uproot my life in a couple of days and move my family permanently out of the United States. I had to take care of a whole lot of shit in an incredibly short time because of you. I didn't get my big payday from the law firm as I was supposed to when I retired. I lost a huge chunk of change from the law firm because of you and Dannie. I was also going to wind down my side business over time or maybe let it be an annuity for my daughter and son-in-law with some great income for them as well. But no, you had to be a big shot and get your rocks off on being a 'player' for the first time in your miserable life. Well, if you think that you can play with the real men then you have to be able to take it as well as dish it out. You really have no idea what that entails. Every action has consequences. You're such an idiot that you never realized that. You two thought you could just waltz in and take what was mine. Bullshit. So now you're paying the price for your actions. Not too much fun, is it?

"So maybe we all have to pay with what is most important to us. There's no question that I worked my ass off to get up the ladder and I was very successful doing it. But you didn't let me finish a great career on my terms. And in addition, the dough was really important to me, and you took that away, too, so you made me pay on two counts."

There was a pause in the commentary, and Rick had the urge to pick up the laptop and throw it against the wall. Steve was waxing philosophical, and Rick had no patience for this crap. Steve was musing about his life and his career as if he were some elder statesman, when in fact, he was no more than a common criminal. Maybe worse than a common criminal because Steve had preyed on desperate people hoping to adopt a child. He preyed on people for one thing and one thing only—money.

Steve finally continued. "Let me finish my thought. We all have to pay with what is important to us. I've already paid. Now it's your turn." Steve let out a snicker, which came out as some very weird sound with the voice distortion. "That's it. You'll have a long time to think about things." With that the screen went dead.

Rick pounded his hand onto the desk and sank down onto his knees.

Steve was definitely taunting him, and it had worked. Rick was no closer to finding Grace, and Steve had put the knife in his heart. There was no ransom request. There was nothing. It didn't seem as if Steve wanted anything except to inflict pain. Just stabbing pain. And it had worked.

All of a sudden, Fannie found herself sitting in Rick's office. She hadn't willed herself to come here. It seemed that she was just "here." She also had no idea of the reason for her visit. She would find out very shortly.

Fannie watched as Rick turned on the computer and then inserted the flash drive. It was apparent that he was agitated. Fannie was surprised by the picture on the screen and the distorted voice. Since she had died in 1975, before computers were a staple, Fannie was continually amazed by what could be done and what was done with computers. Fannie remembered a time before television was invented, when everything was only on the radio. Then you had to use your imagination. Now everything was right in front of you on a screen, but what could be done with a computer was incredible.

Fannie kept one eye on the screen and one eye on Rick. Rick was becoming more agitated as the man spoke. Fannie had no idea who he was. She had no idea what the man was talking about when he said that Rick and Dannie had blackmailed him. The man spoke of the blackmail with authority and with an air of finality. It appeared to Fannie that what he was saying on the screen was true, both from his language and from Rick's reaction.

There had always been questions about Dannie Bevans's death, and no killer had ever been found. Fannie also knew how badly Rick had taken Dannie's death. Everyone had assumed that Rick took Dannie's death so badly because Dannie had been such a good friend to him. She had given him a job in her new law firm at a time when Rick's former firm was kicking him to the curb without a second thought. It was that awful man, Steve Goldrick. He had not been one to be trusted. Not only had Dannie given Rick a job when he needed it for his self-esteem, but she had also put him in a position of authority. It appeared that there was more here than anyone but Rick and Dannie knew. Dannie's lips had been closed by death. In fact, a violent death.

Fannie had always liked Rick. He had been a good husband who was truly devoted to Maizie. Maizie was very much in love with him, and they seemed to be a good match for each other. Fannie could also see that Abby liked him as well and was happy that Maizie had settled down with Rick. For his part, Rick never forgot what Abby had done for him on perhaps the bleakest night of his life. Fannie could see the bond between them.

Fannie didn't want to believe that Rick was capable of blackmail. As the man continued to speak, it began to dawn on Fannie that there was a very good chance that this man was none other than Steve Goldrick. Fannie had never believed in coincidences when she was alive. Now from the other side, she was certain that there were no coincidences. People who were alive didn't have the capacity to see the big picture. As the New Testament said, "Now we see through a glass darkly, but then we shall see face to face." For some reason, the people on earth didn't have the capacity to see or understand all that was going on. They were still seeing "through a glass darkly."

CHAPTER 22

It took a few minutes for Rick to compose himself to come out of his office. He walked quietly through the house and out to the garage. Someone watching him walk through the house and now back his car out of the garage would have thought that absolutely nothing was amiss. Rick looked calm and his actions appeared to be measured, but those actions belied what was churning in both his mind and body. Rick wasn't even sure what he would have said to Maizie if she were between his office and the door to the garage, nor would he have been able to tell her where he was going. He simply didn't know at this point.

Rick drove on autopilot for some undetermined amount of time. He finally pulled into a parking lot of a shopping center and drove into an aisle far away from the stores. He sat there for a few minutes, not knowing what to do, who to call, or if he should just sit there. He needed to get back under control before he saw or spoke to Maizie, or anybody for that matter. He was afraid that he would not be able to hide his upset from her over this latest bombshell. He was sure Maizie would pick up on something, and he didn't know what he would say to her. What was there to say to her? Nothing and everything.

Finally, Rick reached into his pocket for his phone and dialed a number from the speed dial, praying silently that he would not have to leave a message. *God damn it! The voice mail came on.* Rick panicked and hung up. What message should he leave?

Rick sat for another minute or two and tried to think of what to say. Several thoughts went through his mind and he dismissed them all as too complicated or too wordy. He dialed again. When the voice mail came on again, Rick simply said, "Dr. Burke, it's Rick. This is an emergency. I need to talk to you as soon as possible." Nothing fancy, nothing wordy, but this message was as sincere as it was true.

When Rick hung up, he leaned his head back into the headrest, and sighed loudly. He truly had no idea of what to do.

Fortunately for Rick, Dr. Burke was finishing up with a patient and less than five minutes later retrieved the message. He did not like what he heard, both from the content of the message as well as from Rick's voice.

When his cell phone rang, it startled Rick. He saw the name of the caller, and Rick said out loud, "Thank God."

"Rick, what's going on? I just got your message."

"Thanks so much for getting back to me so fast. Is there any chance I can see you? It's about Grace."

"Did they find her? Is she okay?"

"No, but now I have a lead, and it's not good. In fact, it's really bad. When can I see you?"

"Rick, if it's that much of an emergency, I'll wait at the office for you. How soon can you get here?"

"I can be there in ten minutes."

"Okay, come in now."

Rick started the car, and now he was no longer on autopilot. He had a place to go and a goal. The traffic was light, and Rick arrived, found a parking space right away, and hurried into the office. The door from the waiting room to Dr. Burke's office was open, and as Rick walked in, Dr. Burke came out to greet him. He wanted to see Rick's demeanor and how he looked. Dr. Burke did not like what he saw. Rick looked pale, and his eyes were sunken and bloodshot. His expression was one of total upset.

Dr. Burke didn't waste a second. "C'mon in and sit down. What's going on? Do you want some water?"

Rick nodded, and Dr. Burke retrieved two bottles of water and handed one to him. Rick could never see water bottles without thinking of the night he had tried to commit suicide by jumping off the bridge. Abby had managed to keep him from jumping, but when she tried to bring water bottles up to him on the bridge, she had slipped. It always brought a half smile to his face, and he never saw a water bottle without thinking how close he had come to ending it all and how fortunate he was to have met Abby, and then Maizie. That was why today was even more difficult. Rick was going to have to come clean with them and lose their respect and trust.

Rick had seen Dr. Burke in a shirt and tie without his suit jacket on. Today, not only did Dr. Burke not have on his suit jacket on, but his tie was also loosened and his shirt sleeves were rolled up. Rick had never seen Dr. Burke like that, and the thought that flashed through his mind was that somehow Dr. Burke knew that this was going to be a long and arduous session.

After what Fannie had seen on the computer in Rick's office, she desperately wanted to talk to Abby. Fannie wanted to make sense of what she had seen, and she thought Abby would be the right person to bounce this off. Fannie willed herself to be in Abby's presence. Abby was sitting at her kitchen table and was balancing her checkbook. Abby was so clear to Fannie that she felt she could reach out and touch her shoulder, although Abby would not feel it.

"Abby, it's Mom. Can you hear me?"

No answer. Fannie tried again. "Abby, it's Mom. I want to talk to you. It's important that we speak. I don't know why you can't hear me now. I can see and hear you. I really think that it would be better for us to talk about the situation with Grace and Steve Goldrick's involvement than for me to talk to Jason about it. There are things that you would understand much better than Jason. I really wish I knew why you could hear me the last time I came back, but you can't hear me now."

Abby looked up from the calculator. She glanced around the room and cocked her head to the left, as if listening for something. Then she shrugged and went back to her bank statement.

CHAPTER 23

Jason was jogging on the treadmill and watching the Yankees at the same time. When the inning ended and the commercial came on, Jason looked down to get the remote and change the channel. Even though he pointed the remote directly at the television, the channel did not change. He hit the remote with the heel of his hand, thinking that maybe the batteries were starting to die. Nothing happened when he hit it a second time. It also appeared that the volume was now lower, and as Jason looked down at the remote, he heard a voice not coming from the direction of the television.

His head snapped to the right and as he did so, he lost his footing on the treadmill, fell off, and, fortunately, landed in a heap on the couch. Fannie did the celestial equivalent of stifling a laugh, and said, "Jason, are you okay? You have to be more careful. You were lucky the couch was there. You really are going to have to get used to my talking to you and not get so jumpy every time I speak to you. You practically drove off the road one of the times I spoke to you."

Jason looked up from where he was extricating himself from the pillows on the couch. "Jeez, Grandma, you scared me. I don't get why you think this is normal and it should not scare the shit out of me! Oh, sorry, Grandma, didn't mean to say 'shit.'"

"Jason, I thought we already had an understanding between us that I was not a prude in life and I'm still not a prude. I think I told you I was quite a hell-raiser as a young woman. I see that you're watching the Yankees. Are you a big fan?"

"Yup. Been a Yankee fan from the moment we moved back to the States from England. I played tennis as a kid because my dad played and he had no idea of what was going on with cricket. I fell in love with baseball as soon as we got back to America. It would have been so good if we had the internet when we were growing up because we probably could have had the baseball games streamed in."

Fannie didn't quite know what Jason was talking about with all the internet stuff and she didn't really care, so she just let it go. "I was a big Mets fan. I would listen to them on the radio."

"Wasn't TV invented then?" Jason answered his own question. "Of course, it was. *I Love Lucy* and *The Honeymooners* were on TV in the 1950s, and the Mets came into being in the National League in the '60s. So why were you listening to them on the radio?" Jason's tone was truly perplexed.

"I always listened to baseball on the radio from the time I was a Brooklyn Dodgers fan. It was more fun to use your imagination," Fannie said emphatically.

Jason shrugged. "So why are you here now, Grandma?"

"I know that Steve Goldrick is definitely involved with Grace's kidnapping. Before this, I was pretty sure I was right. Now I'm sure."

"Grandma, I asked you if you could tell us where Steve Goldrick is. You told us he's in the Middle East, but we need you to be more specific, so we can find him."

"I'm not really sure if I can do that."

"Why not? You were in the Middle East and now you're here in New Jersey, so you can get around, for lack of a better term. Can you go back to the Middle East and find out where he is? If you gave us some landmarks or the name of a city, that would be terrific."

"I don't know if I can do that. If I know where I want to go, then somehow I can actually get there. But I have no idea how I ended up in Steve Goldrick's house, wherever it was. I can try thinking about going there again, but I truly don't know if it will work.

"I want you to tell Maizie, Rick, and Abby what I said. Even if I can't be more specific, I would think that among you, you should be able to get some private investigator to find him. There must be some trail of where he is. We know he's living in a beautiful place, so he's living in opulence. That rules out certain countries and certain places within each country."

"True, but that's still a lot of territory to cover. It really would help if you can get some more information. Almost anything you give us would be a big help."

"You're right, Jason, but how am I going to read street signs written in Arabic?"

"I've never been to the Middle East, but I presume there are some signs or names that are in English as well as Arabic. You've really gotta try hard, Grandma. Again, maybe there would be some landmark you can give us. You're our best hope."

Fannie nodded, and then realized she had to answer Jason in a way he could understand. "I will try, Jason. I will try very hard, but please make sure you give them the message."

CHAPTER 24

Rick took a long swig from the bottle of water Dr. Burke had given him. Dr. Burke watched him intently, having decided to let Rick start the conversation. Rick fiddled with the cap on the water bottle and then looked Dr. Burke in the eye. There was no good way to start except to jump into the ice water headfirst.

"You remember when Dannie Bevan was murdered under suspicious circumstances in her house, and nothing was taken from the house? Her purse and credit cards were right there on the chair next to her body."

Dr. Burke nodded.

"They never had any leads on her killer, and the case is still unsolved. I had my suspicions about it, which I kept to myself."

Dr. Burke was about to ask why Rick never voiced those suspicions, but then decided against it. He let Rick continue.

"At the cemetery at Dannie's funeral, some guy bumped against me. He looked a little out of place with the rest of the mourners, but it happened so fast that I couldn't put it into any context. When we got home from the funeral and the luncheon, Maizie went upstairs, and I put my hand in my raincoat looking for my keys. The guy had put a flash drive in my pocket.

"When I played it, it made me sick. There was a man in the shadows with his voice distorted who said that he was taking revenge on Dannie for what she and I had done. I was sure it was Steve Goldrick, and the reason I knew it was true was because Dannie and I had blackmailed Steve."

"You blackmailed Steve? Over what?" The tone in Dr. Burke's voice was alarmed.

"Dannie and I somehow got Steve's adoption files from the storage place by mistake when we moved the office. Steve had been running a black-market adoption ring for years and charging desperate couples $100,000 for each baby. Needless to say, he was pocketing the money himself. His secretary, Helen, was a co-conspirator and he was taking care of her very well financially. Sometime during the course of his long and 'distinguished' career doing the black-market adoptions, he even got his daughter and son-in-law involved too."

"So I gather from what you're saying that you didn't go to the authorities with this information."

Rick looked down at his hands and swallowed hard. "No, no, we didn't. Not right away. Dannie had this idea that we would call Steve and tell him what we had, which was boxes of files, which would send him to jail for the rest of his life. Dannie told Steve we'd give him ten days to get his affairs in order, before we went to the authorities."

"For a price?"

Rick croaked the word "yes" without looking up at Dr. Burke.

"And did he pay you?"

"Yes."

"How much?"

"A million dollars in cash. We kept our end of the bargain and did not go to the police or DA for ten days for him to get a chance to gather his assets and leave the country. His secretary, Helen, left the country, too." Rick paused for another few seconds and said in a voice only slightly above a whisper, "I knew it was wrong. It went against everything I had ever done in my life. But for some reason, I never objected, nor did I ever try to talk Dannie out of it."

A few more seconds elapsed, and Dr. Burke had a sense that Rick was going to continue without any prompting from him, so he said nothing.

Rick took another swig from the water bottle, looked down at the carpet, and then finally up at Dr. Burke. "Believe it or not, the money wasn't the driving force for me. I think it was about revenge. I was going to stick it to Steve Goldrick for what he had done to me. I thought I was going to get the last laugh. For once, the high and mighty Steve Goldrick had no recourse but to acquiesce to what we were demanding. We met him in the diner to tell him our terms, and it really was unbelievable. He literally was sweating. I had never seen Steve without his suit jacket on, no less with his tie open and sweat pouring down his face."

Rick even had a somewhat wistful look on his face, and then he said with a slight grin, "That was the only moment of comic relief in an otherwise incredibly intense session. As Steve was storming out of the diner, he bumped into a waiter and ended up with a good part of a plate of eggs on him. It truly was egg on his face."

Both Rick and Dr. Burke laughed a little, but it was laughing from nerves.

"I wanted to tell Maizie about this, I really did. But you can imagine that there was never the right time. You don't just waltz into the kitchen one day and say, 'Oh, by the way, Maiz, I never told you I'm a blackmailer.' I was haunted about Dannie's death, but I didn't know what to do. Steve was in the wind, and if I told the police what I suspected, they'd want to know why I was saying it."

"I guess you and Dannie felt you were insulated by Steve's crimes, and therefore you two didn't have to worry about committing blackmail."

"Yes—what was Steve going to do about it? He couldn't very well go to the police and say he was being blackmailed about the illegal adoptions. Plus, we knew he had to leave the United States and leave very quickly. He had to make some very quick decisions to get out of the country, and he could never return without worrying that he would be prosecuted and the very real possibility that he would go to jail for the rest of his life.

"Wherever he landed, you know he landed on his feet and with piles of money."

"Less the million dollars he gave to you and Dannie. And you truly never thought that he would take revenge in some way on you and Dannie? Steve never struck me as a 'turn the other cheek kind of guy.' He was used to winning. Look at how he practiced law. From what you have described to me in the past, he was a ruthless opponent. He got what he wanted, no matter the cost or, as they say in the Army, the collateral damage."

"I agree that it was an incredibly stupid thing to do, but Dannie was no dope and she was extremely persuasive. It just all happened so fast."

"Rick, I understand what you're saying, but you were distraught on the phone, and I don't think that this was caused by something that happened years ago. What's really happening now?"

Rick's face turned ashen, and he said, "It's Grace. I got another flash drive from Steve, and it's obvious that he is behind the kidnapping wherever he is. He told me in the flash drive from Dannie's funeral that he was going to give me a free pass. I thought he meant that he could have killed me as easily as he had Dannie killed, but he didn't. I guess I wanted to believe that the whole thing was over. It appeared that it was—until now."

"What does he want from you?"

"That's just the thing. He's not looking for ransom. He's looking for revenge in its purest form. He wants to torture me, and he wants me to know it's his doing. He's got Grace, or someone he's paying has Grace, and he has no intention of returning her." The tone in Rick's voice had turned desperate. "What am I going to do? I'm responsible for Grace's kidnapping. I don't know if we'll ever get her back." With that he put his head in his hands in a sign of complete despair.

Dr. Burke got up from his chair and walked over to the couch where Rick was sitting. He put his arm around him and just let him know he was there for him. In his heart, Dr. Burke knew this was going to be a long siege, one from which Rick and/or his marriage might never recover.

Rick finally got a little bit back under control and said, "What do I do about Maizie? I lost Jennifer and Adam, and now I've lost Grace and, because of that, I will probably lose Maizie."

Dr. Burke had gone back to his chair and now stared directly into Rick's eyes. "Look, Rick, I don't have any easy answers. No matter what you do, this is going to be extremely difficult. The first thing you have to do is tell Maizie the truth. You should be prepared that she may fall to pieces because you and Grace are the two pivotal points in her life. She's reeling from the attack and from the loss of Grace, and it's going to be very traumatic that you are the cause of Grace's kidnapping. She probably is going to be enraged at you for a lot of reasons. You don't need me to enumerate them for you. You know them full well in your heart."

Rick was locked into everything Dr. Burke was saying. He was nodding his head slowly. Once or twice, he wiped a tear from his eye with the back of his hand. "There's nothing you've said that I haven't been over in my own mind a thousand times already. I prayed that this day would never come, and we would never have to have this conversation. I prayed with my whole being that I would never have to tell Maizie about Dannie, but most of all about Grace. Maizie may never forgive me for this. That is a very real possibility.

"When I first came to you after Jen and Adam's deaths, I blamed myself for not being there when they were hit by the other car because I might have been able to save them, but I didn't cause that crash. I wasn't responsible for that crash. This is a totally different situation. I am directly responsible for Grace's kidnapping. And it may be the end of Maizie and me. If that's the case, it will be the end of me."

"Look, Rick, we need to discuss how you're going to tell Maizie because you have to tell her, and tell her soon. Then I think you two have to try to get on the same page about what to do about finding Steve Goldrick so you can find Grace."

CHAPTER 25

It was the longest drive in the world for Rick. He had been on some horrible drives in his life that he could remember. As a young lawyer, he had worked very hard as the second chair on a criminal case, and Rick had grown very fond of the client, who was only twenty-two years old. The jury had convicted the client of assault in the first degree, despite some extenuating circumstances. The morning of the sentencing, Rick dreaded going to court to hear what the sentence was going to be because he saw it as the beginning of a downward spiral for this young man, which would probably ruin his life. It had, in fact, ruined his life because he was stabbed to death in prison.

The other drive that Rick remembered as being too painful for words was the night he decided to climb up on the bridge to commit suicide. He was in such agony over the death of Jennifer and Adam that he couldn't stand the pain for another day, yet there was some faint voice deep within him that still wanted to live. That made it even more excruciating because both sides were pulling him in some real life and death tug of war.

Rick arrived at the house and pulled into the garage. He turned off the motor and sat motionless in the car for a few minutes. He had gone over this with Dr. Burke only a short time earlier, but right now it felt as if his mind was a blank and his mouth was bone dry. This could very well be the most important conversation of his life. As an attorney, Rick knew he was good with words and that he could be very persuasive, but at this moment, words seemed to have escaped him and he felt empty. He loved Maizie so much, and yet he knew his actions and his silence had betrayed her. If she couldn't get past this, and if her anger and hurt were too great, there was a very good possibility that he could lose her.

Abby called her Hurricane Maizie. It was a great name, because Maizie could swoop into a room and suddenly everything changed with her presence. She was capable of great love and great emotion. At this moment in time, Rick was quite apprehensive of the great emotion. Rick knew the emotions would only be searing anger and intense disappointment.

The word "disappointment," also triggered something else very powerful in Rick. He knew that Abby was going to be completely disappointed in him. In a very convoluted way, Rick knew he had several separate yet intertwined relationships with Abby. Rick owed Abby his life for not letting him commit suicide on the bridge, so he and Abby had that bond that was only between the two of them. Then, of course, Abby was his mother-in-law, which was another relationship. The third independent relationship was that Abby was Jason's birth mother. Rick was afraid to dwell on what would happen to these three relationships if he and Maizie couldn't work things out. *God, what a mess*, Rick thought. *If you read this in a novel, you wouldn't believe it could be this bad.*

Although he had discussed this at length with Dr. Burke, Rick wished desperately that he could put this discussion off to another time. But he also knew that the longer he put this off, the worse it would be. Up until he received the flash drive, he could say that he had suspicions that Steve Goldrick was somehow involved with the kidnapping, but he didn't know for sure. Now that he knew for sure, every moment he waited before talking to Maizie was only digging the hole that much deeper—a hole he might well never climb out of. He had even toyed with the idea of speaking to Abby first, thinking that she would most probably be the more reasonable of the two of them. Yet he knew in his heart that he had to talk to Maizie first, even though it would be light years more difficult.

He took a deep breath and got out of the car. He walked across the garage and opened the door to the kitchen. As he opened the door, he realized that his life might never be the same again. He was reminded of the saying above the entrance to the Bridge of Sighs in Venice. "Abandon hope all ye who enter here."

Maizie was in the kitchen as he walked in. She took one look at Rick and said, "What's the matter?"

All he could say was, "Maiz, I have something very important to tell you."

CHAPTER 26

It had been a long night—a very long night, with virtually no sleep for either Maizie or Rick. She had indeed run the gamut of emotions, and all of them had been in high gear. Rick was exhausted from lack of sleep but more so from the intense roller coaster of emotions he had been on with her.

Somehow Fannie found herself in the kitchen of Maizie and Rick's house. She didn't know at the beginning of the conversation why she was in the kitchen at this particular time. It happened sometimes, and this was similar to her finding herself in Steve Goldrick's house in the Middle East. She was a quick study, and she had learned that when she found herself in a place she had not wanted to go that she was going to this location for a reason. She had never been a particularly patient person when she was alive, and she was never sure if this newfound patience was a gift or if it was some sort of test or some kind of penance.

She listened as Rick told his story to Maizie and watched as Maizie reacted to what she heard. At first, Fannie was angry at Rick for what he had done, but then she found herself feeling sorry for him since she could see how truly contrite he was. She saw what a terrible burden he had been carrying around inside him for such a long time and what a toll it had taken on him. By the same token, she also saw how betrayed Maizie felt by what Rick had done and the secrets he had kept from her for such a long time.

Maizie's reaction was nothing short of volcanic and violent. At first, she seemed stunned, but then she charged at Rick and pounded him in the chest with her fists. He let her hit him until her energy had drained out of her, and then she slumped down in the kitchen chair and began to sob uncontrollably. Rick stood there and stared at her in disbelief and put his arms around her.

Fannie was almost embarrassed to watch this scene play out, as if she were spying on some act of intimacy between a married couple. She felt helpless as she saw this drama play out over what seemed to her to be a very long night, but she somehow sensed that she was indeed meant to be here in Rick and Maizie's kitchen for some purpose, which was as yet unclear to her.

The only two things Rick and Maizie had been able to agree on was that they would each make a phone call. Maizie would call Abby and ask her to come to the house so that the two of them could tell her what had happened in person. Rick wasn't the least bit convinced that Maizie would be able to hold it together on the phone with Abby when she called her. Rick offered to call Abby himself, but he knew if he called Abby that she would be frantic that something had happened to Maizie. Both Rick and Maizie knew that Abby needed to hear everything for herself and in person. Even if Maizie sounded bad on the phone, which she probably would, since she had been crying and screaming for a good deal of the night, Rick knew that Abby was somewhat used to Maizie's mood swings since the kidnapping.

Rick was emotionally spent after Maizie's outbursts, and yet he had to steel himself for another extremely emotional session with Abby. He was fairly sure that she would not be the emotional volcano that Maizie had been, but he still felt sick about having to tell the whole sordid story to her. Rick had come to realize how much he valued her, and how much it meant to him that she thought well of him.

Fannie was a little relieved that Abby was going to come to the house. She knew Abby was going to be upset, but Fannie also believed that Abby would bring a sense of calm and reason into the house, which at this moment was sorely needed.

Rick was going to make the second of the agreed upon phone calls to Officer Adam Brentano, to ask him to help them formulate a plan to travel to the Middle East and see what they could learn about Steve Goldrick and whether he had Grace with him.

When Maizie went to call Abby, Rick called Dr. Burke to tell him how things had gone. Dr. Burke had told Rick that he could call him anytime that he needed to. Dr. Burke had made it clear to Rick that he knew this was going to be a very difficult and emotionally charged conversation, and so Rick should be prepared for that. He also told Rick that he could call at any time of the day or night that he needed to talk to him.

The last thing he said to Rick was, "Here's my personal cell phone number. My phone will be on, and my wife understands that sometimes I need to deal with emergencies in the middle of the night. This is not the first time it's happened, and it won't be the last time. She understands, and she just goes right back to sleep. This more than qualifies as an emergency. Call if you need me."

It was about 7:30 on Saturday morning when Dr. Burke's cell phone rang. When he looked at the clock by the side of his bed, he was pleasantly surprised that he had slept through the night without a call from Rick. His thought was that Rick would probably call him somewhere before eleven or midnight of the preceding night. His expectation was that Maizie would be hysterical, and that Rick would not know what to do and would need to talk.

The thought crossed his mind that perhaps Maizie had reacted better than they thought. However, after he heard Rick's voice and the fact that the drama had gone on all night, he knew this was going to be a very long and very trying situation.

CHAPTER 27

Officer Adam Brentano liked Rick and Maizie and wished that he had met them under other circumstances. Meeting anyone as the result of a kidnapping was hardly an optimal situation. Despite that, Adam and Rick had gotten along quite well. Since they had spent a lot of time together, the conversation had often meandered around to sports, politics, movies, and novels. When Rick called Adam and told him he had a lead on Grace's kidnappers and wanted to discuss it with him, Adam told him he could be at Rick's house in about fifteen minutes. However, there was something in Rick's voice which made Adam think there was something else going on.

When Adam arrived at the house, Rick answered the door and looked even more haggard than he had remembered seeing him look. He was expecting that Rick would be ecstatic that he had a significant enough lead on the kidnapper to call him. He walked into the house, and Rick shook his hand warmly and asked Adam to follow him into the kitchen. Abby and Maizie were sitting at the kitchen table. Adam took in the scene with a practiced law enforcement eye and saw that Maizie looked worse than Rick. Abby merely looked glum.

Adam had spent enough time in this house with Rick, Maizie, and Abby that he felt comfortable giving both Maizie and Abby a big hug despite the bad vibes in the room. Abby offered Adam a cup of coffee, which he accepted. While she was pouring the coffee and getting the milk from the refrigerator, she asked about Adam's family and how the boys were doing. If Adam wasn't so sure he felt a pall in the room, he would have elaborated on the boys making the varsity team, but he simply answered that they were doing fine.

When Adam had the coffee in front on him and the four of them were all seated around the kitchen table, Rick started the conversation. "This is quite a complicated situation. When we left the law firm in New York City several years ago, by mistake Dannie and I ended up with some of Steve Goldrick's files. Steve was the managing partner of the large law firm in New York City where I worked as an associate. Dannie was a partner.

"Dannie left the firm and started her own firm with Chris McKay in White Plains. She asked me to go with her as a senior associate. This saved me and my career because even though Steve Goldrick promised me that he was going to help me get my job back, he had no intention of helping me. In fact, he was stabbing me in the back with the other partners.

"When Dannie and I were moving files out of storage at the old firm, by mistake we were given some of Steve's closed out files. We found out that Steve Goldrick had been doing black-market adoptions for years and pocketing many hundreds of thousands on the sly. We turned the files over to the DA's office, and Steve left the United States for a country somewhere in the Middle East, presumably where they don't have an extradition treaty with the States.

"I told you when you first came in on this case that Dannie had been murdered under suspicious circumstances in her own house. They never found the killer. Her purse with credit cards and money were still in the kitchen right by her body in plain sight. Nothing had been touched.

"When Dannie was murdered, I had suspicions that Steve Goldrick might have had something to do with it, but no one had been able to get to him to bring him back to the United States for the crimes having to do with the adoptions. I just received a flash drive, which I believe is Steve Goldrick in the shadows with his voice disguised. Of course, there is nothing specific that could prove he's guilty of kidnapping in a court of law, but for our purposes, he's baiting me, and it can only be in relation to Grace. He wasn't asking for money or for anything.

"But for the first time, I think that Steve made a big mistake. He sent the flash drive in an envelope with a postmark from a country in the Middle East. I have since learned that the postmark is from Dubai. This is the first real solid lead we've had, because we need to find him in Dubai, and he may have Grace."

Adam listened intently and said, "I'd like to see the flash drive."

Rick said "Okay, I'll get the laptop."

Before Rick could get up from his chair, Adam said, "If you think that Steve Goldrick is behind all this, why didn't you call the police?"

Rick answered, "As I said, you'll see on the flash drive that there is not enough to arrest him. He speaks in a lot of generalities, but I know he's involved, and he wanted me to know it's him. We need to see what we can find out on our own, without any law enforcement involvement. If he gets wind of this, we'll have lost the element of surprise and our best hope to get Grace back."

There was still something that was not sitting right with Adam, but he had to see the flash drive for himself. Maybe then, things might make more sense. Adam was also uncomfortable that Maizie and Abby were sitting at the table and saying nothing. He knew that Maizie was beside herself about the kidnapping, but it was weird that she wasn't adding to the conversation, nor was she more excited about a good lead to find Grace. Adam couldn't put his finger on it, but he thought that Abby wasn't acting like herself either. They all had been waiting so long for a break in the case that it wasn't making sense to Adam that they weren't acting happier or more excited.

When Rick returned with the laptop and the flash drive, he also had the envelope the flash drive had come in.

"Adam, I don't mean to be presumptuous, but didn't you tell us you were ready to retire from the police department and that you were looking for another career to help you save money for college tuition?" This was the first time Maizie had said anything of substance. "If you are ready to leave the police department, we would love you to go to Dubai and start the investigation. We would make it worth your while to do it for us."

Adam looked up surprised at Maizie's mention of Dubai.

Rick picked up a brown manila envelope from the kitchen counter and waved it in the air before handing it to Adam, who was somewhat puzzled by Rick's actions.

"This is the first time the miserable son of a bitch has made a mistake. I think he was so cocky that he was in control of the situation, or in charge of everything, that he forgot that the envelope with the flash drive had a postmark on it from Dubai," Rick said.

"Let me see it, Rick. You could be right, or it just could be that he gave it to someone and told them to mail it from Dubai."

For a second Rick looked deflated. Adam saw it and said quickly, "This is a real lead. Let's follow it and hope maybe the son of a bitch really did make a mistake. Everyone makes mistakes, even Steve Goldrick. I say we follow this lead and maybe we get lucky. It's better than sitting around with our heads up our asses. I say we make some plans and I'll leave for Dubai. My passport is current."

Rick said, "I'm going with you."

Adam looked him in the eye. "I don't know about that. Steve Goldrick knows who you are. He doesn't know me. That at least gives me the advantage of anonymity. I have a buddy who is a retired US marshal. I'm going to call him and see if he's free to come with me. He can open some doors in Dubai with his international connections."

Maizie spoke up, and this was the most animated Adam had seen her since Grace was kidnapped. "I'm going too."

With that comment, both Rick and Abby laughed out loud, and it broke some of the tension in the room.

"With all due respect," Adam said. "This is not some outing we're going on. We're going into a Middle Eastern country, and we're Americans. We want to fly in under the radar. We don't want to draw any attention to ourselves."

"Adam, Dubai is very westernized. It's very cosmopolitan. They're used to the 'ugly Americans.' This isn't some backwater town. We have to think about this some more before we come to a decision," Rick said.

"Okay, let me speak to my buddy the US marshal and see what he says before we make a final decision."

CHAPTER 28

Fannie didn't like what she had heard from Rick about his involvement with blackmailing Steve Goldrick. Maizie's reaction had been intense to say the least. Fannie understood why Maizie reacted as she had. Rick's confession had struck a blow at the two closest people in Maizie's life. Her child had been kidnapped by some vengeful man who wanted to strike back at her husband. Her husband had lied to her for a long time and probably would never have told her the truth if the kidnapping had not occurred. In her anger, Maizie had screamed at Rick that their life together had been built on a lie.

On the other hand, Fannie also understood what Rick was saying about there never being a good time to tell her despite his good intentions. It resonated with the secret Fannie had never been able to tell Abby when she was alive. Fannie was truly sorry for the pain she had caused Abby, but at the time Fannie could never find the right time to discuss it with Abby, so Fannie did have some sympathy and empathy for Rick and the predicament he was in.

Rick also said that he thought the whole situation was behind him, since years has gone by and he had heard nothing else from

Steve Goldrick. Fannie could also see how much pain Rick was in, both for himself and for causing this much pain to Maizie.

Fannie thought that this fuller understanding of situations, without being judgmental of the people involved, might be the result of "seeing the big picture in the afterlife" as she continued to tell her family. She didn't want there to be this much strife between Rick and Maizie, so she tried to concentrate on something she could "do" to help them.

She truly had no idea of how much "time" had elapsed, as people measure time on earth. However, the next thing she was aware of was being back in the office at Steve Goldrick's house. She exhaled a big breath. She didn't know which she thought was worse, that she was here again or how much she didn't want to be here again.

To calm herself, she roamed through the main floor of the house and looked at the sculptures and paintings. She guessed that the artwork was probably expensive, since it seemed that everything else in the house was also expensive. She cocked her head sideways to look at a few of the paintings, to see if they looked any better from the side, but she remembered that this was called abstract art. What a crock. It didn't look any better or any worse to her if she looked at it right side up or looked at it sideways. She liked pictures of things or people, not splatters of paint on a canvas.

However, something seemed to draw her back into Steve's office, and Fannie was not sure why. She followed her instincts to go back into Steve's office. No one was home, but she had proven to herself last time she was here that no matter what she did Steve couldn't see her. Maybe it was better no one was around to distract her from what she was supposed to "do." Maybe she would have better concentration if she was alone.

She looked around Steve's office, and at first glance, nothing seemed any different from how she remembered it, but she was willing to concede in her mind that the first time she had been there, she was so astounded at being there and finding out that it was Steve Goldrick's office that she couldn't be certain that she remembered all the small details. As she continued to move around the office, nothing struck her, but what kept her in the office was the fact that she hadn't thought about coming here, yet here she was shortly after thinking about Steve Goldrick and the massive problem he had caused Maizie and Rick.

She was about to give up when she realized what she was meant to see. There were two newspapers in English stacked neatly on the desk. The newspapers were the *Khaleej Times* and the *Arabian Post*. Fannie couldn't contain herself. Each newspaper was addressed to a name she didn't recognize, but with a mailing address. Apparently, Steve had assumed a different name and new identity, which was why he had been difficult to find. An address! To Fannie, they were meaningless words on a piece of paper, but this was where the house was, and she could finally give an address to Jason to help them find Steve. Fannie repeated the address as best she could out loud in a cadence to help her remember it. She said it over and over so she wouldn't forget it, even though it was so strange to her. As soon as she was sure she had memorized it, she thought of getting this goldmine of information to Jason as soon as she possibly could.

Fannie was so excited to relay this information to Jason, but at the same time, it nagged at her that she had not seen any trace of a baby or baby things like a crib or bottles of formula at Steve's house. She tried to think things through logically. Maybe it wasn't so strange after all that Grace was not actually at Steve's house. If something happened and Steve was found out, he wouldn't want to have a kidnapped child in his house. Fannie chewed on this for a while.

Okay, so now she knew where Steve was, but they still didn't know Grace's whereabouts. Fannie tried to calm herself. Maybe these were all just steps on a path—the path to Grace.

Jason was sitting in the conference room watching his partner, Jack Moore, give a presentation to the clients. The PowerPoint presentation was going well, but he and Jack had been over it so many times that Jason practically had it memorized, down to the witty remarks and jokes. Jason thought they had sounded better the first twenty-five times he had heard them and tried to stifle a yawn.

He took a mouthful of coffee in an attempt to stay awake and alert. As he looked over the edge of the coffee mug, he had to choke back a startled cry. Standing to Jack's right and in Jason's line of sight was Fannie waving at him, clearly trying to get his attention. Jason shook his head to try to clear what must be the proverbial cobwebs in his mind and looked again. She was still there. Maybe he was just exhausted, and his mind was playing tricks on him.

Apparently, since he didn't react, Fannie took to waving at him much more vigorously so that she looked like she was waving a jetliner in for a landing. Jason didn't have a clue what to do. He figured the safest thing was to ignore her. He looked down at the pad in front of him and pulled his pen out of his pocket as if he were going to write a note. This did not please Fannie, who was very excited over her find in Dubai and not in the least fazed that he was in the middle of a client meeting and was not reacting.

Then a few things happened. First, one of the client's coffee mugs overturned on the conference room table. Unfortunately, for Fannie, that mug did not have very much coffee left in it, and so he was able to grab the paper napkin in front of him and mop up the coffee without too much fuss. The client was more embarrassed than anything else, but in reality, he was caught off guard because his hand wasn't on the mug or anywhere near the coffee mug. Fannie had "helped" to overturn the mug.

That didn't cause as much of a distraction as Fannie wanted; she needed to do something with the computer Jack was using for the presentation. Since she had died long before computers were in common use, she had no idea of what to do with the computer. So she did the next best thing. She pulled the plug literally on the computer and as quickly as possible turned on the lights in the room and then turned them back off. Everyone was so startled and didn't quite have time to react. Jason jumped up from his seat and said, "Maybe 'the gods in the machine' are telling us it's time for a break. Why don't we all stretch our legs, and Jack and I will fix the glitch?"

Jack looked truly perplexed and seemed grateful for a break to figure out what the hell had just gone on. Jason walked over to Jack and said, "Maybe it's a power surge. That's what probably knocked out the lights." He pretended to fiddle with the light switch and of course the lights came back on.

"Who the hell knows," Jack said. "It doesn't appear that I lost any data on the laptop."

Jason said, "Good—I have to go to the men's room." With that he made a beeline out of the room before Jack could say another thing. He made a left turn around the corner in the opposite direction of the men's room. He pulled out his phone from his pocket and pretended to be making a call.

"Grandma, what the hell are you doing? Jack is in the middle of an exciting client presentation."

"Oh, yeah, it looked real exciting. You were practically falling asleep, and the man across the table from you was playing some game on his phone."

"Grandma, you can't just barge in like this. This is an important client for us. Couldn't you wait until it was over?"

"I tried to get your attention so that they didn't have to stop the presentation, but you were Mr. Important and wouldn't acknowledge me. You think what Jack was saying is important. Well, it's nothing like how important the news I have for you is."

Jason realized there was no point in arguing with her. She wasn't going to listen to him anyway. She was a woman on a mission.

CHAPTER 29

Jason had written the address in his phone hoping that Fannie's pronunciation was close enough to the real address that they could make sense of it. Fannie wanted him to leave the meeting now and go tell Rick and Maizie. "Grandma, the presentation is almost over. I can't just walk out."

"I don't see why not. You're not doing anything but sitting there. You're bored and drinking coffee. This information I just gave you is far more important."

"Ah, you're sort of right, Grandma, but what am I going to tell my partner? That my grandmother who's dead and has been dead for a long time is talking to me in the middle of an important client presentation and that I have to get up and leave? That will go over really well. They'll have me institutionalized."

Fannie frowned and sighed out loud. "Jason, I love you, but you can be so stubborn sometimes."

Jason was about to argue with her, but he had learned that was a futile effort. The old adage of "If you can't beat them, join them" came to mind. "You're right, Grandma. You're absolutely right. But just remember whose grandson I am. The apple didn't fall far from the tree."

Fannie rolled her eyes. "Touché." A small smirk crossed her face. "How much longer are we going to have to endure this?"

"Not that much longer. I promise you. I've heard this many times, and he's almost done. It's not root canal, Grandma. It might be a little boring, but we need clients."

"A little boring. A little boring! A little boring is a Mets game when they're losing 7–0. We're bordering on insufferable."

"That's a little strong, don't you think?" Jason realized that, even as the last word was coming out of his mouth, he didn't see Fannie anymore. He turned 360 degrees, but he couldn't see her. He caught himself, realizing how crazy he must look turning in a circle in the hallway and no one else was there.

As much as he wanted to "get the hell out" of the meeting and over to Maizie and Rick's house, he knew that there would be no way to explain it to his partner, Jack, or the clients. Since he knew the presentation almost by heart, he really did know they were almost at the end. Even though this could prove to be a good client with some serious bucks coming into the firm, Jason was secretly hoping they wouldn't have too many questions, and then he could legitimately "get the hell out of there."

There were a few questions from the clients, and normally he would have stayed around to bullshit with them, but today, Jason stuffed his materials and legal pad into his briefcase. He did a few quick handshakes and then headed purposefully toward the door. Jack would have questions as to why he didn't stay to talk to him about the postmortem. He could handle those later.

As soon as he got off the elevator and went out the door to the parking lot, he hit Rick's number on the speed dial on his phone. The phone rang a few times and went to voice mail. "Rick, it's me. Call me. I think I have an address for that bastard, Goldrick. I just got out of a meeting, and I'm on the way to your house."

Jason debated about whether to call Rick's office or the house next. It was late enough in the afternoon that Rick could have been on the way home, and that's why Jason thought he'd catch him in the car. Lately it seemed to Jason that there was no pattern with Rick anymore. He was distracted and not at all like himself. Jason could understand after all that had gone down with this horrific situation. He also thought he was picking up something between Rick and Maizie. Again, understandable after what they had gone through and were still going through, but Jason couldn't help but feel that there was an undercurrent of tension between them. He truly didn't know what to do. He didn't know if he should broach the subject of the tension between Maizie and Rick, and he didn't know how to start. What if he said something to Rick and Rick thought he was crazy or was offended? He didn't want to start anything, if there was nothing there. But on the other hand . . .

CHAPTER 30

Jason tried the house next, and Maizie answered the phone. "Hi, Maizie, it's Jason." He didn't give her a chance to say other than "Hi" back to him. "I have the address for Goldrick from Grandma. I don't know how exactly how she got it, but it's some crazy Arab name I can't even pronounce. I'm on the way over to your house. I tried to get ahold of Rick, but he's not answering his cell. Do you know where he is?" Jason finally stopped to take a breath.

Maizie's whole tone of voice perked up from when she answered the phone. "Oh my God, Jason, this is so wonderful! If we find Steve Goldrick, we find Grace!"

The thought flashed through Jason's mind as Maizie was speaking that he never even thought to ask Fannie if she had seen Grace. He really felt stupid. He felt the air come out of the balloon a little.

"Jason, did Grandma see Grace? Is she okay?"

"Ah, Grandma didn't say that she had seen Grace." Jason was quick to add, "It's okay, Maizie. Think about it. We certainly didn't expect Grace to be at his house. Steve didn't do the actual kidnapping. The bastard wouldn't get his hands dirty. He

obviously paid someone to do it. He's too smart to have Grace
at his house." Jason surprised himself that he was that quick to
react because only seconds earlier he was feeling like a total idiot
that he hadn't thought to ask Fannie if she had seen Grace at
Steve's house.

Maizie didn't say anything at the other end of the phone.
When she did say something, her voice was a little shaky.

"It's okay, Maizie. This is the best lead we've had. Let's talk
to Adam and get him over to Dubai. We're going to get Grace
back. I can feel it now. Where's Rick?"

A very quiet Maizie answered, "I don't know." She sounded
like she was holding back tears.

To fill the empty space, Jason said, "Call him again on the
cell and at the office. I'll be at your house in a couple of minutes."
Jason really couldn't tell if Maizie was going to cry because they
finally had a lead or because she had thought Grace would be at
Steve Goldrick's house and they would find her. "Maizie, it's going
to be okay. Hang in there. Find Rick and get him to come home."

After she hung up the phone, Maizie slumped down into a
chair and began to sob. She didn't know what she was sobbing
about, but her body was wracked in sobs nonetheless. This was
slow torture. She wanted to be hopeful, but it was so hard. She
didn't want to give up hope.

CHAPTER 31

Steve Goldrick sat in the air-conditioned porch, which overlooked the pool. He was waiting for his daughter, Gabriella, and there was no way he would go out in the afternoon sun. This godforsaken hellhole. Yeah, he was living in opulence, and yeah, he wasn't in jail, but this was another kind of jail. He hated everything about this place. He really did feel sorry that Gabriella and her family had to be here as well, but it was unavoidable. If they hadn't left the United States, Gabby would certainly have ended up in jail. No matter how many attorneys they hired or how much influence he brought to bear, she would be tried and convicted for her part in the black-market adoptions if she ever returned to the United States. He had never actually asked Gabby what she thought of Dubai. If he thought about it, she didn't complain about it very much. *Maybe since she's younger, she's more adaptable*, he thought. *It's just that she has a hell of a lot longer to stay here than I do. Perhaps when her mother and I die, she'll decide to move somewhere else, but her options are extremely limited.*

He also felt very bad for Peter, who was now living his life in Dubai. There are so many great things about American culture that Peter would miss. No matter how they tried to mimic things here, it still wasn't the same as being in the United States. For the most part they socialized with Americans, because Peter was in a school mostly comprised of American kids. The bad thing was that most of the American kids were here for a relatively short term, while a parent worked for a multi-national corporation, and then they went home. Unfortunately, Peter had already watched several of his good friends come and go. Steve wasn't sure if Peter had asked his parents why if they were Americans, they could never go to the United States, even for a visit or a vacation. Steve couldn't bring himself to ask Gabby if she and Peter had already had that conversation. College was in the not-too-distant future, and it would probably have to be in Europe and not the States because neither Gabby nor Dave could take him to see US colleges or take him to school to begin his college career.

Gabby whizzed into the porch and kissed Steve hello.

"Didn't hear you come in."

"Rasa saw me drive up and opened the door. Is that iced tea?" Steve nodded yes.

"Anything in it?" Gabby asked.

Steve made a face and answered, "Just some ice and lemon. Nothing more, nothing less. You checking up on me?"

"No, but you can't drink yourself into oblivion. I know you hate it here, but you refuse to see anything good here. Clearly, it's not the United States, but Dubai has its own charm, and you should try to see some of the positive things here. Yes, it's a completely different culture, but you act as if you're living with a group of cavemen. I know you're brilliant, but you need to stop looking down on everyone and everything here."

Steve held up his hands as if to deflect the words. "Okay, okay, no more lectures. I really have curbed my drinking. I'm not even using the 'sun coming over the yardarm' as the time to be able to have a drink. Haven't had anything in over a week." Steve changed the subject. "Wait until you hear this. I always wanted to learn to ride, but I never had the time to do it. I found a place for private lessons, and I'm starting next Thursday. They always talk about the Arabian horses being so wonderful, so I'll see. And then the coup d'état. I did a training session yesterday. Boy, you should see this trainer. What a body on her!"

"So do you like the training or the trainer?" Gabby asked skeptically.

"Both."

"Yeah, but in what order?"

"Doesn't matter, does it, as long as I keep doing it. After the first session, I needed to put the Aleve in the iced tea. Or maybe even intravenously. These are pretty old muscles."

"I'm not sure I'm wild about your riding a horse at your age either. If you fall off, you're going to break something. All you need is a broken hip."

"I never think of myself as old, and so I'm going to do what I want. I want to try new things. You'll be surprised when I come home looking like Lawrence of Arabia."

"Oh, God, why do I even ask? So why did you want to see me in the middle of the day—and all alone?"

"Well, you know that even though I'm supposed to be in retirement, I just told you I like challenges. I still have some things I want to do that don't involve riding a horse or sweating my brains out with the trainer. I still need those brains."

Gabby nodded while watching her father like a hawk. His face didn't give away if this was going to be something heavy or something tangential. However, the fact that she was here alone with her father and he had specifically requested this meeting made her wary.

"I have an opportunity for you. I still have my connections all over the world, even if I play it much more low-key now. I like making things happen. I like it better that I can still make things happen, even from the other side of the world." He stopped for a moment and sipped his iced tea. "I can put my hands on a very cute, very healthy white baby who needs to be adopted. I thought you and Dave might want to take her."

Before Gabby could say anything, Steve leaned forward and reached for an envelope on the table, next to the pitcher of iced tea. He handed Gabby the envelope and said, "Open it."

To say that Gabby was taken back was a large understatement. She hesitated for a moment and then leaned to take the envelope. Inside were about ten pictures of a very cute chubby baby with dark hair and light eyes. "Oh, she really is a cutie. Is she an American?"

"Yes. Two American parents. Looks very healthy to me."

"How did this 'opportunity' come to present itself to you, especially now that you're out of 'the business'?"

"You know, things just come to you some time."

Gabby wasn't buying that answer. "That's a bullshit answer. What really happened?"

Steve sidestepped the question and tried a new tack. "I thought you always wanted a girl. Now I practically drop this beautiful child into your lap, and you're suspicious. I always wondered why you never had a second child, but your mother said she'd kill me if I asked." Gabby didn't say anything but looked down at the pictures in her hand, so Steve pressed on. "Don't you want a daughter? This child is so cute. I'm surprised that you're even hesitating. She's healthy, and you don't have to be pregnant. Ready-made. You're a great mother to Peter. You're not doing the travelling you were doing when we were running the business. You have plenty of time on your hands, and you have help in the house. All you have to be is a mother. Sounds pretty good to me."

Gabby was hesitant, but Steve's hard sell was making her nervous. "I'd have to talk to Dave about this. Why is this such a secret? Dave was working with me in the business, so it's not as if he didn't know what was going on. Plus let's face it, I'm getting older, too, and Peter will soon be going off to college."

"Gabby, Dave will do whatever you want. You know that. And as I said, you're not running around the globe and money is certainly not an issue."

"Dad, I can just feel that you're not coming clean with me. You're being secretive and you're pushing too hard. I think I'll pass on this unless I know the real story. And there is a story." In truth, Gabby was intrigued by the pictures of this gorgeous child, but she had a feeling she was being manipulated. She kept her poker face and then decided to play the trump card. "I don't know, Dad. I think this could be a real hassle and more than I want to deal with. You didn't even tell me where the baby is. I think I'll pass, as intriguing as this may be." She put the pictures down pointedly on the table and got up to leave. She knew that she could call him from the car or when she got home and tell him she wanted some time to think about it, but she was trying to flush out the truth.

Steve let out a big sigh and said, "Wait. There is a little more here. This baby is in the United States. She's actually my great-granddaughter, and I think we ought to keep her in our family. Who better than you?"

Gabby opened her mouth, closed it, and swallowed hard. She finally said, "She's what?"

CHAPTER 32

"Look, Adam, I won't interfere with your job, but there is no way that I am staying here when my daughter is in Dubai. We've been sitting here for what seems like an eternity doing nothing but waiting, and now that we have a real lead that can help us find Grace, nothing can stop me from going."

"Hold on a second, Maizie, don't fly off the handle. We need to think about this." Adam looked at Rick when he finished speaking and was clearly looking for support.

Maizie shook her head no and then said even more emphatically, "I'm going."

Rick looked at Adam for a second and then said, "Maiz, let's hear what Adam thinks and kick this around before we make any final decisions."

Maizie turned on Rick in a nanosecond and all her pent-up fury at Rick for causing this situation was unleashed. "Haven't you done enough? This is all your fault. Our baby has been kidnapped and we're living a nightmare that never ends all because of you! I don't give a goddamn what you think or how you want me to be reasonable. My mind is made up!" She screamed this last sentence at Rick and stormed out of the room.

The three other people in the room all looked as if they had been slapped. No one said anything for a few seconds until some of the shock wore off. Abby looked distraught and said, "Let me go talk to her." With that, she got up and walked out of the room.

Adam said, "Does she mean that she's trying to talk Maizie out of going?"

Rick shrugged a weary shrug and said, "I don't know. Right now, she's not going to talk to me, so let's see what Abby can do. She's the voice of reason and the peacemaker."

"No offense, Rick, and I get it that Maizie is beside herself. But first I need to ask you some questions. First, has Maizie ever met Steve Goldrick? In the firm in New York City or at some charitable event? I don't want to take a chance that by some bizarre coincidence, she should run into him in Dubai and he recognizes her."

Rick looked drained, but he answered nonetheless. "I don't think so. I was already out of the firm when I met Maizie, so there wouldn't have been any reason for her to be at the old firm. We didn't go to any charity events until after we were married, and by then Steve was long gone out of the country."

Adam said, "This might be our best lead to Grace, and I don't want to blow it on some chance meeting and we lose the element of surprise. I would much rather that you let me go to Dubai and do my job without worrying about all this extraneous crap. It's a distraction I don't want.

"I have a friend who just retired from the US Marshals Service, and he wants me to go into business with him. We've been kicking this around between us. He thinks we will have enough business doing sophisticated surveillance both at home and abroad. He has a lot of contacts in the Middle East, which would be helpful to us in Dubai. It's just better that the two of us go to Dubai without having to worry about anything else rather than Steve Goldrick.

"I have another problem with this. Is it possible that once she gets to Dubai that she goes to Steve Goldrick's house and rings his doorbell? I'm worried about all of this."

"Look, Adam, right now I have no answers. You saw with your own eyes the state Maizie is in. Let's see what Abby says after she talks to her and maybe calms her down a little. Why don't you contact your buddy and make some plans? I'll call you as soon as I have a better handle on things here. No matter what, we still want you to go."

"Okay, I'll call him. I just have to think about this some more if Maizie is adamant that she has to go to Dubai."

CHAPTER 33

Adam called his friend, Greg, the retired US marshal, about the job to go to Dubai. He decided he would take two weeks of vacation from his job on the police force, and then upon his return, he would decide what to do about putting in his retirement papers with the police. He was going to say he was taking his son to see some colleges this week. He just felt it was better while he was still employed by the police department not to say he was going to a foreign country to do surveillance. It would be a little difficult to say why he needed the vacation time quickly, but he figured he could talk his way out of it by saying that adolescent boys weren't exactly known for planning ahead. He would say he decided to take advantage of the fact that the kid was willing to look at colleges.

Adam could feel Maizie's desperation, but he felt he had to be the one with the cool head. He called Rick the following day and asked if he could come to the house to speak to them. He had grown fond of the three of them, and he saw how the longer this situation went on, the greater the toll it took on all their relationships. He wanted to help them, and he was going to take another run at Maizie now that he had some time to reflect on things away from the cauldron of emotions in their house.

He arrived at the house with a peace offering and a smile, even though that was not how he felt internally. When he rang the doorbell, Rick answered the door. Adam took a quick appraisal of how Rick looked and decided he did not look worse than Adam feared. Rick was showered and shaved, although the ever-present circles under his eyes were perhaps a bit deeper.

"I brought some breakfast, thinking maybe it would put us all in a better mood. These are some of the best scones, bagels, and muffins on the planet," Adam said as he pointed to the huge bag in his arm.

"C'mon in, buddy. Glad you wanted to come back to talk to us." Rick led Adam into the kitchen where Abby was making coffee and putting out placemats, silverware, and plates.

"Morning, Abby." For the first time in all the time he had spent in the house, Adam went over and kissed Abby on the cheek. He surprised himself that he did, and he clearly surprised Abby. Maybe he had crossed some line from being a professional to being a friend, but he didn't care. "I brought some really wonderful stuff. Maybe it will put all of us in a better mood."

Abby said thank you and squeezed his hand, but rolled her eyes.

"Where's Maizie? How did your conversation go with her yesterday after she uh, uh, 'left' the room yesterday?" Adam stammered.

"About as you would expect. There's so much going on in her head all at the same time. It's like she has a tornado raging inside her, and she exploded. Rick called the doctor, who prescribed a tranquillizer for her last night. We didn't even have to fight to get her to take it. I think she knew she was out of control. What you saw went on here all day. At least, the tranquillizer knocked her out and she got some sleep. I'm not sure you're going to be able to convince her not to go to Dubai. You've really never seen Maizie once she's made up her mind about something."

"I get that. That's not why I came, but there are certain things we have to agree on before I agree to take this job. I need some assurances from Maizie."

Rick heard the change in Adam's words from yesterday. When they spoke yesterday, Adam had agreed to take the job with his friend. Now he was saying there were conditions before he would take the job.

"Maizie is upstairs. I'll get her. Why don't you start eating something while you're waiting for her to come down? I think I hear the shower. I'll tell her you're not here to convince her not to go to Dubai." Rick walked out of the kitchen to get Maizie.

When they were alone in the kitchen, Adam sat down with Abby at the table and busied himself with his scone. He looked up and said to Abby, "You might be in the worst position of anyone in this house. You're walking a tightrope here with your daughter, your son-in-law, and your granddaughter. While everyone has the same paramount interest of getting Grace back safe and sound, all the other stuff going on makes it that much more difficult, especially on you."

A sad half smile crossed Abby's face. "Thanks for saying it. It's true. I have the very tough vantage point of being able to see everyone's position. It's so difficult. We all just want this to be over quickly and for Grace to come home. Unfortunately, what we originally thought was 'quickly' has long since passed."

Rick returned to the kitchen and said that Maizie was getting dressed and was coming down. A few minutes later, Maizie walked into the kitchen with none of her usual energy or presence. She said a quiet hello to Adam and poured herself a cup of coffee. She refused any of the food that Adam brought, but she did take an orange out of the refrigerator and sat down at the table and proceeded to peel it.

Adam waited a few more agonizing seconds. Finally, he said, "Look, Maizie, I heard you yesterday. I know how important this is to you, but we need to get a few things straight between us and you have to understand the risks. I'm not willing to take this job unless you do."

At the mention of the fact that he might not be willing to take the job, Maizie's head jerked up and she looked directly at him.

"I want you to understand and assess the risk. You have to think about the fact that you could jeopardize this entire thing. We know that Steve had some guy put the flash drive in Rick's pocket at Dannie's funeral. If he was that close to Rick that he could put something in his coat pocket, he was certainly close enough to see you. We don't know if it's the same guy from the cemetery who snatched up Grace. If it is, then he knows what you look like as well. We pretty much believe Steve is behind this kidnapping based on the tape. Then I'll bet anything that he had your house cased before the kidnapping. That means Steve could easily have had pictures taken of you."

When Adam said "taking pictures," Rick said, "Oh, shit. When we were at the cemetery at Dannie's funeral and walking to the grave, I saw some guy taking pictures from his car. I remember thinking that it was some creep looking to make some money from a sensational story about Dannie's murder. I think he was the guy who put the flash drive in my pocket. I forgot about the picture taking because the video eclipsed that in my mind."

Adam continued. "Let's assume that Steve Goldrick knows what you look like. If you insist that you want to go to Dubai, against my advice, you have to agree to a few things. First, we will find a nice, but not five-star, hotel that's off the beaten path. You will stay there, and you will stay inside the hotel. You will not go out sightseeing or shopping or to a movie. We'll arrive at different times on different flights.

"Second, you must give me your word, and I really mean this, that you will not attempt to contact Steve Goldrick in any way. You won't try to call him or email him. Most importantly, you will definitely not drive by his house or attempt to ring his doorbell. You won't go anywhere near where he lives.

"We shouldn't be there that long, but if you can't contain yourself, then I will pack up and go home immediately and we're done. Done for good.

"I will be in touch with you morning and night while we're there to let you know what's going on." Adam stopped speaking abruptly and then there was dead silence in the room.

Maizie bit her lip, and her eyes welled up with tears. "Yes, I can do that."

"I have your word, Maizie?"

"Yes."

Rick then said, "If Maizie's going to Dubai, then I'm going with her. I can't sit here in the States while she's there."

Adam let out an exasperated sigh. "What the hell is the matter with you? We're trying to do covert surveillance and now you want to go? You're the very guy that Goldrick wants to hurt. You have the bull's-eye on your back. If he should see you, any element of surprise we have is gone."

Maizie countered. "Maybe Mom should come with me." The words hung in the air.

Rick looked directly at Abby as Maizie finished talking and caught her eye. She rescued me once. Should I let her do it again?

CHAPTER 34

Gabby walked back to where she had been seated only a few minutes ago and sat back down heavily in the chair. She looked at her father, who hadn't said a word after Gabby's outburst of a few moments ago. "What exactly do you mean that the baby is your great-granddaughter and that you can lay your hands on her? What the hell have you done?"

"Well, I haven't really done anything."

"Dad, this is total bullshit, and you know it. You can't dance around this with me. You've got to tell me the truth. I thought you and I were always honest with each other. The fact that you're trying to play me is very upsetting."

"Yeah, I guess you're right. You're my daughter, and you were my partner. I was just trying to protect you."

"Dad, I'm not going to pull every detail out of you. You want me to adopt a baby who's your great-granddaughter, but you're not telling me how it is that you happened to 'lay your hands on a baby' whom you want me to adopt." Gabby made the sign for parentheses in the air around the words, 'lay your hands on a baby.' "I need the truth and I need it now."

Steve looked uncomfortable and looked down at his hands. Gabby had no intention of moving from where she was sitting in the room, nor was she going to prompt him to get the story. Rasa rapped lightly on the door and asked if they needed anything. Gabby waved her away. Rasa knew that when Steve was in a meeting or on the phone that any slight movement that she should go away should made her scurry away as fast as she could go. She never knew what it was that he did, even though she was curious. She realized that it would be better for her job, and probably better for her in the long run, if she knew as little as possible. He paid her well and he was always polite to her, but he was never friendly.

Steve took a sip of his iced tea and it appeared that he was trying to buy time as he gathered his thoughts. Gabby's stare was nothing short of withering, and she wasn't moving a muscle.

"Okay, so here's what happened."

To Gabby, it sounded a little bit like "Once upon a time," and she hoped she wasn't going to hear something akin to a fairy tale from her father.

"You remember Rick Singleton, right?"

Gabby nodded.

"Well, he and that bitch, Dannie Bevan, blackmailed me."

"I know, Dad, ancient history, and why we're here in Dubai. Get to the real point of the story." Gabby's tone was now exasperated.

"Rick benefitted from the blackmail. He bought a big house, and he became a partner in that law firm after Dannie's death. He got off scot-free while we're here in this hellhole. Things got better for him. Nobody sticks it to me and gets away with it. Nobody."

Steve paused, and Gabby still didn't say a word. She was beginning to have suspicions, but she was trying very hard not to jump to conclusions because none of the conclusions looked to be very promising.

"Anyway, Rick got married, and they had a kid. It just seemed that maybe this was a way to make him pay a little."

"Pay how?"

"Things were just going so perfectly for him, and he had never felt the pain of my wrath. I decided to have the baby kidnapped so that he could feel some pain."

"You kidnapped his baby?" The tone in Gabby's voice was incredulous. "You actually thought there was something to be accomplished by kidnapping a child? Are you out of your mind? Dad, this is completely and totally different from getting paid by people to adopt babies. Can't you see how crazy this is? You sound like some vengeful god from mythology. These are real people and a real baby we're talking about."

Gabby had been quiet for a while, but now that she had started speaking, or maybe now that she was close to screaming, it was a whole torrent of words and emotions that were being poured out.

"Now you tell me you want me to adopt a baby that's been kidnapped. This just gets crazier and crazier. Where is the baby now? Please tell me she is not in this house."

"No, she's still in the United States."

"You have got to give her back—back to her parents. Why are you even hesitating?"

"Because I'm not sure that's what I want to do. Frankly, I want you to adopt her. She's my great-granddaughter."

CHAPTER 35

Adam flew into Dubai International Airport on Emirates Airlines ahead of Maizie and Rick. The airport was huge and sprawling, constructed of steel and glass. He had quite a walk to get to the car rental. As he did, he passed aisle after aisle of shops. He could just as easily have been walking through a mall in Los Angeles because every store in an LA mall was also here in Dubai. In doing some reading about Dubai, he had read that the rents were exorbitant in the airport. He had also read that this airport was a hub for travelers going from Europe to Africa or to the Southern Hemisphere. Because of that, Adam probably heard more than twenty different languages during his walk through the airport.

The flight had been long and boring. He usually was able to sleep for at least part of the flight, but he was so keyed up that he barely slept. His back hurt and all his muscles felt tight. He had a bad headache both from the lack of sleep and from the lack of moisture in the plane. In fact, this whole job was giving him a headache. He felt out of sorts and thought maybe he should go directly to the hotel and get some sleep.

He didn't have a weapon with him, which was also making him unhappy. It would have taken too long to get the permits and permission to fly weapons into a foreign country without being in law enforcement. Adam didn't want to take a chance that anyone would check with his police force about his bringing a weapon into Dubai if he said he was on the police force. He didn't want to blow his cover that he was supposed to be looking at colleges with his son.

Technically what he was going to do in Dubai was against the law and that he probably should have notified law enforcement in New York for them to approve his surveillance. It would never be approved, so there was no point in opening a can of worms. However, this autonomy gave him freedom he would not otherwise have playing by the rules of law enforcement or as a police detective. He also knew that he was going to put in his retirement paperwork when he returned home and take up his friend's offer to go into business with him.

Adam had made a call before he left New York to a contact who would be able to provide him with a weapon while he was in Dubai. He was not supposed to have a weapon since officially he was not in the military or on the police force in Dubai, but after all these years on the police force, he was too uneasy not having one, especially in a foreign country.

The fact that Maizie was insisting that she was coming to Dubai was a big problem in Adam's mind. It was possible that the baby was in Dubai, but he didn't think so. It was difficult to get an infant out of the country, and whoever had the baby didn't have her birth certificate. It was just easier to keep the baby in the United States.

Once Maizie made up her mind that she was coming, then Rick really had no other choice but to come. Adam didn't think Rick really wanted to come, despite his having said so early in the discussions. Rick probably would have been fine to let Adam handle things. But Adam really had a lot of reservations about controlling Maizie. She was beginning to feel like a loose cannon.

He continued mulling over the situation. He had done the

best damage control he could under the circumstances. He had warned her that if she left the hotel while in Dubai or did something stupid like trying to get in touch with Goldrick, then he was done. He told her he would pack up and leave, but he still wasn't convinced in his own mind that she would follow his instructions.

"Look, Maizie, I really don't think Grace is in Dubai with Steve Goldrick. It is much easier to keep her here, rather than try to fly with a baby that's not yours. There literally are a million places where she could be in the United States and no one would be any the wiser. Taking her out of the country is way too complicated. Steve Goldrick is too smart to have a kidnapped child in his house."

"But suppose Grace is in Dubai and you find her. I want to be there. I have to be there," Maizie had said. Adam remembered that Maizie's tone had been more than emphatic.

He also thought that Rick was so worn out by the situation that he didn't have the energy to fight her. Rick was a good guy, and Adam liked him. He didn't think he had anything to worry about with Rick. He just wasn't happy with the clients being in Dubai.

Even though he had pounding over his right eyebrow, Adam changed his mind about going directly to the hotel. As he drove out of the car rental place, he pulled over to the side of the road and punched in a new address on the GPS.

After a few minutes of driving, he said out loud to himself, "Okay, I'm going to be at Goldrick's house in a minute. The house will be on the right." As he drove past slowly, he noted certain details about the house. He said out loud again, "Wow, it's some house. Huge and set back a little from the street. Big gates around the property, and there have to be security cameras that are not all that visible. "

Adam circled the block to see the house a second time. Now he continued to say out loud the things that were going through his mind. "Well, Mr. Goldrick, you certainly set yourself up in luxury when you left the United States. Hard to make the case that crime doesn't pay, when you see the size of this house. You certainly reaped the benefits of your crimes."

Adam turned off the street and drove for a few minutes in silence as he now headed to the hotel. He pulled into the underground parking lot for the hotel. *Okay, finally here. I'll check in and get some sleep and start afresh tomorrow.*

CHAPTER 36

The conversation took place in Russian.

Vladdina picked up her cell phone when she saw that it was Fatima calling. The two sisters were close, and it was only because of their relationship that they had decided to go through with Steve Goldrick's plan. They would not have trusted anyone else.

Fatima was agitated at the other end of the phone. "I have not heard from him at all."

"Well, is he still paying you?"

"Yes, the money comes in on time, just as he said it would. He has never missed a payment."

"So why are you upset? He's paying you as he said."

"Yes, but I don't know how much longer this is going to go on."

"When you agreed to do this, did he say how long the job was going to be?"

"No, he didn't but . . ."

Vladdina broke in and cut her off. "I don't understand why you are worried. You just said that he's paying you exactly as he said, so that's a good thing. This is far more money than you could ever have expected to make, and all you're doing is taking care of a baby. You're not doing laundry, cleaning a house, or doing ironing. It's an easy job. And you're being paid well."

"But what if he stops paying?"

Vladdina let out an exasperated sigh. "Then we'll worry about that when it happens, but as I said, it will probably never happen."

"Why do you say that?"

"Because this baby is important to him. In the meantime, just enjoy not having to do very much and enjoy collecting that money."

"Even the money he sends to take care of the baby's needs is too much. It's more than I need for the baby's expenses."

"So that's even better. Every week you get paid, and you get extra money for the baby. That's more than you could have hoped for. You need to calm down."

Vladdina hesitated to tell Fatima the next part, but she felt she should. "Maizie and Rick are going to Dubai. I'm not sure why they are going. They have a detective working on the case, and he is going to check things out. I think he is going to spy on Mr. Goldrick. It seems a bit crazy since they seem to know that the baby is not in Dubai."

"How do you know this?"

"They told me they have a lead about the baby, and they are going to Dubai. I am going to stay in the house while they are gone."

"Is this bad for us?" Fatima sounded more distressed, and that was why Vladdina had hesitated to tell her. However, Vladdina felt it was better to tell her in advance than have Fatima find out later and flip out.

"I don't think so. They are not going to find the baby in Dubai, are they? I'll let you know when I hear some more from them. You need to calm down."

CHAPTER 37

Fannie was sitting in the kitchen unnoticed during both conversations about Maizie and Rick going to Dubai with Adam. She had seen Maizie storm out of the room during the first conversation, and she saw Maizie's reaction when Adam said he had certain conditions for Maizie to agree to or he would not take the job.

Fannie thought to herself, *That's my granddaughter. She definitely got those genes from me and from Abby.* Abby had been just as stubborn when she was young, but Abby had matured and not just aged. Abby now certainly had a much better perspective on things. She seemed to have acquired the proper perspective about when she should stand firm and when it was wise to compromise.

As to me, Fannie thought, *it's hard to know if I was right all the time. Now in the light of eternity, I'm pretty sure I wasn't right all the time, but as I look back, it was very difficult for me to admit when I was wrong. Sometimes I dug myself into a hole it wasn't easy to climb out of. I just hope that Maizie didn't climb down into the same kind of hole about insisting to go to Dubai, especially since I'm pretty sure that Grace is not there.*

Fannie wished that Abby was going to Dubai as well. She thought that Abby would be a calming influence on Maizie in an extremely difficult situation. Fannie could also see the tension between Maizie and Rick, and she wasn't sure if their being in close quarters in a pressure-cooker situation in a foreign country was going to make things any better. She also wished that Abby could hear her. It was easier to talk to Abby from the other side than it had been to talk to Jason and have him relay the messages to the other three people.

Fannie thought about being with Jason. She had some things to tell him. She also wished he would calm down when she spoke to him. At one point she had even wondered if she could drop a Valium into his coffee before she spoke to him. It just wasn't that easy to move inanimate objects from the other side. It could be done, but it was hit and miss. Fannie really didn't know where she would get a Valium.

Two days earlier, she had seen Jason out on a bike ride but had decided against speaking to him while he was on the bike for fear that he would fall off and break his collar bone. Fannie vividly remembered Jason having fallen off the treadmill one of the times she had spoken to him.

Now that the plans were firming up for Dubai, Fannie needed to speak to him. Jason was not as athletic as Rick, but Fannie gave him credit for his perseverance. Sometimes his athletic efforts were almost comical, and Fannie didn't always understand his choice of sports. He had recovered very well after all the surgeries after his car crash, but he still had a limp.

Jason had a friend who had told him how wonderful and what great exercise kickboxing was. So today Jason was taking his second kickboxing class. The kickboxing class was held in a cavernous gym that had once been a warehouse. The gym had a fresh coat of paint, and some walls had been built to separate the various classes from each other. There were huge posters on the wall of men with ripped muscles performing various martial arts moves. There were no amenities as some of the upscale gyms had like saunas and juice bars. The space was clean and new, but spartan was the word to describe the place.

Now that Jason was in his second kickboxing class, he had a misguided sense of his own prowess. As the class wound down to its final minutes, the instructor asked his class of beginners to pick a partner and spar for two minutes.

This was one activity that Fannie could just not understand at all. It made no sense to her to try to kick people. *What possible use could this activity have in real life?* She waited as patiently as she could through the last half of the class, and now, just when she thought the class was over, the participants were going to spar. If she could have let out a huge sigh, she would have. She stood with her back to the wall of the gym and waited.

Jason turned toward her as he moved around his opponent. Fannie gave him a little wave. He did a double take, and as he looked at her a second time, he stopped paying attention to his opponent. He should have moved away or blocked the kick. He did neither because he was distracted by her. The kick caught him in the stomach, and he doubled over and went down in a heap on the mat. His opponent was horrified and apologetic and ran to help him up. The instructor hustled over to help as well. Jason had the wind knocked out of him. He lay there on the mat trying to catch his breath, but he couldn't take a deep breath because of the pain.

After a few moments, the instructor helped Jason up off the mat to a chair. One of the other students brought over a bottle of water. The instructor stayed until he was sure Jason was okay. The other class members left and Jason gathered his things but waited a few more minutes so as not to have to answer the same question if he was okay over and over.

As he slowly walked to his car, he heard Fannie's voice. "Are you okay, Jason? Looks like you took quite a shot."

"Jeez, Grandma, what were you doing in the gym?"

"I was waiting patiently for you to finish your class."

"Next time will you please wait somewhere else? You can get me killed."

"I just don't get the point of kickboxing. When will you ever use that?"

"It's just for fun."

Fannie couldn't contain herself and her response. "Well, it certainly looked like you were having a lot of fun lying in a heap on the mat. I have something important to talk to you about.

"You know that Maizie is insisting that she has to go to Dubai. I think it's a very bad idea, especially since I saw no evidence of Grace in Mr. Goldrick's house. You need to tell Maizie that."

"Look, Grandma, I think we all agree with you, but Maizie is insisting that she has to go. Rick doesn't want her to go and apparently neither does Adam."

"Well then, you just have to tell her what I said and talk her out of it."

The expression on Jason's face looked more pained after Fannie's remark than it had when he had been kicked. "You're kidding, right? Have you ever tried to talk Maizie out of something once she's made up her mind?"

"Jason, I couldn't be more serious. Tell her I'm saying this. And you need to talk to Abby and tell her to talk Maizie out of this."

"I know they have all tried. It's a waste of time and energy."

"Jason, it isn't going to do any good to argue with me. Make sure they know it's me who's saying this."

"But Grandma—" Before Jason could say anything else, he looked again, and Fannie was gone.

CHAPTER 38

Rick decided that he had to go to Dubai with Maizie. He didn't want her to go, and he didn't want to go. However, since the die appeared to be cast, he decided that he had to make the best of what he felt was going to be a long, arduous, and fruitless task. He had a tablet loaded with three new books, his play list of music, and two movies for the plane trip. Things were tense between him and Maizie, so he felt that it was better if he stayed calm and had activities to divert his attention from the long and boring flight. He tried to convince himself that getting irritated or antsy wasn't going to make the plane go any faster or shorten the trip.

What hurt Rick the most was that he felt the gap between him and Maizie widening by the day. He would never have believed that anything like that could happen to them. He loved Maizie so much, and now it seemed that the two people closest to him, Maizie and Grace, were absent from his life. He was afraid to let himself use the phrase "lost to him", because he wasn't ready to give up on either of them. He couldn't imagine going forward in his life without either or both of them. He was going to do everything in his power to fight for them.

They had the perfunctory conversations about getting into the car taking them to the airport, checking their luggage, and getting through security at the airport. When they finally boarded the plane and took their seats, Rick put his hand on Maizie's on the seat between them. There was no reaction from Maizie. He squeezed her hand and turned to look at her, sitting only a few inches from him. He thought he got a little smile from her. Maizie said, "I'm going to try to get some sleep."

Rick said the first thing that came into his mind. "Maiz, this is not over. We will get through this." He hadn't mulled over what he was going to say, but now that he thought about it, what he said was true. He felt that what he had just said applied to the situation with Grace as well as the problem with Maizie.

Before they left, Rick had sought out Abby to talk to her alone. He now mulled over the conversation as he could recall it, and it was very vivid in his mind.

"Abby, I don't want to put you in the middle of this, and I'm very aware that Maizie is your daughter and your first loyalty is to her. You know that if I could go back and change the past, I would. Obviously, I can't. In a million years, I would never have imagined that Goldrick would kidnap Grace or anything remotely close to that. You see this stuff on TV, but you think it never happens in real life.

"I feel I'm losing Maizie. She's drifting away from me, and I don't know how to reach her anymore. Maizie and Grace are the two most important things in my life, and I can't think about losing either or both of them. This has all the markings of what happened when I lost Jennifer and Adam. I just don't know what to do."

Abby looked at Rick and saw the pain written all over his face. "Look, I know this is a horrendous situation for everybody. I've thought about your pain and the similarities to your losing Jennifer and Adam and that just makes it worse for you. You know that what you did with Dannie was wrong, but you certainly never could have imagined anything like this coming out of it.

"I have been speaking to Maizie, since it's clear that there's a rift between you. I've been telling her not to do something foolish or make any decisions when everyone is under incredible stress, but you know her. We call her Hurricane Maizie for a reason. I've told her that she needs to tone it down and not do anything stupid. Things look one way now, but I think they will look very different when this crisis is over. Right now, she can't see anything except that her heart is broken without Grace.

"Honestly, Rick, I have been trying with her. I'm not sure how much of what I say that she hears. You're getting her wrath for everything because she blames you. You can't reason with her; you can only tell her how much you love her. I'll continue to talk to her, but who knows."

Rick was so happy to hear that Abby was talking to her. It also seemed to him that Abby didn't hate him. However, Abby's last words in the conversation, "I'll continue to talk to her, but who knows," made him feel sick.

CHAPTER 39

Adam had things to do before Maizie and Rick arrived in Dubai. Even though Dubai was cosmopolitan and wealthy, Adam's first priority was to arm himself.

Adam's friend Dylan who was in the US Marshals Service frequently went in and out of the Middle East for his work. He knew people—lots of people and all kinds of people. Adam had called him about this job in Dubai not only for advice about the place itself but also for contacts in the city. Dylan had arranged with a contact of his for Adam to be able to get a weapon. Adam could dispose of it in any number of places like the sewers before he had to return home. He had given Adam a phone number and first name only for the contact. He had also arranged a place for the meeting that was not in the seediest part of town so that Adam wouldn't become a crime statistic while picking up the weapon.

The next task involved a meeting with a guy who was connected to the local government. Adam wanted a copy of the building plans for Steve Goldrick's house. In the United States, anyone could walk into a local building department in any town or city, pay the required fee, and get a copy of the building plans for any residential or commercial building, no questions asked. Real estate agents, builders, developers, attorneys, prospective buyers, and architects did it all the time. No one thought twice about the requests.

Adam had no idea what the locals would think about a request for building plans for a house here in Dubai. He didn't want to take that chance. He didn't know how far Steve Goldrick's influence extended, and he didn't want any request to somehow get back to Steve Goldrick and set off alarms. He wanted to fly under the radar, especially Steve's radar.

The GPS in his car said he was only a few blocks away from the cafe where he was to meet the next contact. His phone rang and the voice at the other end asked where he was. The voice told him where to park the car, and in a few minutes he was sitting in a cafe with tablecloths on the tables and fancy water glasses and expensive and heavy cutlery.

Adam had only had to walk several blocks from the car, but the heat was so oppressive that his shirt was wet by the time he got to the cafe. In the summer, it was not unusual for the temperature to get up to 120 degrees during the day. Adam felt the heat coming at him like waves. What little breeze there was did nothing to cool him off. The air itself was stifling.

When Adam said the name of the man he was supposed to meet to the maître d', he walked Adam to a table toward the back of the restaurant. Sitting by himself was a small balding man dressed in a dark suit with a vest, despite the heat. Adam looked like he had the hose turned on him, and yet this man, who had several layers of clothes on him in over well over 100 degrees temperature, looked like he just stepped out of the shower. Once Adam shook hands with the man and sat down at the table, Adam mopped his face and both temples with his cloth napkin. At this moment, Adam didn't care if this was a breach of some kind of Dubai etiquette, but the sweat was getting in his eyes and stinging like crazy.

The man introduced himself as Aziz, and Adam didn't know if this was his first or last name. Adam guessed that Aziz was a man in his late fifties and perhaps had been educated in Britain, based on his pronunciation of some words. Aziz mentioned a few items on the menu that he suggested were very good, but he also said almost everything on the menu was good. The menu consisted of various goat and lamb dishes. Adam quickly noticed that there was no beef on the menu at all. There were a lot of dishes made with roasted peppers and onions and side dishes of couscous and hummus. Based on this introduction to the menu items, Adam surmised they were having lunch together.

Not wishing to cross some Dubai line of etiquette, Adam was willing to play along. The food on other tables looked good so if Aziz wanted to have lunch, so be it. This lunch was going on the expense account, and Maizie and Rick were going to foot the bill, as well as Aziz's fee. Adam also had no idea when during lunch he was supposed to bring up business and the real meaning for their lunch. Aziz appeared to have been well-educated and well-travelled, and the conversation was lively and interesting.

It did not appear to Adam that Aziz was trying to pry into why he was in Dubai. He only asked if Adam had ever been there before and if he would like some recommendations of restaurants. He asked Adam if he had been to the tourist spots and mentioned which ones he thought were worthwhile and which he thought Adam could pass on. Aziz named the Burj Khalifa, which had the highest view in Dubai, the Dubai Fountain, the Ski Dubai, which had desert snow and ice skating, and the Dubai Aquarium and Underwater Zoo.

Finally, when they ordered coffee at the end of the meal, Aziz asked Adam what building or buildings he would like the plans for. Adam gave Aziz the address, and Aziz wrote it down on a pad that had almost magically appeared from his pocket. He quoted the price to obtain the documents.

"I can have the documents you request by tomorrow. I know that sometimes people are loathe to give a stranger the location of the hotel at which they are staying. I would be happy to leave the documents here with the maître d'. I will call you to tell you that they are here. You can come and verify that they are the documents you requested and then you can leave an envelope with the payment in cash with the maître d'. He has done this for me many times, and it works very well with my customers."

"Thank you, Aziz. That seems like a great arrangement. I appreciate your discretion in this matter."

"It has been my pleasure. I enjoyed having lunch with you today. If you return to Dubai again, even if we don't have business together, I would be pleased to have lunch with you again."

"Thanks, that's very nice of you. I enjoyed myself too."

"Oh, and Adam, one more thing. You need to get yourself a hat. Too hot to be outside without one." With that, Aziz stood up from the table, bowed slightly to Adam, thanked him for lunch, and left the restaurant to go out in the blazing heat in his three-piece suit. Adam watched as Aziz carefully put his hat on before he left the restaurant.

He looked at his watch. It had been almost an hour and twenty minutes since he arrived in the restaurant, but it wasn't a waste.

CHAPTER 40

Maizie and Rick's flight had been delayed about an hour and a half. Rick had slept for a few hours during the flight, but he had too much on his mind to sleep for the entire time. He was keyed up because who knew what might happen in Dubai. He had fallen back to sleep for about two hours before the plane landed, so he didn't feel completely sleep deprived. Maizie, on the other hand, had slept most of the flight. Rick wasn't sure if she had taken a sleeping pill or if all the nights of bad sleep or no sleep had finally caught up with her.

They were having a driver pick them up, and they saw a young man with a sign that said "Singleton" near the baggage claim carousel. He helped them get their luggage off the carousel and wheeled both suitcases toward the doors leading out of the terminal.

"It is not too far a walk to the car. If you prefer, I can go get the car and bring it to the front of the terminal."

Rick wanted to stretch his legs after having been in the plane for so long, and Maizie seemed refreshed after sleeping for most of the flight, so they decided to walk to the car. After having been in the climate-controlled air of the plane and then the terminal, when they exited the terminal, the air that greeted them was oppressive. Since they had made their choice to walk, they decided to stick with it. By the time they reached the car, they looked a little bedraggled and sweaty.

The driver opened the car door for them to the back seat but told them to wait a minute before getting in the car. He then quickly ran around to the driver's side and turned the air conditioning on full blast. After a minute or so, he told them it was okay to get in the car. As the driver put the luggage into the trunk, Maizie turned to Rick and said, "I get it that New York may not be the garden spot of the world, but why the hell did he pick a place that's like an oven? What about all the beautiful places in Europe?"

"I think for two reasons. He wanted to be halfway around the world, but more important is that Dubai doesn't have an extradition treaty with the United States. Dubai will not deport him back to the States for his crimes. It's supposed to be a glitzy place, where everything is new and the buildings are gigantic and made of glass and chrome. I'm sure that would appeal to Steve as well."

"So he's stuck here for life?"

"There are far worse places to be. We don't know where he first went when he left America. He might have come directly here or made a stop or two to decide where he would ultimately end up. He knew law enforcement was on his tail, so he didn't have a whole lot of time to get out of the States. The partners at his old firm went ballistic when they realized that he was gone and what he had done.

"We know he didn't show up for work on a Friday, and then for a few days after that until the firm sent people looking for him. His secretary, Helen, covered for him on that first Friday that he was out of the office, and then she disappeared sometime over that weekend, too. He's living under an alias here as well.

"Steve also had to get his daughter, son-in-law, and grandson out of the country. Gabriella and Dave were an integral part of the adoption scam. They had to get out of the country fast before they got arrested. Steve probably knew that based on the seriousness of the crimes and how long it had been going on that a judge might not grant bail. All of them would be considered flight risks, so a judge might have remanded them to custody without bail. He had to act fast and get them all out of the country."

"Miserable bastard. I hope he rots in hell," came the quick response from Maizie.

"Maybe with all this heat, Dubai is God's waiting room for hell."

CHAPTER 41

Abby looked at her cell phone right after it pinged that there was a text. Maizie had texted her that they had arrived in Dubai and that the weather was extremely hot. Abby sighed. She had been over this a million times in her mind. It was infuriating that nothing had really changed. She still didn't think that they were much closer to getting Grace back either. That was the most discouraging thing of all. She tried to keep those thoughts at bay.

A part of her understood why Maizie wanted to go to Dubai in case Adam found Grace, but that seemed like a remote possibility. Maybe it was just to do something and not just continue to sit and wait endlessly. However, in her heart of hearts, Abby thought it was futile to go to Dubai for Maizie and Rick, especially since Fannie had said she saw no evidence of Grace or any baby things in Steve Goldrick's house. Abby also saw Maizie becoming more and more upset about a lot of things, and that worried her.

Abby still had tremendous affection for Rick. He had made a horrible mistake with Steve Goldrick, but no one could have foreseen the depth of Steve Goldrick's need for revenge. She could see that Rick was suffering on two fronts. He was suffering incredible guilt about what he had done and its impact on his family. She also could see that Rick was humiliated that his mistake had come to such public scrutiny. As she had thought this through, she realized that most people make mistakes and that was enough punishment from the consequences of the mistake, but most people didn't have the dirty laundry of the mistake aired the way it had been with Rick.

This kidnapping had shed light on all the relationships in all their lives. She and Rick had genuine affection for each other that incredibly had nothing to do with Maizie and, in fact, predated Maizie. Rick was also very worried that his relationship with Abby would be so badly jeopardized by the kidnapping that he would lose that relationship as well. She so hoped that things would not come to that, but Maizie was not making things any easier on Rick. She just hoped the bonds were strong enough.

Meanwhile, Jason continued to be the only person Fannie was communicating with. No one on this side had any idea why Abby could no longer hear her mother, and Fannie seemed just as baffled from the other side. Jason's psyche seemed not to be adjusting all that well to his conversations with Fannie. He was rattled every time she spoke to him. He had fallen off a treadmill, almost drove his car off the Thruway, took a body blow in kick-boxing, and jeopardized a client presentation, all because Fannie had spoken to him. Abby would have hoped that by now Jason might have gotten a little more used to it, but that did not seem to be the case.

Since the wind was howling and whipping the rain in all directions, Abby decided not to go home after seeing clients and slog through the miserable drive across the Tappan Zee Bridge. She would stay at Maizie and Rick's house tonight. As she pulled into the driveway, she was surprised not to see Vladdina's car in the driveway, since she was staying in the house while they were gone. It wasn't all that late, but considering the weather, Abby would have thought Vladdina would have been tucked into the house by now. *Well, no matter*, Abby thought. *I have the keys to the house and the alarm code.*

In the short distance from the car to the back door, Abby was drenched as her umbrella was turned inside out by the gusting wind. She turned on a few more lights in the kitchen and looked around. Everything appeared to be in order. The lights in the kitchen were on a timer, so they were on. Abby figured she ought to walk through the house and make sure everything was fine and there were no leaks anywhere in the house.

Before she took off her raincoat, she decided to take in the mail, which would certainly be soggy even if the mailbox was closed. The newspapers had been put on a hold while Maizie and Rick were away, but as Abby opened the front door to get the mail out of the mailbox, she noticed four circulars in the driveway she hadn't noticed when she drove in. Abby cursed the retailers as she put her hood up over her head and ran out into the driveway to retrieve them. On one, the plastic cover had held, but the other ones had landed in the driveway in such a way that the water had leaked in and the circulars were a soggy mess.

Abby tried to grab the mail on her way into the house with her other hand, but there was too much mail to do it. She left the circulars on the front porch and then was able to have hands free to grab the mail. Since there was so much first-class mail and junk mail, the mailbox couldn't close, so the mail at the top of the box was very wet and the mail below was soggy.

Abby brought the mail into the kitchen and separated it by first class mail and junk mail, which she brought to the recycling bin in the garage. "God, that's a lot of mail," she said out loud. Maybe Vladdina hadn't been staying in the house, as she was supposed to have been.

CHAPTER 42

Adam and Greg pored over the plans to Steve's house that Adam had received from Aziz. They looked at all points of entry as well as the electrical and HVAC system. They looked at the number of windows in the house and their elevation to see if it would be easier to get into the house through a window rather than a door. They matched up the plans with the pictures they had just taken of the house to see how the bushes and vegetation might provide cover. Their original idea was to carry out a home invasion on Steve's house to get him to talk and tell them where he had Grace stashed away. As they reviewed the plans, they found out that the alarm system had been hardwired into the house. This was certainly going to make a home invasion much more difficult to carry out.

The second plan under consideration was to carjack Steve on the road, but this was also a complicated scenario, since they not only had to find an opportune place to carjack him, but they also had to do it in a place and at a time when no one was around to identify them or call the police. They had to carry out surveillance to figure out his patterns of leaving the house.

They came up with a third plan, which they decided was the most feasible. Adam called Rick and said he wanted to meet them at their hotel. Adam introduced Greg only by his first name. The hotel room had a sitting room. Maizie and Rick met them there, and they were visibly nervous. Greg and Adam accepted the proffered cup of coffee and jumped right in with the explanation.

Adam did most of the talking with Greg adding an occasional comment here and there. He said that they had considered three plans and explained why they agreed on the third plan. They were going to wait until Steve was on his way into the house as he got out of his car in his driveway, jump him, and kidnap him, hopefully in the dark. Adam pushed a manila envelope across the table toward Maizie and Rick. "Here are the pictures we've taken of the house."

Adam continued the explanation. "We're pretty sure he doesn't have Grace at his house. That would be reckless, and he is certainly not that. We think she's in the United States somewhere because otherwise he'd have to get a passport for her. That would be messy without a birth certificate. There are a million small towns across the country where she could be.

"When we tell you that we have Steve and that he's talked and told us where Grace is, I want you both ready to be on the next flight out."

Maizie was about to interject, when Adam held up his hand to stop her. "Let me finish. He obviously will know you sent us, but I don't want any complications with your getting out of the country. It would have been better if you had never come here so there was no record of your having entered or left the country, but that's water under the bridge now.

"You realize we are going to have to verify the info Steve gives us. He's enough of a snake that he could tell us where Grace is and then have her moved right after that. That's why we're going to have to hold onto him until we can get someone to wherever Grace is and get her. Depending on who's holding her is who we send to pick her up. I think you should call Jason and Abby and have them ready to leave immediately once we know. Tell them to bring her birth certificate with them."

"Suppose it's that degenerate that kidnapped her in the first place? Jason and Mom are no match for him," Maizie asked.

Now Greg answered. "We don't think that some muscle guy who grabbed her is going to have her. We think this is about punishing you, rather than hurting Grace. Steve knows this is his great-granddaughter, and we're betting he is not going to let anything happen to her. She might be with some family or a couple that he's paying to take care of her."

Adam continued. "It could take us days or a week or more until we find the right opportunity to grab up Steve. Hopefully, he talks right away, but he might not. Once we have the info, we have to act on this immediately. We also can't let him go until somebody gets Grace back. By then you will be out of the country, and we will disappear some other way.

"Please call Jason and Abby and get them on alert that they could have to leave today, tomorrow, or in a week. If they have some problem doing this, we need to know immediately, because we have to find a back-up person, and that might not be so easy. We need to have someone ready to act as soon as we have the information."

Adam finished up. "We're going to go now, since we have a lot of things to do today. Call us as soon as you've spoken to Abby and Jason. I think Abby will do just fine with this. I don't know Jason as well, so let me know if he's okay with the plan."

When Adam and Greg left, Maizie and Rick sat back down to digest what they had just been told.

Rick was the first one to speak. "You realize that no matter what country we're in or the reason for doing it, kidnapping is illegal. I think they weren't prepared to tell us about these plans until now because it involved kidnapping and probably involves some violence against Steve if he doesn't cooperate and talk right away. I think they sanitized the version they were telling us."

Maizie nodded in agreement. Her reaction was much more muted than Rick would have expected. The reality of this was becoming very real to Maizie and they were halfway around the world. Maizie's voice was barely audible.

"I hate that bastard, Steve Goldrick. He has put us through hell, and he's enjoying it. Otherwise, there would have been some ransom demand. I don't care if they beat the hell out of him. He's just plain evil. I never thought I, or anybody we know, would be in this situation. But we are. We have to do whatever is necessary to get Grace back."

"Maiz, there's another issue. I can see Abby being willing to go wherever she needs to go pick up Grace. I just hope Jason can do this. Even with Abby being there, Jason is so freaked out every time Fannie communicates with him. This going to get Grace back is a much more serious and difficult situation. I hope he can handle this."

Maizie listened to Rick's every word, without blinking. A few seconds elapsed before she said anything. "I think it will be better if I talk to him. I don't think he will try to weasel out of going when he hears my resolve. I will get him to understand how vitally important this is and that he's going to have step up."

CHAPTER 43

Maizie and Rick called Abby and put her on the speaker phone. They explained the three possible plans Adam and Greg had outlined to get Steve, and they explained that Adam had decided on the third plan.

"Abby, Adam has asked that you and Jason be ready to go to whatever place Steve tells them Grace is, if it's in the United States. We'll be coming back immediately once Steve gives them the information, but we're going to have to deal with plane schedules, possible delays, and the flying time to get back into the country. Adam wants you two on the move as soon as he has the information.

"Plus Adam and Greg are going to detain Steve until you get Grace back. Adam is afraid that if they let him go before we get Grace, that Steve will make a call and have her moved somewhere else. He's certainly enough of a slime bucket to do that."

Abby had been silent on her end of the phone, but when Rick finished, she said, "Of course, I want to get Grace back and I'll do anything to help. But why aren't you going to involve law enforcement once you know where Grace is?"

Rick cleared his throat and said, "We don't want to involve law enforcement, if possible, because they are necessarily going to ask a lot of questions about who has been holding Grace, and where and how we got this info.

"You can understand how this could get really messy. We just want you to go in and get Grace."

Abby said, "Suppose whoever is holding her doesn't want to give her up? What are we going to do then? And, don't you want this person arrested?"

Rick looked at Maizie and shrugged before he answered Abby. "If it comes to that, then you will have to call the police. We're betting that the person will be so surprised that you're there that the person will give her up and flee. You might even want to say that to the person. That you'll take Grace, and the person can disappear with no questions asked. No police, no arrest."

Abby answered that she didn't think it was the best plan, but that she was willing to try if that's what Adam thought was the best solution. Abby's last question was, "Does Jason know about this plan and is he okay with it?"

Maizie jumped in. "Mom, we decided to talk to you first, so that if Jason calls you, he'll see that you're on board and he can count on you. We're going to call him now. Do we think that he will freak out when he hears the plan? Yes.

"But he'll probably be okay if you're going to be with him. I'm going to talk to him myself, because I think he's less likely to say no to me. Rick and I are going to double team him. We also are going to impress on him that if you and Jason say no, Adam then has a huge problem of trying to find someone else. We don't know who's available and who's willing to go."

Rick finished up with this thought to Abby. "After we talk to Jason, I would say you should expect a call from him. He may say yes on the phone to us, but you know he's going to need someone to bolster his confidence. He often talks a good game but then he'll be throwing up. He's going to need someone to keep up his courage.

"Once again, Abby, I'm calling on you to save me. More importantly, you'll be saving Grace." When they hung up, Rick shook his head. "Your mother is really something." Rick pulled Maizie to him and hugged her. Maizie didn't pull away. "Her daughter is really something too."

The next call was to Jason. They knew it would be a harder sell. The call to Jason didn't even go as well as they had expected, and their expectations were low.

"You want me to do what?" That was Jason's initial reaction with a lot of skepticism in his voice.

Maizie and Rick had Jason on the speaker phone, as they had with Abby. As she said she would, Maizie took the lead.

"Jason, we need you to do this. We're not winging this; we're doing this on Adam's advice. We explained the logistical problems of our getting back to the States quickly, and Adam doesn't want to hold Steve any longer than they have to. They can't let Steve go without our getting Grace back first. Steve might not be telling the truth about where she is, or he might have her moved. We just can't take that chance now that we're so close to getting Grace."

"I get that, Maiz. I do. But this is not a job for Abby and me. This is a job for the police. Some thug took Grace at gunpoint. I assume that whoever has Grace is going to be an equally dangerous person. He probably also will have a gun. Do you think we're going to be able to waltz in and say, 'Give us Grace,' and that person is just going to fold? That's ridiculous."

Now Rick jumped in. "Jas, Adam is going to find out not only where Grace is being held, but by whom. Adam thinks it's going to be one person, maybe a woman who wouldn't attract attention by having a baby with her. It's been over a month since Grace was taken, so Adam doubts that it's some thug taking care of her."

"Okay, suppose it's not just one woman, but a husband and wife. One of them could easily have a gun."

"That's the information that Adam and his partner are going to find out for us. Exactly who has her and where."

Now Maizie picked up the ball. "Jas, none of this has been easy. We know it's not a perfect solution, but it's the best solution we have right now. We'd rather not have the police involved because we don't know what Adam and his partner are doing to get the information out of Steve. Frankly, I don't care what they do to him. But we don't want the police asking a lot of questions about how we go the tip about Grace and then their contacting the police in Dubai. It could really get messy. Everything about this has to fly under the radar."

Jason let out a huge sigh on the phone. "Is Abby okay with doing this?"

"Yes, she is. She understands that it's not perfect, but it's what we have to work with."

"Maybe I should call to talk to her."

With that comment, both Maizie and Rick almost laughed out loud.

"Jas, we're family. This is what families do. They help each other, even when it's difficult," Maizie replied.

"Okay, let me think about this and call Abby."

When they hung up, Rick said to Maizie, "I think you better call Abby and make sure she's totally willing to do this. If she has any reservations, we better address them now. If Jason hears that Abby has any reservations, he will bolt. Let's call her now so she definitely knows he's going to call her, and make sure she's 100 percent with the plan."

CHAPTER 44

Adam and Greg took turns watching the comings and goings at Steve Goldrick's house. For the first two days, nothing much happened. Steve and or his wife were home because lights went on and off in various parts of the house when it was dark, but there was no actual sighting of Steve outside the house. A woman, who possibly could have been a housekeeper, came at the same time and left at the same time every day. She often left the house in the middle of the day and returned with bundles that appeared to be groceries. On the third day, an elderly woman, who matched the pictures they had of Steve's wife, came out of the house, got in her car, and drove off. She returned about an hour and a half later with her hair "done."

Adam said to Greg, "Maybe we should think about grabbing his wife if we can't grab him. It might be messier, but we'd at least get his attention. Are we sure he's even in the house or even in town?"

Greg answered, "You need to be a little more patient. The guy is up there in age. Maybe he's sick or he's old and he doesn't go out much. We must wait this out some more. It's a gorgeous house, but maybe he'll get bored staying home, or maybe he'll have a doctor's appointment."

Each day, Adam would report to Rick and Maizie, but there was precious little to report. Adam was getting very antsy, but when he spoke to Rick and Maizie, he took the tack that Greg employed that sometimes stakeouts went quickly and sometimes they didn't.

Finally, on the fourth day, Steve emerged from the house wearing what looked to be gym clothes, during Adam's shift. Adam let out a howl of delight in the car. He called Greg and said he was going to follow the car and see where Steve was going. Maybe this would provide the opportunity to grab him. Adam told Greg he'd call him back when Steve got to his destination to see if the gym or wherever he was going looked promising. Unfortunately, the gym parking lot was busy with people coming and going and the gym itself was near stores.

Adam got the idea while he was waiting for Steve to finish at the gym that by the time he finished it would be dark, especially if he made any other stops before going home. Adam called Greg to come meet him with the van. Greg and Adam waited in the parking lot. Finally, Steve emerged from the gym looking sweaty and spent. He was walking slowly to his car. Steve had begun to look his age. His gait had the look of an old man. They were about to get out of the car and van to grab him when two other men came out of the gym. Greg and Adam had to hesitate and lost their opportunity.

Greg called Adam on his cell phone and said, "Too bad. We missed him but we should find out if he comes here more than once a week. Hey, wait a second, our boy just made a left turn. Looks like he's not headed directly back to his house. Maybe Allah will smile on us after all. Let's see where our prize is headed now."

After about two miles and a few turns, Steve pulled into a parking lot where there were only a few stores. It didn't appear to be the greatest of neighborhoods, and now it was fully dark outside. Steve pulled up in front of a cigar store. The whole area was dimly lighted. No one else appeared to be around, and the cigar store had a small neon sign in the window that said "Open."

"After all that good work in the gym, now our boy is going to pollute his lungs with the demon tobacco," Adam said sarcastically into his headset. "This is the place to get him."

Greg pulled the van to the left of Steve's car so that he was next to the driver's side door. Steve opened the door and as he got out, Greg gave him a vicious punch to the head. As Steve crumpled from the blow to the head, Greg caught him before he fell and whisked him toward the back of the van where Adam had opened the back door to the van. Adam yanked Steve into the van by his shoulders, and Greg shut the door. In a matter of seconds, Adam had the unconscious Steve tied up and had put a hood over his head. He covered him over with a rug and then jumped out of the van and walked casually back to Steve's car. Both the car and the van drove carefully and slowly to a place outside the city.

On the way to their destination, Adam called Maizie and Rick and said they now had the "package" in their possession. He told them he would call them back when they had the package situated and when they had some concrete information. "Look, it could be that we have the information quickly or it could take some time. I have no idea how cooperative or stubborn he will be. No way to know. I'll let you know when we know."

CHAPTER 45

Maizie and Rick called Abby every day. The conversations were brief because there was little, if anything, to report until Adam and Greg grabbed Steve. Abby could hear the anxiety in Maizie's voice, but she thought perhaps she still heard a small spark of life in the relationship between Maizie and Rick.

She didn't want to worry Maizie or put more things on her plate, but she felt she needed to raise this concern. "Maiz, wasn't Vladdina supposed to stay in your house and watch things for you?"

Maizie seemed a little taken aback by Abby's question. "What do you mean? Vladdina is supposed to be watching the house, taking in the mail, and checking the voicemail. Stuff like that. She's not there?" asked a skeptical Maizie.

"No, it doesn't appear that she's been here. The mail was in the mailbox, and there were circulars lying in the driveway. Do you want to give me her cell phone number? I'll try to call her."

Maizie relayed this problem to Rick, who seemed equally surprised that Vladdina was not at the house. Maizie gave Abby Vladdina's cell phone number and also said she would text

Vladdina. Since there was a time differential of seven hours, Maizie asked Abby to call Vladdina and see what she could find out.

When they hung up, Abby called Vladdina, but the phone went right to voicemail. She left a message and then texted her. Abby was also a little surprised by this, because her impression of Vladdina was that she was a very responsible person.

••••••••••••••••••••••••••

The truth was that after Vladdina's last phone conversation with Fatima, Vladdina was bothered by what she heard. Fatima seemed restless and disturbed. Even though Steve was faithfully depositing all the money he said he would into Fatima's account, Fatima was upset that the situation with Grace had gone on as long as it had. When Steve did communicate with her, it was infrequent, and he would never commit to what was happening or any end point to her custody of Grace.

When Vladdina called Fatima the day after their last phone call when Fatima seemed upset, Fatima did not answer her cell phone, nor did she respond to Vladdina's texts. By the end of the second day, Vladdina was very concerned. *Could something have happened to Fatima? Could she have taken sick or fallen and be unconscious? Could someone have hurt or even killed her?* These and a host of other dire scenarios played on an endless loop in Vladdina's head.

After three full days of no response whatsoever from Fatima, Vladdina was beside herself. Fatima was a very shy and quiet person who kept to herself. Vladdina could not imagine that Fatima would suddenly change into an outgoing person who made a lot of friends. Especially with the circumstances under which Fatima was taking care of Grace, Vladdina also could not imagine Fatima talking to a lot of people or making friends. Even if Fatima had made some friends, Vladdina had absolutely no idea of who they were or how to contact them.

On the morning of the fourth day, Vladdina made a decision. She packed her bags and got in the car to drive to Virginia where Fatima was staying. She had no idea what she would find, so she drove even faster and with more determination. After all, she was the one who got Fatima into this mess in the first place.

So far, nothing in this situation had turned out the way it was supposed to. Everything was to be quick and neat. Now everything was unraveling, and the money, which was originally so appealing, seemed like a curse.

CHAPTER 46

Steve woke up with a raging headache. As he opened his eyes, his sight was a little blurry, and he shook his head a few times to try to clear his vision. When it finally did clear, Steve looked around the room, but nothing looked familiar. In fact, quite the opposite was true. He had no idea where he was or what room he was in.

As both his mind and his vision cleared, he tried to jump up from the chair to explore where he was. That's when he realized he couldn't get up because his arms and legs were tied to the chair. He was about to scream, but something in his head told him not to. It told him to assess the situation.

He still had the raging headache, but he tried to ignore it and think back to the last thing he could remember. He could remember coming out of the trainer's office and the gym and going to the cigar store. He didn't remember going into the cigar store at all. Try as he might, nothing else came to him. He had purposely kept a low profile in Dubai and barely knew anyone there. Therefore, his being tied to a chair in an empty room didn't make any sense to him.

He might have drifted off for a time, but again with the headache and lack of noise in the place, he wasn't sure. Suddenly, the door to the room banged open and two men wearing masks that looked like Edvard Munch's painting, *Scream*, walked into the room.

"Well, well, look who's awake and with us."

The voice was slightly muffled behind the mask, but it was no voice that Steve could recognize. Steve blinked but didn't say anything.

The second man, also wearing the same kind of mask now spoke up. "So, Steve, do you know why you're here?"

Steve wanted to sound like a tough guy in response, but when he tried to answer and growl back at them, his voice was dry and cracked. "I have no idea who you are and what you want with me, but you probably have the wrong guy," Steve rasped in response.

"Not likely, since we know you're Steve Goldrick, and we wanted you and grabbed you. I'll ask you again. Do you know why you're here?"

It was a common tactic in interrogation. Get the subject to talk. Find out what he knew and intimidate him. If the subject talked, the interrogator not only found out what the subject knew, but see if he knew anything about other useful subjects. The interrogator also got to see if the subject was scared or panicked.

"No clue, why I'm here or what you want. My name isn't Steve Goldrick. Don't even know who this Steve guy is." Steve was now beginning to think that these were just thugs who kidnapped him for the money. Even though he was getting old, he still thought of himself as a tough guy. Steve might have been a tough guy in his former life in court, but in this situation, there was no judge within miles. He had never been in a situation like this, tied up and dealing with two men who knew who he was and wanted something from him.

"Don't play games with us. We know you're Steve Goldrick."
The speaker continued as if he hadn't heard the denial. "So, Steve,
we can do this the hard way or the easy way. It will be up to you.
It's really in your best interest to cooperate with us and give us
what we want."

Steve gave a slight nod to indicate yes, but these two bozos
had not yet actually said what they wanted from him. He was
still thinking they were looking for money.

The second guy spoke. "We know you masterminded the
kidnapping of Grace Singleton. We want to know exactly where
she is so we can get her back."

For a second, Steve was actually taken aback. He didn't have
much respect for Rick Singleton since Rick had tried to commit
suicide. He hadn't thought Rick had the balls to hire someone
to kidnap him. Steve forced a fake laugh. "I don't know anything
about kidnapping. I don't even know who Grace Singleton is.
Why would you think some old guy like me just living out my
final days would get involved in something like that? You really
must have the wrong guy."

The second guy spoke again. "Don't do this, Steve. Don't
make it hard on yourself. Just give us the info and you go home."
There was a pause. "All in one piece."

"I just said, I don't know what you're talking about."

With that, the first guy backhanded Steve across the face.
Steve had been looking at the second guy and never saw it
coming. He was rocked back in the chair. The ring on the first
guy's hand left a welt on his face almost immediately.

"We're not screwing around. You are not in control here, so
you will do what we say."

It took Steve a few seconds to catch his breath.

"So where is she?"

"Even if I knew who Grace Singleton is—which I don't—
why would I tell you? You kidnapped me, so you probably will
kidnap this Grace too."

"You want to play games with us? We know you had her kidnapped. So don't try to play innocent with us. You're going to get hurt bad if you don't tell us."

Steve looked up defiantly at the second guy. The second guy punched Steve in the face, and his nose began to bleed.

The three men in the room stayed very still and stared at each other for a few seconds.

"Is this worth it? You're going to tell us where she is. If you tell us now, we don't hurt you. If not . . ."

Steve shook his head no. The second guy hit him in the face again. Now his mouth was bleeding, and he spat the blood onto the floor.

The second guy looked at the first guy and caught his eye. He motioned with his eyes to the door, and both men walked out into the hall and shut the door.

"He's an old guy. He's over eighty years old. I thought he would fold after I hit him the first time. What do you want me to do? I can hit him a few more times to see if he gives up, but if he's stubborn, he might just take it."

Adam frowned. "I don't know. What do you think we should do? He is old and, we have to be careful that the guy doesn't have a heart attack. We certainly can't risk that we kill him or we're totally screwed."

"Let me go hit him a few more times. I'm going to get him up out of the chair and knock him down a couple of times. Wait ten minutes and then come in. You can be the good cop. Maybe then he'll talk to you since I've been the one pounding on him."

CHAPTER 47

When Steve didn't come home after his session with the trainer, Steve's wife, Torrey, began to get worried, especially now that it was dark. Steve hated everything about Dubai, so it wasn't like he had friends to visit or that he went on outings or shopping trips by himself. When it was an hour and half after the end of his training session and Steve hadn't called her or picked up his cell phone, Torrey couldn't stand it any longer and called their daughter, Gabby.

Gabby agreed that it was not like her father to be wandering around alone. "Did you call the trainer and see if he's okay? Do you have her number? Could Dad have overdone the training and had a heart attack?"

Torrey was so rattled that she couldn't think of the woman's name or where she worked. Gabby said she'd be right over. When Gabby arrived at the house, she could see that her mother was becoming hysterical.

"Mom, can you think of the name of the gym where Dad goes? We can start by calling them."

"I, I can't remember the name. What are we going to do?"

As Gabby thought about it, she realized that if her father had taken sick at the gym, they would have called the house. For right now, it was at least a start. Hopefully, the trainer was still there and could tell them what time Steve had left the gym.

"Does Dad have an address book? He might have the name of the gym or the trainer in the address book."

Torrey said yes, and they went into Steve's office to try to find it. This was a time when Gabby was thankful that her father was not totally hooked on technology. If he were, he would have had all the names and numbers on his cell phone instead of on paper in a book.

It didn't take them too long to locate the address book in his desk. Just as Gabby hoped, the gym name and the trainer's name were listed in the book.

Gabby called the gym and explained who she was and what time her father had the appointment. The receptionist at the front desk said the trainer had left for the day, but that she made the appointments for the trainer. The receptionist confirmed the time of Steve's appointment. The receptionist said she didn't remember seeing Steve leave, but Gabby knew the training session was for an hour.

By now more than two hours had elapsed since the end of the training session. There really was cause for concern since no one had heard from Steve and he was not answering his phone. Gabby had called her husband, Dave, when she was on her way to her parents' house. Dave walked into the house just as Gabby was finishing up on the phone with the gym.

Gabby explained what had happened so far and suggested that Dave go to the gym to see if Steve's car were still there.

"Mom, did Dad mention to you that he was going anywhere else after the gym? That he had an errand to do or he wanted to buy something?"

Torrey said he had hadn't mentioned anything to her. "Dave, if you don't see Dad's car at the gym, then maybe we should call the police and see what to do. Do we file a missing person's report? I have no idea."

CHAPTER 48

Rick paced back and forth in the sitting room in their hotel room. Maizie wanted to tell him he was making her more nervous, if that were possible, but she walked into the bedroom and plunked herself down on the bed. They hadn't heard anything from Adam and Greg after the text telling them that they were in possession of "the package," and this part of the waiting was proving to be even more painful and frustrating. After staring at the ceiling for a few minutes, Maizie found herself reciting prayers from her childhood. Then she decided to talk to Fannie.

"Grandma, I know you love us and have been trying to help us. For some reason, the only person who can hear you is Jason. I don't know why, but I have faith that you are there for us in whatever way you can. Please help us now. We are so close to getting Grace back and we can't fail now, not if you help us.

"I know I'm not a perfect person, but I do try to lead a good life. If we get Grace back, I will try to find it in my heart to forgive Rick so that we can be a family again. He made a huge mistake blackmailing Steve Goldrick, but he has paid such a horrible price for that mistake, and I know that he never meant for any of this to come back to hurt me or Grace. All of this happened before Rick and I were married, and certainly way before Grace was born.

"I don't know if you can answer me in some way. Even some sort of sign from you would be great. We're so far from home, and it's so scary to think of all the things that could possibly go wrong. I really wish I was given the opportunity to know you while you were on this side. I love you, Grandma, and thanks for all your help so far."

□□□□□□□□□□□□□□□□□□□□□□□□□

Meanwhile, about ten miles away, there was anything but a love fest going on with Steve, Adam, and Greg. As Greg walked back into the room, Steve's head was down and drooping onto his chest. Greg banged the door open with a resounding boom of the metal door. Its boom startled Steve, and he jumped within the confines of his bonds.

"So, old man, we gave you time to think about this. Just give me the information we wanted and this whole thing is over. You don't get hurt anymore and when we have Grace, then you go home."

Steve eyed Greg up and down as if he were appraising a prized horse. Even though not much bothered Greg, he was still glad he had on the Edvard Munch mask. Greg was a huge and powerful man and his biceps bulged under his T-shirt. He had been careful never to get a tattoo, even though they had been wildly popular when he had been in the Marshals Service. It was always best to remain anonymous in his line of work. A tattoo could ultimately come back to haunt, hurt, or even get him killed, if a subject remembered a tattoo and could identify him in later years.

Greg moved to within two feet of Steve, making Steve look up at him, which made him appear even larger.

Steve said, "So what assurances do I have that if I tell you where Grace is, that you are going to let me go?"

Greg felt himself smirk behind his mask. He wanted to say to Steve, "Now we're getting somewhere." At least Steve had stopped denying that he didn't know anything about what they were talking about and that he didn't know who Grace was. A chink in the armor. A good first step.

"Look, I already told you that we don't care a rat's ass about you. You give us the info, we verify it, and then you can go home."

Steve looked skeptically at Greg.

Greg countered quickly. "You are not in a position to negotiate with us. You are not in control of this situation. You've admitted that you know Grace, and you know where she is. There's no point in your having broken bones or worse."

Steve cursed himself that he had made such an amateur mistake. The truth of the matter was that his muscles ached from being tied up, his face felt like it had swelled from being punched, he still had a headache, and he badly needed some water. These all added up to his having made a stupid mistake. Maybe the revenge he wanted had already been taken and he didn't need it to go on any longer. Steve wasn't sure he could hold up to another beating. In his own mind, he was still a tough guy who hadn't wimped out as soon as he had been kidnapped. He could show Gabby at least, who knew the story about Grace, that he still had it.

‗‗‗‗‗‗‗‗‗‗‗‗‗‗‗‗‗‗‗‗‗‗‗‗‗‗

Shortly after Maizie had her "talk" with Fannie, she sat bolt upright in the bed as if she were part of a spring-loaded toy. She was sure she heard the word, "Richmond." Maizie looked around the bedroom to see if Rick had come into the room or if someone else had come in. She was alone in the room, and she was sure that she had not dozed off. She definitely had heard the word.

It took Maizie a moment to make sense of it, but then she realized what happened. She jumped off the bed and ran into the sitting room, where she startled Rick. Maizie said in a breathless voice, "Richmond."

Rick looked at Maizie like she was crazy. "What?"

Maizie said it again, this time with emphasis. "Richmond."

"What are you talking about?" Rick asked.

Maizie told him about her "conversation" with Fannie just a few minutes earlier and how she heard the word "Richmond." Under other circumstances, Rick would have been skeptical at best. However, he had seen Fannie at work in the past and he was not inclined to doubt her.

"Maiz, you think that Fannie is saying Grace is in Richmond?"

Maizie nodded yes. "Do you think we should text Adam about this? Maybe it would help them with Steve. Since we haven't heard from them after they told us they took Steve, this could be info they could use against Steve since he's obviously not cooperating."

Rick thought about this for a minute and then said, "How exactly are we going to tell them we know about Richmond? We've never said anything about Fannie to them. For sure they are going to ask and want to know how we got this information. They will think we're nuts. To someone who is an outsider to the family, this is really going to sound crazy."

CHAPTER 49

Vladdina had been driving for what seemed like endless hours. Her shoulders felt cramped, and her right leg was beginning to feel numb from being in one position on the gas pedal. As much as she didn't want to stop, she desperately needed some coffee or tea to keep her awake and she had to go to the bathroom. The sign said there was a rest stop in two miles, and when she pulled in, she saw the signs for McDonald's and Dunkin' Donuts. Vladdina had become Americanized in many ways, but American fast food was not one of them. She sighed as she pulled the car into a parking space and uncoiled her aching body as she got out of the car.

At least she could get tea and an egg sandwich at Dunkin' Donuts. If she kept the eggs as plain as possible, without all the things Americans wanted to put on a perfectly good egg, she wouldn't hate it. McDonald's was a different story. The combinations of food slopped together not only made her wonder about Americans and their eating habits, but it also made her stomach turn a little. The idea of putting mayonnaise, ketchup, and pickles on some sort of ground beef so you couldn't taste the beef really made her wonder if there was any hope for the American palate.

And why did it have to be done in minutes? What made it special merely because it was done quickly and came off looking like wrapped-up plastic? That she would never understand.

She decided she would take a few minutes and eat in the restaurant. Another thing she still could not understand about Americans was the fascination of eating in the car while driving. Vladdina had seen many people try it only to end up with mustard or ketchup on their shirts or coffee all over their clothes and burns on their hands as well. She bought a newspaper and forced herself to read the front page while she was eating, both to slow herself down and to take a few minutes to stop worrying what had happened to Fatima and Grace.

This was not how things were supposed to turn out. It was supposed to be simple and quick, and no one was supposed to get hurt. It frightened Vladdina that Maizie had been hurt in the break-in to take Grace. She was led to believe that the whole thing would be over quickly and not go on for almost a month. None of this was how things had been explained to her. It sounded so simple, and she thought it would be quick money for her and Fatima so that they could go back to Russia to live well with a lot of money and be able to help their parents. But this was turning out to be a disaster. Not being able to get in touch with Fatima made her apprehensive and bordering on frantic.

The few minutes of a break in Dunkin' Donuts made her feel better physically, but the thoughts of all the things that had possibly gone wrong with Fatima made her so afraid. It just was not like Fatima to deviate from the plan, and even stranger that she was not picking up her cell phone or answering her texts. Either something had spooked her or something bad had happened to her. Vladdina was afraid to consider either possibility in her mind for too long a period, so she was back in her car and headed to Fatima's apartment. She really didn't know what she would find. Right now it didn't seem to her this was going to end well.

CHAPTER 50

"I need some water and the bathroom," croaked Steve.

"Yeah, and I need the rest of the information first. Tell me where Grace is and who has her."

"Water and the bathroom first." Steve tried to sound like he was giving an order, but his voice sounded weak even to him.

"For the last time, answer the question, or I'm going to knock your teeth down your throat. There is gonna be pain for you for no reason, you stupid shit. Don't you get that?"

Greg was out of patience with playing games with Steve, and now he was going to let loose on him. Just as Greg was about to knock Steve out of the chair, Steve finally relented. It might have been fear or exhaustion or it might have been a survival instinct that made him realize he didn't have any cards left to play with Greg.

"Okay, okay, I'll tell you. The kid is in Richmond, Virginia."

"Where in Richmond and who's got her? I'm not going to drag this out or you're going to pay for wasting my time and this aggravation. I'm asking you for the last time, where in Richmond and who's got her?" Greg screamed right into Steve's ear.

"It's an apartment. 210 Justice Street. Good name for what I did to them."

Steve's smug tone and obvious enjoyment of the situation infuriated Greg and he backhanded Steve in the face. "You low-life bastard. I ought to beat you some more just for that. Who's got the kid?"

"Some Russian woman. Her name is Fatima. I'll tell you the rest, but I need water and I gotta pee."

Adam had been standing in the next room with the door open. He let Greg handle the interrogation because these methods or worse would never be allowed by any police department in the United States.

Greg walked out of the room and shut the door. Adam said, "Do you believe him or is he screwing with us?"

"I wasn't sure until he said that Justice Street was a good name for what he had done to them. This miserable bastard had been enjoying putting these people through hell. I want to kill him myself. I have kids. Imagine if this was my kids or your kids."

"Okay, I'll go call Maizie and Rick. I want them out of the country now, and I want Abby and Jason on their way to Richmond ASAP." Adam bolted outside the building to call Rick and Maizie where he had better cell service and where Steve couldn't hear anything. They could find out the rest of the information from Steve, but for now they had the two most important pieces of information they needed.

Rick answered his phone on the first ring. Rick said he was putting Adam on speaker phone so Maizie could hear as well.

"Okay, we got the information out of him. He's a twisted bastard. Grace is in Richmond, Virginia. The address is 210 Justice Street. Some Russian woman named Fatima has her."

Maizie started crying when she heard that they had an address for Grace. Because of that, the rest of the information was a blur to her. However, Rick heard what Adam said loud and clear.

"The Russian woman is Vladdina's sister. Vladdina is our babysitter. I can't believe that bitch is involved. I thought she loved Grace—and us. I want to kill her. She acted all worried about Grace having been kidnapped, and now we find she's right in the middle of this."

Maizie seemed to come out of her fog as she heard Rick talking about Vladdina. "Oh my God, Vladdina is involved! I can't believe this."

Adam jumped in and said, "Look, we'll figure out how to deal with her later. Right now, we don't want to tip anyone's hand. I want you on the next plane out of Dubai so there are no complications. Got it?"

Maizie and Rick said yes in unison.

"Get this info to Abby and Jason and get them on a plane to Richmond. I think they can get a direct flight from either JFK or LaGuardia to Richmond.

"Make sure they have Grace's birth certificate and the police reports of the kidnapping with them in case this woman tries to put up a stink. I've told you I would rather that Abby and Jason don't have to involve the police because of all the back story, but if they have to, then they need to show the proper papers."

Rick said, "What are you going to do with your 'package'?"

"Well, first of all, we want to get some more info out of him. Then when we can verify that you have Grace, we'll leave and make a call for someone to come get him after we're long gone. We will slip away. He's never seen our faces.

"And one more thing. When he told Greg that it was great that the name of where they had Grace was Justice Street, and Steve thought that was fitting, Greg wanted to kill him. Greg is a professional or else he might have. Steve is a sanctimonious bastard, and he deserves whatever he gets. I don't think there would have been an end in sight with this kidnapping unless we did something and found out where Steve was and grabbed him. He's been enjoying your misery."

CHAPTER 51

When Maizie and Rick hung up the phone with Adam, the hug they gave each other was long and powerful. To Rick, it felt like relief from a millstone around his neck that was going to drown him. He felt that Maizie was truly hugging him back and that soon they would have Grace and be a family again. For Maizie, it was also relief that the nightmare was going to end soon, but for the first time in what seemed like a very long time, she felt the love she originally felt for Rick instead of unbridled anger.

Maizie said to Rick, "Grandma came through for us. She said the word 'Richmond' to me. She somehow communicated this to me, even though lately the only one who has been able to hear her is Jason." Maizie continued, "I'm going to call Mom and tell her. Why don't you call Jason? They can coordinate with each other about going to Richmond. Then we can call the airline and get the hell out of here."

Throughout the many problems that had occurred in their lives, Abby couldn't have named a time when she was more relieved than when Maizie called to tell her the news about Grace. She had been worried on so many levels. First and foremost, she desperately wanted Grace's safe return. Then she was worried about Maizie's mental health if something happened to Grace. She was worried how Rick would cope if something happened to Grace and he lost a second child.

Abby was still worried about what would happen to both Maizie and Rick if they got divorced. Maizie was her daughter, and Abby certainly didn't want her to be unhappy. Because of the bond between Abby and Rick that preceded Maizie and Rick's marriage, Abby would have felt a profound loss if Rick were no longer in her life. Then there would have been the complications with Rick being Jason's brother, and Jason's two daughters, who were Abby's grand-daughters. The bonds were many and so interwoven that it gave Abby a headache to try to think of dealing with all these problems.

Abby had a host of questions, and Maizie told her as much as she knew. Abby was also shocked about Vladdina's involvement with the kidnapping. Apparently, they had all been taken in by Vladdina and her veneer of concern. Abby told Maizie that it seemed that Vladdina had not been staying at the house as she was supposed to. Whether she was on her way to Richmond to meet up with her sister or had fled the country, Abby had no idea. However, it might present yet another possible impediment to getting Grace back. Maizie was upset by this news but was more elated about getting Grace back, so Abby didn't think Maizie was understanding all the implications.

"Maiz, let me talk to Rick before you hang up. I want to tell him how happy I am about this great news." Abby wanted to make sure one of them understood that there could be more problems lying in wait in Richmond because Maizie didn't seem to be focusing on what Abby was telling her.

Maizie promised to call Abby as soon as she had any more information from Adam, but she was very insistent that Abby and Jason get on their way to Richmond as soon as possible.

Maizie said to Abby, "I can't wait for you to tell me you are holding Grace in your arms. You'll have to FaceTime me as soon as you have her. Rick is on the phone with Jason now, so as soon as he hangs up, you should call him and make the plane reservations. Adam wanted me to remind you that you should take Grace's birth certificate and the police reports with you. I left them in a folder on Rick's desk with Grace's name on the folder. We're going to get on the plane to New York as soon as we can. I'll text you the flight information once we have it. Hopefully, we can be home tomorrow and see Grace the next day!"

Abby finished the call with Maizie and then Rick. She breathed a sigh of relief with this news about Grace, but she also had a certain amount of trepidation about going to Richmond to, in effect, snatch Grace back from the woman she had now learned was Vladdina's sister. Abby didn't know what to expect. Would Vladdina be there when they arrived? Would there be someone else there with Fatima? No one had really discussed the possibility that the man involved in the home invasion might be at the apartment in Richmond. Was he a boyfriend or husband of Fatima? Was he just a hired thug doing a job and getting paid for the kidnapping? Did he bring Grace to Fatima or had Fatima been in New York? And perhaps worst of all, had Vladdina been the go-between? Had she taken Grace from the man and brought her to Fatima? After all, Vladdina had called in sick the day of the kidnapping. It did prove the theory in Abby's mind that there are no coincidences.

And then there was Jason. Abby loved him dearly, but he was a little bit of a loose cannon. He was excitable, which sometimes bordered on hysterical. He often overreacted and then had to backtrack. Jason would not have been Abby's first choice to go on this "mission" to Richmond. Abby would have preferred that it were Rick or someone with a personality similar to Rick's. Abby didn't want to make this trip alone, but she wasn't sure Jason was the best copilot.

Abby said out loud, "Thanks, Mom. I knew you would help us. Now just help us for a few more days to finish this up and get Grace back."

Fannie smiled.

CHAPTER 52

"I gave you what you wanted. Let me go," rasped Steve.

"How fucking stupid do you think we are?" Adam answered. "When we get Grace back and you have answered the rest of our questions, then you can go home—or you can go to hell for all I care. When we know you haven't double crossed us, then you can go. In the meantime, you can have some water and you can go take a leak. That's it."

Adam turned and walked out of the room. Greg walked behind Steve and said, "I am going to put this bag over your head and then untie your hands. You are going to get up slowly from the chair. If you make one false move, try to take the bag off, or try anything, I will beat the shit out of you, and you will never go home. You got it?"

Steve nodded yes, and they began the slow trek to the bathroom, such as it was in an abandoned building that they had rented for a few American dollars. The owner didn't care what they did in there as long as he didn't find a dead body, and payment was made in advance in cash in American dollars. Steve was old, and he had been tied in one position for a number of hours. His muscles were screaming as he tried to get up. He got halfway up from the chair and fell back into it. Greg had to help him up the second time to get him out of the chair.

When they returned from the bathroom, Greg shoved Steve back in the chair. He handed him a bottle of water, which Steve downed almost in one gulp. Then he handed Steve a paper bag with the McDonald's logo on the front. Inside was a cold burger and some French fries looking like they were glued together. The look on Steve's face was nothing short of contempt, but Steve hadn't eaten since yesterday before he went to the gym. As bad as it was, it was food, and it was identifiable American fast food. In Steve's mind, it wasn't some Arab food he couldn't identify and had no idea whose filthy hands touched it.

Halfway around the world in Richmond, Vladdina passed her second McDonald's restaurant since she had entered the city limits. Since she had taken a few minutes to eat at the rest stop with the McDonald's and Dunkin' Donuts, she had passed a few other rest stops with the same two restaurants. She even hesitated to call them restaurants.

The GPS on her phone said she had to go another mile and then make a left turn onto Justice Street. Her heart rate quickened when she realized how close she was to Fatima's apartment. This part of town looked to be all residential and tree lined—not magnificent houses, but nicely maintained apartment buildings. There were a few high rises, but mostly the area had garden apartments and low-rise buildings; it was very middle class and very neat. She didn't think this looked like a bad area, and Fatima had never mentioned that it was a high crime area or that she was afraid to go outside. In fact, Fatima had even told her that she had taken Grace out for walks in the stroller and to some park nearby.

Vladdina found the building and saw a few cars parked in front of the building. She found a parking space in front of the building as well. She couldn't remember what kind of car or what color Fatima's car was. As much as she wanted to know what had happened to Fatima, she was afraid to get out of the car. It took a few seconds, but finally she mustered her courage and got out of the car. Fatima's apartment was on the third floor. That she remembered. She walked up the stairs and saw the apartment door. She rang the doorbell and called out to Fatima with a few words in Russian. No answer. She waited a few seconds and rang the doorbell again and immediately knocked on the door as well. Still no answer.

There was no point in trying to call Fatima on the cell, since she had not answered in several days. She tried the door handle, and, to her surprise, the door was unlocked. She pushed in the door and looked around the living room. It looked okay, and the room didn't appear to have been ransacked. On the face of things, everything seemed to be in place. She called out Fatima's name again, but to no avail.

Vladdina walked into the bedroom, and again everything seemed to be in place, but then she opened the closet first and then the drawers. Everything was empty! Now she made a more thorough search of the apartment and realized that there were very few baby things left in the apartment—no stroller, no crib, and no boxes of diapers or jars of baby food.

She sat down heavily on one of the dining room chairs. What should she do? There was no one to call for help.

Fatima was gone and with her Grace!

CHAPTER 53

Abby and Jason landed on time in Richmond. The flight had been smooth and it hadn't been completely filled, so under other circumstances it would have been a pleasant flight. Abby was doing what Rick and Maizie wanted her to do, but she had serious reservations about this trip. There were too many unknowns and too many things that she thought could go wrong. She still thought that they might very well have to call the police to sort this out. That potentially being the case, Abby thought it was risky not to involve them from the beginning.

However, Adam also thought it was the right thing to do, and presumably he had far more experience in criminal matters than she did. The long-ago blackmail of Steve Goldrick by Rick and Dannie Bevan seemed far removed from this kidnapping. Abby thought Grace's kidnapping was a crime that could stand on its own and be prosecuted on its own.

Jason, who liked to talk and engage people, was equally quiet on the flight. Abby wasn't sure if he were picking up on her mood or if he were mulling over his own reservations. Normally with Jason, if anything was on his mind, it was very shortly on his lips with very little filter. Abby smiled to herself. It was probably some gene Jason had inherited from Fannie. Fannie had always been impetuous like that. If she had a thought or an opinion, of which she had many, she was going to express it. Abby thought that she had been the recipient of many of Fannie's thoughts and opinions, which had often gotten both of them into trouble.

Abby looked down at the iPad in her lap and realized she had read a total of seven pages during the whole flight. As she glanced at the newspaper in Jason's lap, she saw he was still on page two and he was at that moment staring at the seat in front of him.

"We're close to landing. How far is Fatima's apartment from the airport?" Abby had given the tasks of renting the car and mapping out the trip to the apartment to Jason. This not only kept him occupied but also kept him from obsessing about the trip in general.

"Looks to be about twenty to twenty-five minutes from the airport." Jason looked as if he were going to continue talking and then stopped.

"What were you going to say?" Abby prompted him.

"Suppose we get there and she won't give up Grace? What do we do then?"

"We tell her we are giving her the opportunity to give up the baby and leave, or we are going to call the police who will arrest her for kidnapping. I would think that would be a pretty potent threat. We don't know her status in this country. Is she here legally? Is she here on a work visa, which maybe has expired? Or maybe she's not here legally. I don't think that she wants to be involved in any way with Immigration and Customs. That's what Adam thinks is our best tool, along with the element of surprise."

"What do we tell the police if we have to get them involved?"

Abby sighed and answered as if she were talking to a child who had asked the same question multiple times and to whom she had given the same answer multiple times. "We have agreed that we will explain that I am Grace's grandmother and you are Grace's uncle. Her parents are on their way back to the United

States because they were pursuing a lead about her kidnapping out of the country. That lead overseas gave us a tip that Grace is in fact in the United States and right here in Richmond. Her parents are on their way back to the United States from overseas, or they would be here in Richmond right now. That should certainly cover it.

"If need be, and the police want to detain us with Grace until Maizie and Rick get here, that's fine, but at least we will have Grace and she will be safe. We'll be at the end of this long nightmare that never seems to end."

Abby looked at Jason for his approval, and he nodded his head yes. She prayed that they could get Grace without any need for intervention from the police, because she had a bad feeling that Jason was not going to hold up to more stress in this situation.

The trip to the apartment took a little more time than Jason had predicted because of traffic, but Abby felt her heart rate increase as they neared the apartment. Even though she didn't want to spook Jason as he was driving, she wanted to say something to Fannie and have Jason hear it, especially because if Fannie answered and spoke to Jason, she didn't want him to freak out and have an accident.

"Mom, it's Abby. I don't know if you know that Jason and I are here in Richmond to get Grace. We still need your help until we have her safe and sound. If there's anything else you can tell us or can help us with, please do so. We're so close to getting her back in large part because of your help. We need to finish this and get her back. Thanks, Mom."

Abby took a sidelong glance at Jason, but he was keeping his eyes on the road.

As they arrived at the apartment, Jason pulled into a parking space and cut the engine. He turned to look at Abby and said with more confidence than Abby felt, "Let's do this. Let's get her back."

In a later session, Steve Goldrick had also told Greg the apartment number after having earlier given them the street address. As they arrived on the third floor, Abby was repeating over and over to herself the mantra, "Help us, Mom. Help us do this without a problem."

They found the apartment and rang the doorbell. No answer. They rang the doorbell again and knocked on the door and called out Fatima's name. Still no answer.

"Maybe she's out and we should wait for her to come back," Jason said. "There was no guarantee that she was going to be here when we came."

Just as Jason finished speaking, a young woman opened her apartment door carrying a laundry basket. "Are you looking for Fatima? I saw her carrying a suitcase and baby stuff out of the apartment a few days ago. She told me she was going on a trip."

"Did she say where she was going or for how long?" asked Abby.

"Nah, she doesn't say much. She mostly keeps to herself."

"Was she taking the baby with her?"

"Yeah, looked that way. She was carrying the port-a-crib and baby stuff. I can't tell you anymore than that. Sorry." With that the woman continued walking.

Abby and Jason stood there in stunned silence. Where had Fatima gone? Where had she taken Grace? Had she taken her out of the country? Perhaps even back to Russia?

Abby felt sick. They had come this close, and Fatima and Grace had been here, but they were gone.

Jason looked bereft. "I guess we better call Adam and tell him what happened. I don't know if this was some double cross by Goldrick. Maizie and Rick are still in the air. You know they are going to call us the minute they land."

CHAPTER 54

As she drove further away from the apartment, Fatima wasn't sure whether she should leave Richmond or where exactly she was going. Her thoughts were all jumbled in her head. She wanted no part of this kidnapping anymore. She was supposed to take care of Grace, and she had done that. This was all Vladdina's fault. Vladdina had made her a part of this by telling her how easy it would be and how much money they would make. Then they could go back to Russia and help their parents and younger siblings and not have to worry about money.

Vladdina had been calling and texting her, but Fatima was so angry that she wasn't answering her. This whole thing was supposed to be over quickly. As she thought back to the conversations about it, she couldn't remember exactly how long it was supposed to last, but this was over a month and there didn't appear to be an end in sight. She was afraid of the man at the other end of the phone. He was polite to her on the phone, and she couldn't put her finger on it, but he scared her. Vladdina didn't seem to understand it either. All she kept asking Fatima was if the man was making the payments. It seemed to her that all Vladdina cared about was the money. Fatima was also afraid that she would be found with Grace and go to jail. As to the money, the man was making the payments exactly as he said he would. The money was very good. It was far more than she needed to take care of Grace and for her own living expenses. She was saving a lot of money to be able to bring back with her to help her family.

She didn't understand how American banks worked, but every so often she withdrew the money from the account where the man was making the deposits and moved most of it into a different account in her name alone. She wasn't sure if he could somehow take the money back from the first account, so she didn't want to take any chances. Fatima wanted this whole ordeal to be over. Right now she wanted to go someplace where no one could find her. She especially didn't want the man sending the money to know where she was. She wanted to slip away and never be found. Every time she looked at Grace, she felt guilty. This beautiful baby really should be with her parents. But Fatima didn't know what to do. So right now she kept on driving.

·························

As Fatima continued her drive to "somewhere," Abby and Jason walked slowly back to the car. "Do you want to call Adam or should I?" Abby asked.

"Nah, you call him," came the glum answer.

Adam looked at his phone and saw Abby's name come up on the screen. He answered on the first ring. "You got her?" He listened as Abby recounted what happened. "Shit, shit, I can't believe this. Let me think about this for a minute, but you might be right that there is no way that this low life could have tipped her off. We've had him under wraps since we took him. No way he could have communicated with her. Even though it was reluctantly and not right away, he told us the truth about where she was. You're telling me the neighbor confirmed this Fatima woman was there with the baby. Now she's in the wind."

Abby said, "Maizie and Rick are still in the air, but you know they are going to call me the second they land. They are going to be devastated. We all are."

"Look, Abby, let me talk to Greg, but I don't think we should let our package out of our custody so fast until we have a chance to think things through. He might know something he hasn't told us. Do you think the sister, what's her name, would talk to Maizie and Rick? The two women are probably together and maybe Maizie and Rick can convince them that it's over and to give up the baby. How long before Maizie and Rick are supposed to land?"

"I think a few hours. The plane was delayed taking off."

"Okay, Greg and I will talk, and I'll get back to you. I think we have to tell Maizie and Rick something other than that Grace was not at the apartment in Richmond. I can't even imagine how upset they're going to be. I don't envy your having to tell them."

"I feel sick myself. I don't know how I'm going to tell them this when they are so hopeful that Jason and I have Grace. This might be the worst phone call I've ever had in my life. Call me back. Right now Jason and I are just sitting in the car. We don't know what to do. We don't know if we should just head back to the airport."

"Wait until I call you back before you do anything."

CHAPTER 55

For what seemed like an eternity to Abby and Jason, they sat in the car in stony silence. There was nothing to say. They were so close to getting Grace back. They were at the very place where she was, and they failed—not because of anything they had done wrong but because of bad timing. They were just a little too late, and that was enough for everything to fall apart.

Finally, Abby said out loud, "Mom, I don't know if you saw what happened. We missed Fatima and Grace by a few days. We have absolutely no idea of where they have gone or where to even start looking for them. Please, Mom, if ever there was a time we needed your help, this is it."

Jason had turned in his seat to look at Abby as she spoke to Fannie. "What do you think? Will she help us?"

"Honestly, I have no idea. I believe with my whole heart that she will help us if she can. But by the same token, I have no idea how much she can do from the other side."

As Abby finished talking, the phone rang. Both of them jumped and looked at Abby's phone, as if it were going to be Fannie on the other end. It was Adam.

"Okay, Greg and I have been talking about what to do. I am going to call Detective Williams in Rye Brook and tell him you got a tip about Grace and that's why you went to Richmond. I'm going to ask him to make a call to the chief of police in Richmond and fill him in on what's been going on. Then I think you should go to the police station in Richmond and explain things to him as well. Detective Williams will tell him an Amber Alert has already been issued.

"We don't know what kind of car this Fatima has, but we do know the car Vladdina has. You can probably give him a better description of Vladdina than I can. I would bet that the two women are together. Detective Williams can also send the pictures that we have of Grace to the police chief.

"Greg is going to make some calls to his contacts in the Marshals Service to see what they can do with Homeland Security and the TSA to get these two women on the 'no fly list.' At least we keep them in the country. If they go back to Russia, we are really up shit's creek without the paddle.

"Give me some time, and I'll call you back with the name of the police chief and what we can do. Greg will make his calls as well. If you want to start driving to the police station now that's okay, but don't go in yet until I have a name for you. Otherwise, you'll get stuck at the front desk with someone who won't know what the hell is going on."

Abby said, "Do you think that Steve had anything to do with Fatima's taking off? Could he have tipped her off to run?"

"I don't think so. We've had him here with us under wraps, so I don't think there was any way he could have called her or communicated with her. Now it's possible that he said something to her before we got him that spooked her, but that's gonna be hard to get out of him. He may not even realize what he said to her. By the way, was the apartment where she had Grace a nice place?"

"Yes, why do you ask?"

"After we got the most important pieces of information from him and he realized that he wasn't going anywhere for a while, then he got a little bit chatty. Wanted us to see what a big and important guy he was. How generous he was. He told us how nice the apartment he was renting for her, like that was supposed to impress us. At least he didn't have them in some hellhole. Okay, give me some time and I'll call you back with the info."

Jason heard the whole conversation with Adam on the speaker phone. "Well, let me get the address for the police on the GPS, and I guess we should start heading there." Jason turned on the engine, and the navigation screen came up on the display on the dashboard. He tried to move the display to the next screen, but nothing happened. Then something happened that shocked both Jason and Abby.

It seemed as if Fannie's voice were coming through the GPS. Instead of the mechanical voice of the GPS, it was Fannie's voice. Both Abby and Jason jumped in their seats.

"Jason, it's Grandma."

Before Fannie could utter another word, Abby cut in with a voice that was a weird cross between agony and excitement. To Abby, it didn't even sound like herself. "Mom, I can hear you! It's been so long since I've heard from you. I've missed you so much!" With that Abby's voice cracked and the tears were rolling down her face.

Jason, on the other hand, truly looked like he had seen a ghost, even though there was nothing to see.

Fannie sounded a little flustered as well. "Abby, you can hear me? It's not just Jason who can hear me?"

"Yes, yes, I can hear you. Mom, I meant it when I said I really missed you. You know that as much as you were often a pain, I really loved you so much. It's been a few years since I heard from you. It was that time we were all at the beach house in New Jersey. It seemed you came to say goodbye." Abby was still weeping unabashedly as she was talking and her words came through her tears.

"I have no idea why I was never able to talk to you directly after that day at the beach house. I thought that I had come back to make amends to you for what I did, about, about, about Jason was completed. I, er, did what I came to do, and so I thought my time back in this world had ended.

"I don't know why it was that Jason was the only one recently who could hear me, especially since it was Maizie and Rick who were the two in the most need of my help. I told you before that I have never quite understood how this works. I only know that it works.

"Frankly, Abby, I'm very glad to be able to talk to you directly. Now Jason, don't take this wrong, but you are a little difficult to talk to. You're way too skittish. Everything upsets you. Have you ever thought about taking a tranquilizer once in a while?"

Jason would have preferred, at the precise moment that Fannie was speaking directly to him, to either be invisible or to crawl under the front seat of the car. He didn't know if he was or was not supposed to answer Fannie.

Fannie didn't really give him much of a chance. She dismissed him with, "Well, no matter now, Jason. Let me continue to talk to Abby and you just listen.

"Abby, I feel strong and vibrant today for some reason. I did see you go to the apartment and that Grace and that woman were not there. What kind of names are Vladamus and Fatinamus?"

"It's Vladdina and Fatima. They're Russian names. But go ahead, Mom, about Grace." Abby noted quickly to herself that in these past few minutes Fannie sounded like her old self—her old self when she was alive—the opinionated and self-assured Fannie who thought she was always right—about everything. It reminded Abby of the old saying, "Not always right, but never unsure."

"Well, right now I don't know where they went, but I will try to find out and find out quickly. As I said, today I feel strong, the way I did when I came back to help you and Rick last time.

"Tell Maizie and Rick that Grandma Fannie is on the case. Tell them I will find these women, and I will help them find Grace. Tell them to be strong for a little longer. It's going to work out. I can feel it."

With that, there seemed to be no more voice coming from the GPS. Abby smiled as she wiped the tears that were still flowing.

Abby looked at Jason who was as still as a statue. He didn't even appear to be breathing.

CHAPTER 56

Abby knew the phone call from Maizie and Rick was inevitable as soon as the plane landed, and she was dreading it. The only positive thing she had to tell them was that she actually heard Fannie and that Fannie sounded strong and said she was on the case. That was true, but it sounded lame to Abby as she thought about saying it out loud.

Right now she wasn't sure anything was going to matter to Maizie and Rick once they heard that she and Jason didn't have Grace. As Abby thought about it, she wasn't sure she would feel any differently if she were Grace's mother. The problem was she couldn't reproduce the feeling of talking to and hearing Fannie in mere words to Maizie and Rick.

As they drove to the police station, Abby felt she had to say something to Jason about the conversation with Fannie. "So what did you think of the conversation with your grandmother?" She felt the question was broad enough that she had given Jason a lot of leeway.

Jason thought for a moment and said, "I can't help it. It really freaks me out every time she talks to me. I was so glad you could finally hear her. She's dead, you know."

Abby didn't know if Jason realized how funny, yet almost innocent, his comments were. Of course, she knew Fannie was dead. Everyone knew it, and that was why it was so incredible that Fannie was talking to them from the other side. And she hadn't heard from Fannie in a few years. "It seems to upset you when she talks to you. Why is that? You know she's only trying to help us find Grace."

Jason thought about it and stuttered his response. "You know, you know, she's dead, right? You act like she's been sitting in the next room, and it's the most normal thing in the world."

"Okay, I grant you that it certainly is not the norm to talk to someone who's dead. But, Jason, Grandma has been talking to you for some time now. Every time you hear her, you act like you're going to have a heart attack. She sounds like a normal person when she talks to us. We're not at a séance or in a haunted house with the wind wailing or ghosts flying by.

"Do you think you could take a step back and focus on the fact that she loves us and wants to help? That was her reason for coming back last time and helping us find Grace is her motive this time. Does that help you cope with it?"

The response was less than a rousing endorsement. "Yeah, I guess so."

CHAPTER 57

Abby knew her phone was going to ring as soon as Maizie and Rick landed and they could turn their phones back on. Maizie sounded almost breathless as she blurted out, "Mom, do you have Grace?"

Abby heard the sob on the other end of the call, as she said no. For a second Abby wasn't sure if Maizie had hung up, but then she heard Rick say hello and she realized Maizie must have handed the phone to him.

Obviously, Rick realized as Maizie broke into tears that things had not gone well. "Abby, what happened?"

She explained all that had transpired with the empty apartment, and her conversations with Adam. "We're headed over to the police department now, but we're waiting to go in until Adam calls us back to tell us to go in because they have paved the way."

Rick sounded defeated, and Abby could identify with that emotion.

"Where's Maizie?"

"She's sitting next to me, because we're still taxiing to the gate, but she's crying pretty badly. I hope I can get her off the plane. Is Adam really sure that that bastard didn't stall and then somehow communicate with her to leave? If that's what he did, I swear I will kill him myself!" Rick hissed.

"No, Adam and Greg both felt that they had him incommunicado the whole time and that there was no way he could have tipped her off. The other very troubling thing is that Vladdina is gone as well. They're in this together. To me, that's even more upsetting. Fatima never met you, but Vladdina was almost a member of your household, and she knew you and Maizie. How could she do such a thing to you? She betrayed you and betrayed your trust for money. She put you through hell for money! I want to kill her myself."

"This whole thing makes me sick. We really thought Vladdina liked us and loved Grace. It's hard for me to even imagine anyone kidnapping a baby, but for it to be someone we brought into our house is just unimaginable to me. Of course, now we realize why she was supposedly out sick the day Grace was kidnapped."

"Rick, Adam suggested that maybe you should try to call Vladdina and appeal to her sense of decency. Tell her you know she was involved, but now it's time to give Grace back."

Rick sounded defeated again. "I can't imagine that this would do any good. She's just evil."

"I don't know. Maybe if you tell her you know she's been involved, but she could just drop Grace off at a police or fire station with no consequences. It's something to think about. You might just persuade her to do the right thing."

"I sincerely doubt it, based on what's gone on so far. She knew exactly what she was doing. It was all about the money." Rick sighed deeply.

"Wait a minute. I have an idea! Suppose I call her, and the police track her cell phone? What's it called? I've seen it on TV. They triangulate the call. We could find her! Let me call Adam and see if he can talk to the police about doing this. I'll call you right back after I talk to Adam."

Through the tears, Maizie heard what Abby said about

triangulating the call. She said in a whispered tone, "Do you think there's a chance it could work?"

At that moment, Rick didn't have time to stop and answer Maizie. He was on a mission to call Adam and ultimately find Grace. Adam saw Rick's number come up on his phone and knew he had to answer, even though it was going to be an awful conversation. "Hi, Rick. I'm really very sorry that it didn't work with Abby and Jason getting Grace. I can't imagine how bad you must feel."

"Hold on, Adam. Abby told me that you think we should call Vladdina and try to persuade her to do the right thing. I'm sure she's with Fatima and Grace. What would happen if we got the police to triangulate the call, and they pick her up? We'd get Grace!"

Adam let out a long whistle on the phone. "It just might work. I called Detective Williams and told him what was going on. He was calling the chief of police in Richmond. I'm waiting for a call back. I don't know if we can convince the Richmond police to do this based only on our call to them. I think Detective Williams was also going to email them the police reports and all the documents on the kidnapping. With the documents, hopefully the police chief can be persuaded. Let me call Detective Williams again. I'll get back to you after I talk to him."

At this point the plane had mostly emptied out. Maizie's eyes were red, and she had a wad of tissues in her hand. The flight attendant looked at Maizie and then eyed Rick. She directed her comments to Maizie. "Are you okay, honey? Is everything okay here?" The implication was that maybe Maizie was being forced to leave the plane with Rick against her will.

As Rick stepped out into the aisle and reached for the carry-on suitcase, the flight attendant stepped between them and whispered to Maizie, "You don't have to get off the plane with him. You can stay here, and we'll get security to escort you off the plane."

In the midst of all the chaos and misery, Maizie broke out laughing. The thought of Rick hurting her was so absurd to her, that she started laughing. "I know this is going to sound crazy, but we got some bad news about our daughter. That is why I was crying. It had nothing to do with Rick. I was just upset, but I certainly thank you for caring enough about what happens to me. Your act of kindness to me is just so touching at this time when I was so upset."

CHAPTER 58

Detective Williams had been persuasive, and that along with the police reports about the kidnapping that had been faxed to Chief Redmond in Richmond and the information provided in person by Abby and Jason about Vladdina's car got them to put an alert out for Vladdina's car. Abby was so grateful to this man for being supportive that she didn't know if she wanted to cry or hug him or both. Meanwhile, Rick and Maizie were getting their luggage from baggage claim and had booked the first flight they could get to Richmond. Chief Redmond had brought in one of his techs to work on triangulating the call. Since Maizie and Rick couldn't get on a flight for several hours, after a few calls back and forth with Adam, they decided not to wait until Maizie and Rick got to Richmond to call Vladdina. It was decided that Abby would make the call and see if she could engage Vladdina on the phone.

While they were setting up the equipment, Abby said she needed to use the ladies' room. It was more a chance to gather herself before she had to make the call. Her thoughts were racing. Sure, she wanted to do everything to get Grace back, but she was truly fearful that she could say something that would make matters worse, and they would lose any opportunity to get Grace. At this moment, she was pacing up and down in the hallway near the ladies' room.

"How do I get myself into these situations?" Abby was talking out loud to herself and maybe to the universe. "I don't know how to do this. I don't know anything about kidnapping or what to say to Vladdina. I always liked her, but I don't know her that well. I hope she will relate to me." She asked herself again, "How do I get into these situations?"

This time it was Abby's turn to jump when she heard Fannie's voice. She heard Fannie's voice as if Fannie were standing there talking to her.

"Abby, you get into these situations because you are very capable and because you love Maizie and Rick so much that you will do anything to help them. Anything. Sure, it's a burden, but it's also a blessing. People need you and depend on you. You somehow rally by drawing on incredible inner strength. You're a special person and people see that in you. I saw it in you from the time you were a little girl.

"I think you have to do this because I don't think Maizie or Rick could do this. Maizie is too volatile. Rick would probably be too emotional or angry to carry on a conversation with Vladdina. You'll be able to do this; I know you will. My money's on you."

"Do you really believe this, Mom, or are you just saying this to try to make me call Vladdina?"

Fannie didn't hesitate in her answer. "I truly believe what I'm saying to you. Besides that, once you have passed to the other side, truth *is*."

"Is what?"

"Truth *is*. You can only speak the truth. Lies are a part of evil, which exists in the physical world. Evil falls and succumbs to the Light here."

"Will you help me, Mom? I think I'm going to need help."

"I will do whatever I can to help you. I'm always with you,

NOËL F. CARACCIO   219

Abby. I don't know why you haven't been able to see or hear me until very recently, but I am with you. C'mon, go make the call. You can do this."

"Okay, Mom, I believe you. Let's go make the call. Stay with me."

Abby walked back down the hallway to the room where Jason and the tech sat. Jason looked like he was seasick and was very pale.

The tech introduced himself to Abby. His first name was Quinn. "May I call you Abby?"

"Of course. I'm very nervous about making this call."

"That's completely understandable. I've done this many times before. All you need to do is talk to her. You know her, right? From what Jason just told me, you liked her before you found out what she did. Try to block that out for a minute. Tell her you know she's involved with the kidnapping but that she has a chance to make this right. Tell her it's okay. She's not going to get in trouble if you get Grace back.

"The important thing is to just keep talking. If she wants to answer you, so much the better. Don't get angry with her or accusatory. Keep reassuring her it's okay. The object is to keep her on the line. The longer she's on the line, the more chance we have to trace the call.

"Do you want a minute to collect yourself? I'm going to get one of the detectives to sit in with us. So take your time."

"Do you think I could have some water? All of a sudden, I can't swallow—my mouth is so dry."

Quinn smiled. "Everyone feels that way. There's a cooler right over there filled with water and soda. Help yourself." With that, Quinn smiled an encouraging smile and walked out of the room to get the detective.

Abby walked over to the cooler, and Jason walked over to it as well. "It's going to be fine, Abby. I can feel it." He squeezed her hand.

CHAPTER 59

Abby wished the cooler contained wine or vodka instead of just water and soda. *It's probably good that there is nothing stronger than soda*, she thought, *because everyone would be guzzling the alcohol and God knows what would come out of their mouths.*

Detective Borgman walked into the room behind Quinn. Quinn had a certain boyish look to him, which probably belied his age. Detective Borgman was probably twenty years older than Quinn. Abby thought he looked like a cop on any police show on TV. While Quinn was encouraging in his manner and his speech, the detective was much quieter and, after introducing himself, didn't have anything else to say. He went to take a seat over near the equipment that Quinn was going to manage.

"Okay, ready to roll? Quinn asked. "Here's how it works. Your phone number has been loaded into the equipment. You will talk to Vladdina on your phone, so it sounds normal to you as you talk to her and normal as she hears you. We'll have headsets on, so we hear everything said on both sides, and the conversation is being recorded. To Vladdina, it will seem you are calling her on your cell phone and your number will come up on her screen. Nothing out of the ordinary to her.

"You can look at anything in the room or look out the window. You shouldn't look at us because it will distract you. When we have enough to trace the call, I'll snap my fingers or tap on the desk to tell you we have enough. If you're getting information out of her or she's coming around to telling you where Grace is, you can keep her talking."

"How long do I have to keep her talking?"

"Not long. Twenty to twenty-five seconds will do it. I'll put the headset on now, and whenever you're ready, just dial the number."

Abby nodded and took another long drink of water. Jason got up from his chair and walked to a chair in the corner of the room out of Abby's line of sight.

Abby took a deep breath and dialed Vladdina's number. She didn't know whether to hope Vladdina would or would not answer the phone. The phone rang three times, and a tentative voice answered the phone.

Vladdina didn't recognize the phone number. The only reason she decided to answer it was that it was perhaps someone calling about Fatima.

"Vladdina, this is Abby, Maizie's Mom." Abby took a breath but decided to plow forward so Vladdina didn't hang up. "Vladdina, I stayed over at Maizie and Rick's house because the weather was so bad, and I saw that the mail hadn't been taken in for a few days and there were some circulars lying in the driveway. So I realized that you hadn't been at the house."

Vladdina only answered, "Yes."

The thought that flashed through Abby's mind was that Vladdina was going to play it close to the vest and not give up anything right away, which was probably good because she could keep her talking for a few seconds longer. Every second counted. "So Vladdina, are you still in New York at your house?"

"No, I'm not. Something came up, and I couldn't stay at the house. So are you staying at the house?"

"Yes, I am. I was trying to find out if you are okay."

"Yes, I am fine."

"Vladdina, you know Maizie and Rick are in Dubai, right?"

"Yes, I know that."

"And you know why they are in Dubai, don't you?"

"Yes, to help find Grace."

"Vladdina, Maizie and Rick are very fond of you. They feel that you are part of their family."

There was a long pause when Abby stopped speaking. Abby heard a sound in the room that distracted her. She saw Detective Borgman rip the headset off himself and bolt out of the room. She looked at Quinn who gave her a smile and a thumbs-up. He also gave her the signal with his hand to keep talking. He gave her the thumbs-up sign for a second time.

Since Vladdina had not answered Abby in those few seconds, Abby continued. "Vladdina, we know that your sister, Fatima, was involved in Grace's kidnapping. Do you know anything about that? Can you help us find her and Grace?"

Again, there was silence at the other end of the phone.

"Vladdina, can you get in touch with Fatima and help us find Grace?"

Abby realized that the call had been terminated. She looked hopefully at Quinn. He had a big smile on his face.

"Abby, you did great. Not only did you keep Vladdina on the phone long enough for us to track the call, but you also saw Detective Borgman bolt out of the room. That's because Vladdina is about three miles from here! He and a team of officers are on their way to pick her up, presumably with Fatima and Grace. Boy, you did a great job."

Abby sank back into her chair. All of a sudden, her legs felt a little wobbly. She mumbled under her breath, "Thank you, Mom. Thank you."

Jason rushed over to hug her.

CHAPTER 60

Vladdina didn't know what to think or what to do. The call from Abby completely unnerved her. *How does Abby know about Fatima?* If she knew about Fatima's involvement with the kidnapping, then it was a simple deduction for her to figure out about Vladdina's own involvement. After all, Fatima would have no possible connection to Grace unless she had been involved.

Vladdina wanted to get on a plane and go back to Russia. But she hadn't expected the situation to get so out of hand. She expected that Fatima would renege and finally answer her phone. She would never have guessed that Fatima would have bolted either. Vladdina couldn't get on a plane now because her passport was in her apartment in New York. Even if she had her passport with her now, she couldn't just go back to Russia and leave Fatima—especially since she had gotten Fatima involved in the kidnapping in the first place.

As she went back over the brief phone conversation in her mind she just had with Abby, she wasn't sure whether she had let on whether she was still in New York or where she was. She was mostly sure Abby had said she was at Maizie and Rick's house in New York, far away from her here in Richmond.

When there came a sharp knock on the door, Vladdina was so startled that she couldn't get up from her chair to answer the door. The first knock was also accompanied by a booming voice of a man identifying himself as being with the Richmond police department and telling her to open the door immediately.

It was only a matter of seconds before the booming voice on the other side of the door, screamed, "Vladdina Petrovia, open the door immediately, or we're going to break it down."

"Okay, I will open the door. I'm coming."

As soon as she opened the door, two uniformed police officers pushed their way into the room and grabbed her roughly by the arm. The burly one pushed her against the wall so that she was facing the wall and his big hand was against her back. The second police officer checked the bathroom and yelled, "Clear."

A man in a suit said he was a detective. "Vladdina Petrovia, you are under arrest for kidnapping and for endangering the welfare of a minor. You have the right to remain silent. Anything you say can and will be used against you in a court of law. You have the right to an attorney. If you can't afford an attorney, one will be appointed for you by the court. Do you understand these rights as I have told them to you?"

"Yes, but what is this about?"

"It's about the kidnapping of Grace Singleton. You know that. Where is your sister, Fatima, and where is Grace?"

"I, I don't know."

"Listen, this is going to go a whole lot easier on you if you cooperate and tell us where they are. The district attorney can make it better for you if you cooperate now. We know you're involved with the kidnapping, so it's better if you don't try to play games with us. You gotta be smart about this. So you need to tell us now where your sister, Fatima, and Grace are."

"I really don't know what you're talking about." Vladdina was trying to think, but she was so scared with the police coming to find her and this detective was yelling things at her. It was all happening too fast. The only thing she could think of right at this moment was to say nothing.

"All right, then, have it your way. Cuff her and get her out of here."

°°°°°°°°°°°°°°°°°°°°°°°°°°

Back at police headquarters, Abby's hands were shaking after the phone call was over. Jason said, "I'll call Maizie and Rick and tell them the good news. Just sit for a while and calm down."

"Do you think we should wait to call them until the police come back with Grace?"

"Well, I can at least call them and tell them the police are going to pick up Vladdina. That's something to give them hope after we came up with an empty apartment and no Grace. It's a solid lead. The police think the three of them are together. Why else would Vladdina be in Richmond? When the police come back with Grace and Fatima, then we make another call. I just want to tell them something good after all the bad news we've given them. Unless you want to call them? You were the one who made the call and kept Vladdina on the line."

"It's not about taking credit, Jason. Think about it from Maizie and Rick's viewpoint. They are most certainly going to jump to the conclusion that the three of them are together. We certainly thought it was so. For another few minutes, I say we wait until we know for sure that the police have Grace."

Jason shrugged and said yes, but Abby could see that he was humoring her. At that point, Abby was so emotionally exhausted from the highs and lows of the day that she was going to give in. But there was something in her that was resisting. She didn't see the point of putting Maizie and Rick on any more of an emotional roller coaster than they had already been on today.

Abby wasn't exactly sure how long they were sitting in the room after the phone call ended. She hadn't checked her watch to see what time the call ended.

Some more time passed and then Detective Borgman came into the room with Quinn following him. Without preamble the detective said, "Okay, we have some good news. We've got Vladdina in custody. But she was alone. There didn't appear to be any sign of the baby being in her hotel room. No baby clothes or baby things like a crib or stroller. The hotel manager said she checked in alone, and he never saw her with anyone. He never saw a baby.

"Look, she's definitely scared. That's what we need. If she's scared, then there's a good chance we can get her to talk. She knows more than she's letting on now. When the seriousness of this situation begins to sink in, I think she will talk. We're even going to bring in one of the women detectives to talk to her, so maybe she will open up to her. This is a good solid lead.

"Maybe you folks want to go home, and we'll call you as soon as we get anything out of her. It could take a few hours. Here's my card, and give me your cell numbers. We will certainly keep you advised of any developments. You have my word."

Abby and Jason must have looked exhausted and dejected. Quinn picked up on the vibes. "C'mon, we can talk some more and then I'll walk you out."

As they walked down the hallway, Quinn walked them into a conference room. "Honestly, this is a very big break. When you first saw Fatima's empty apartment, you must have been devastated. You had no idea of where to start looking. The outlook must have seemed so bleak to you. Vladdina could have been anywhere, instead of just a few miles from here. She knows where her sister and the baby are, or she knows how to get in touch with her. That's light years ahead of where we were three hours ago."

Quinn was much more of a people person than the detective, and his explanation gave Abby and Jason much more hope. His next offer surprised them.

"If you want to call your daughter and son-in-law, I will get on the phone with them and explain things. If you think it would help for them to hear it from the police, I'm more than happy to talk to them. It sounds like they've been through enough and hearing it from an independent person might be good for them."

Abby and Jason agreed, and Abby dialed Maizie's cell. Fortunately, Maizie answered her phone shortly before they got on the plane to Richmond.

CHAPTER 61

Abby and Jason checked into two rooms at the Hilton and reserved a third room for Maizie and Rick who had been delayed in the airport in Dubai, then were on a nonstop flight to New York for fourteen hours and forty minutes to cover the almost 6,900 miles. They waited two more hours to get on the flight to Richmond. Abby and Jason said they would pick them up at the airport so that the endless trek from the other side of the world would finally come to an end.

They also realized as they walked out of the police station that they hadn't had anything to eat since before their flight left LaGuardia Airport that morning. As they got in the car, Abby said, "Oh my God, we never called Adam back to tell him what was going on. He must think the worst has happened. You drive and I'll call him."

Adam was just about to leave the warehouse when his phone rang. Adam was more than relieved to hear what Abby had to tell him about Vladdina being in custody. Even though they didn't yet have Grace back, Adam felt this was huge and perhaps the last step. "Let me know when you get her back. If I don't answer, leave a message because I might be in the air."

Adam put his mask back on and went into the room where Greg was looking at something on his phone and Steve was apparently talking to him, although Greg was paying no attention. Adam motioned for Greg to follow him into the other room. "What the hell is he babbling about?"

"Who the hell cares. I'm reading a book on my phone. I can tune out a hurricane if I want to. He really loves the sound of his own voice. It's all about how great he was and all the cases he won. Like I give a crap. So what's up? You got a call."

Adam explained what had transpired in the States. "I think we can wrap this up here now. How do you want to handle it?"

"You should get out of here now and get on a flight anywhere—anywhere you can make a connecting flight back home. Just get yourself out of Dubai, but not directly back to New York. I'll wait here for a few more hours with our 'houseguest' and then I'll take off. My connections will take me by car out of here. Then I'll probably go to Europe and take some time off.

"Since we mashed up his cell phone and dumped it, do you have a burner phone? When I'm a couple of hours away, I'll make a call to his house and tell them where he is and then dump the burner. They can come pick him up. He's already complaining that he gave us the information and that we should release him. I told him if he asks me again, I'm going to put a gag in his mouth. At least he stopped asking me, but he still is talking to me. I haven't answered him in God knows how long."

"Okay, I can pack up my stuff and be out of here in five minutes. I'll take all the garbage, and you take your own stuff. Thanks, man. We make a good team. I really think we should finish our discussion about going into business together. We can talk about this when we get home."

They gave each other a high five and a quick hug. Adam started to pack up his things into a duffel bag. He looked around the room to see if there was anything else in the room except for the plastic bag of garbage. It wasn't that they cared about being neat or picking up after themselves, but they had each learned from various jobs and missions in the past that you do not leave one scrap of paper that could allow someone to connect them to this place. Even the crumpled-up McDonald's wrappers and Styrofoam cups were carefully loaded into the plastic garbage bag. No one would know they had been there. The owner of the building had been paid in cash and told to stay away.

In a few minutes, Adam said, "I'm ready to go. Take care of yourself. Here's the burner phone. Call me when you're outta here."

"Go; we did a good job. I'll call you."

Adam smiled, nodded and headed for the door. Greg heard the car start outside.

He sat down in the room and continued reading the book on his phone. He looked at his watch and realized he only had to wait about three and half hours and then he'd be out of here. This was going to be a big payday, and he hadn't taken a punch or been shot at. He looked at the closed door to the room where Steve was still tied up.

Adam was a decent guy and had been in law enforcement solely and exclusively in the United States, where there were rules and plenty of them. Greg realized that he had been in the Marshals Service and had been all over the world. The rules didn't necessarily apply in many places in the world. The only rule was do the job and survive to go home.

Maybe he should finish the job and do justice. Maybe he should finish off Steve. Adam would never have to know. This bastard Steve had caused so much pain for no reason. He was never going to be brought to justice for the kidnapping. Adam had also told him the back story of why Steve was living in Dubai and all that money Steve had made in the black-market adoptions. Steve was never going to be brought to justice for those either. Maybe there really was a way for true justice to be done. He had several hours to consider the answer.

CHAPTER 62

Detective Carol Powers had just finished an hour-long bike ride. As she was putting her bike in the garage, her cell phone rang. It was a police department number. Since this was her day off, a call from the department meant something was up. She listened to the voice at the other end of the phone and nodded and said only six words. "Yes, I'll be in right away."

She took a quick shower and called her husband at his job to tell him she was going in to work and why. Since it was already late afternoon, she told him not to wait for her for dinner. It could be a long night.

She said hello to her co-workers as she walked into the police station but didn't stop to chat with anyone. She headed straight for Detective Borgman's desk. He was waiting for her. "This is what we know so far," he began.

He gave her all the background they had and said that he had sent the grandmother and uncle back to the hotel and that they were waiting for the parents to arrive. "I can let you talk to the grandmother and uncle and ask them to come back if you want, but they seemed pretty fried, so I sent them home. These people have been through a hell of a lot today."

"Do you have any doubt as to what they are telling you is true?"

"No, no doubt, especially when you hear what they said coupled with the reports from the PD in New York. You can talk to Quinn, too, if you want, but I don't think he thought anything was fishy."

"Rather than drag them back here, I think I'll talk to them on the phone. I want to hear the story in their own words."

"Okay, no problem. Here are their cell phone numbers."

This was how Detective Powers had been successful. She listened to her co-workers, absorbed what they had to say, but then wanted to hear and verify things for herself. Sometimes the smallest detail could change the whole course of an investigation. She didn't want to confront this suspect or, in fact, any suspect unless she felt comfortable with all the details.

After close to a half hour on the phone with Abby first and then Jason, Detective Powers was ready to speak to the suspect. She thought about waiting for the parents, but the grandmother and the uncle answered every one of her questions without hesitation or inconsistency. If she did not get what she needed from the suspect now, she would have another crack at her after she talked to the parents.

She grabbed a tape recorder, a pad, and a pen and walked into Interrogation Room 4. Sitting facing the door was a young woman who looked to be in her late twenties or early thirties, with dark hair and penetrating blue eyes, who was sizing up the detective, even as the detective was sizing her up. This young woman was quite attractive.

Det. Powers took in the young woman handcuffed to the table and noted that she also looked pale and frightened. Leaving her sitting in the room alone wondering what was going to happen to her and worrying about her future in a country not her native land was a good thing.

"Vladdina, I'm Detective Powers. I'm here to talk about the

kidnapping. Our main goal is to get the baby back as soon as possible. You can help me do that and in the process help yourself. Let's just you and I talk and see if we can do that."

Although Detective Powers had not spoken with Maizie and Rick, she wanted Vladdina to think she had. She had a number of details from her conversations with Abby and Jason to make it seem she had spoken to Maizie and Rick. Maizie and Rick were the best connections to Vladdina and maybe that connection to them would help move her in the right direction.

"I've heard nice things about you from Maizie and Rick. They like you and they thought you were good with the baby. They thought you loved Grace and wouldn't do anything to hurt her. They wanted you to be a part of their family. I guess something went wrong. It might have been a mistake in judgment, and things didn't turn out the way you thought they would. But it's not too late to fix that. You and I have a chance to fix that now."

Detective Powers would start out friendly, just two women talking trying to clear up a problem. If she didn't get anywhere, then her whole tone and demeanor would change. But for the time being, she would try to befriend Vladdina.

"So what do you think, Vladdina? Can we work together on this?"

"I, I don't know what to say."

"Well, how about we start at the beginning, and you tell me how this kidnapping came about in the first place. As I said, Maizie and Rick like you or they wouldn't have wanted you to take care of Grace. You love the baby, don't you?"

A single tear ran down Vladdina's cheek. "Yes, I love Grace and I don't want anything to happen to her. Maizie and Rick must hate me now, even if they liked me at one time."

"Well, let's see if we can help get Grace back. Your cooperation and telling the truth will help them, help Grace, and help you."

To Detective Powers's relief, Vladdina was not going to sit there and deny that she had any part in the kidnapping. That was a huge hurdle to overcome. Things would go easier and faster this way and hopefully getting Grace back would come more quickly as well.

Vladdina told the story of the kidnapping and how she got Fatima involved to take care of Grace. She explained that she believed that no one was going to hurt Maizie or Grace during the kidnapping. She also explained that she was shocked to hear that Maizie was hurt badly enough to have to go the hospital. As she told the early part of the story, she said that she agreed to the kidnapping because she thought that she would help her family in Russia with the money she and Fatima would earn and that they were doing it for selfless motives.

Detective Powers had heard all kinds of stories from criminals about why they had committed various crimes. Some of the stories were heartbreaking, some were evil, some were to get rich, and some were purely dumb. It reminded her of the adage that where you stand on any given subject depends on where you sit. Detective Powers wanted to shake her head that Vladdina could actually believe she was doing the kidnapping for altruistic reasons.

Vladdina told Detective Powers that all the contact with the man paying the bills had gone through Fatima. With hindsight, Fatima admitted to Vladdina that the man paying the bills had never been very specific as to how long Fatima was to care for the baby. Fatima had been led to believe it would be a short time. Vladdina didn't know the man's name, and she thought that Fatima didn't know who he was either. After she got through that much of the story, Vladdina broke down in fits of sobbing about how sorry she was about what had happened.

Detective Powers had been doing this long enough to know that a suspect crying didn't necessarily mean that they were remorseful about the crime or what they had done to the victim. Some suspects cried because they were caught and knew they faced jail time. So while it looked like Vladdina was crying because she was sorry about the kidnapping and her role in it, she could be crying for her own selfish motives or to gain the sympathy of Detective Powers.

The first red flag to Detective Powers was that Vladdina claimed not to know the name of the man paying the bills. Detective Powers questioned her a little more on that subject without really getting anywhere, so she decided to leave that subject and circle back to it later.

CHAPTER 63

Abby and Jason met Maizie and Rick at baggage claim. They looked like the walking dead to Abby. As she did the math in her head, she realized that they had been awake for more than twenty-four hours and had probably been in the air for more than eighteen hours. Added to that was the emotional strain and the roller-coaster ride of ups and downs of thinking they were going to finally have Grace back.

As Abby hugged Maizie, she felt Maizie clinging to her as she had as a child.

"Mom, I'm so glad you're here. I need you. I really don't know how much more of this I can take."

Abby hugged Maizie back. "It's okay, Maiz. It's going to be okay. The police have Vladdina in custody, and they told us they were going to bring in a woman detective they say is great to talk to her. The police think this woman detective can get her to talk."

Maizie seemed reluctant to let go of Abby.

"C'mon, let's get out of here," Abby said. "You two must be so exhausted. Have you had anything to eat?" With that, Abby gently turned Maizie around and put her arm around Maizie's shoulder and guided her away from the baggage carousel. She also managed to get a hold of Rick's arm and leaned in to kiss him. Rick looked equally wiped out.

Jason said, "Just tell me which are your suitcases and I'll are grab them and we'll be out of here." Jason then put his arm around his brother's shoulder. "We're going to help you through this, bro. You were all there for me after my car wipeout and my ordeal in the hospital. Now I'm here for you. It's going to be over soon. I can feel it."

Rick didn't even have the energy to agree or disagree. He was too spent physically and emotionally. Right now, he needed someone to take care of him. Fortunately, the luggage came off the baggage carousel quickly, and the four of them headed out of the terminal to the car.

As they drove back toward the hotel, Jason said, "There's a restaurant in the hotel. Have you two had anything to eat in the last twenty-four hours that hasn't been airline peanuts, pretzels, and soda? We can eat something quickly and then you can go to bed."

Rick answered first and said, "I'm dead tired, but I am a little hungry. What about you, Maiz?"

"I'm not hungry. I want to go to the police department and see Vladdina."

Abby purposely was sitting in the back seat of the car with her arm still around Maizie. It was Abby who answered, because the tension in the car was palpable after Maizie's statement.

"There's no point in going to the police station now. They're not going to let you or anyone else see Vladdina while she's in custody. We can call Detective Borgman and ask him what's going on or we can call Detective Powers, but that's all we can do now. She may still be questioning Vladdina, so I don't know if she will talk to us now. She said she'll call us when they had some definitive information."

"No, I want to go to the police station now. I want to confront that bitch. I want her to look me in the eye and have her tell me why she did what she did."

Abby let out a sigh and answered Maizie as she would a child. "We are not going to the police station now. As I said, they are not going to let you or anyone see Vladdina right now. When we get to the hotel, we can call the detective. Jason and I both have his cell number."

They arrived at the hotel and went up to Rick and Maizie's room. Abby dialed Detective Borgman's cell phone number and he answered. She explained that she had Grace's parents with her and that they had just arrived from overseas. She put the phone on speaker and Rick introduced himself and Maizie. For some reason, he felt a rush of adrenaline.

Detective Borgman was patient on the phone as he recounted all that had transpired over the last few hours, even though he was sure Abby and Jason had briefed them already. He told them about Detective Powers and that she was interrogating Vladdina right now. "As soon as she's finished with the interrogation or if she takes a break and has some concrete information, I will tell her to call you immediately. Give me your cell phone number. I already have Abby's and Jason's."

Maizie had been quiet during the conversation, and Rick had done most of the talking and the questioning. Now as the conversation was ending, Maizie said in a quiet but firm voice, "I want to see Vladdina."

"Sorry, ma'am, but that cannot and will not happen. You will be able to be present when she is arraigned in court if you want to attend the proceeding."

"I really need to see her."

"No, that's not possible. So if there is nothing else, I will have Detective Powers get in touch with you when she has some information. Good night."

CHAPTER 64

Greg had tried to concentrate on his book after Adam left, but now his mind was spinning. This bastard Goldrick had walked away scot-free from all his crimes, and from what Greg had learned from Adam about the black-market adoptions and now this kidnapping, it appeared that pattern was going to continue.

He had never answered to anyone for his actions. He hadn't answered to a court of law, he hadn't answered to his partners in the law firm, and he certainly hadn't answered to his victims. His house in Dubai was large and opulent, so apparently he had indeed profited from his crimes. From all that he had been bragging about to Greg about his career, even though Greg was barely listening, it seemed that Goldrick had made out extremely well financially. The only thing that seemed to bother him was that he could never set foot in the United States ever again. If he tried to enter the United States, he would probably set off alarms and be taken into custody as a fugitive. He would spend his remaining years in a prison.

So if Greg left the warehouse now and called Steve Goldrick's family in a few hours, they would gladly come retrieve him, and he would go home to his family, big house, and lifestyle of the rich and famous. No consequences. No consequences whatsoever except for a few bruises and welts and that he had to eat a few McDonald's hamburgers.

Greg continued to grapple with this. *Where was the justice in all this? How did this despicable person get to walk away from all his actions?*

The other question pinging around in Greg's mind was whether he should be the one to administer the justice. Who appointed him as judge, jury, and executioner? On the other hand, if he didn't administer justice now, would justice ever come for Steve Goldrick?

Greg got up and paced back and forth in the outer room. He had killed people before. It wasn't a pleasant thing, but sometimes it was necessary in furtherance of the mission or the cause. Did justice itself qualify as a mission or cause?

He hadn't signed on to do anything except find out where this baby was, do what was necessary to find her, and help her parents get her back as quickly as possible. These parents had been in a living and seemingly endless hell, while Steve Goldrick went on with his life as if nothing had happened. That wasn't even a correct assessment. Steve was enjoying the misery of these parents while exacting his own vicious brand of revenge.

That's when it clicked in Greg's mind and it all jelled. Steve Goldrick had nominated himself as judge, jury, and executioner, and now it was high time that someone perform those functions on him. Greg unholstered his gun, took out the clip, and reinserted two bullets in the chamber. He put his mask back on and strode into the room where Steve Goldrick was tied up. He purposely banged the door open on his way in.

Steve startled. "So are you finally letting me go? For God's sake, you've had all this information, you've checked it out, so let me go."

"Shut up. You're not going anywhere. You've done nothing but cause pain and misery to people in a profession where you were supposed to be helping people, not ripping them off. Now you've caused untold pain to these parents by kidnapping their child. Were you ever going to give her back or were you going to keep her forever? You are one sick bastard. And you need to pay for what you've done.

"No court has made you pay so far. Because of that, you were just emboldened to do more and inflict more pain. It's time for this to stop."

For the first time, it dawned on Steve that this huge man standing before him might really kill him. Fear spread through him like a fire licking at kindling. It caught and spread.

"What are you talking about?" Steve was desperately trying to regain some measure of control. He was trying to be the tough guy. But it wasn't working with Greg, and Steve could see that. "Look, if it's money you want, that can be arranged. Tell me how much and where it's supposed to be paid, and I can have it done."

"You still don't get this, do you? It's not always about money, you fool. It's about paying for the evil things you've done in your life. A court can't get to you, but I can. I can make you pay, not with money, but with your life."

Greg had his hand on his sidearm and pulled the gun out of its holster. He did this in full view of Steve.

Steve's whole countenance changed. He went pale and his voice came out as a croak. "Wait a minute. We can work this out. Let me pay you."

There was a panic in Steve's voice as the realization dawned on him that he very likely was going to die—and in the next few minutes, in this miserable warehouse, all alone. No one would even find his body. The rats would eat him. This wasn't how Steve Goldrick, one of the once most powerful lawyers in New York City, was supposed to die.

He tried again. "Wait, you don't have to kill me. I've got lots of money, and you can have it. You don't have to kill me. Take the money and walk away."

"Shut up! You've done despicable things to a lot of people, and you were going to get away with it. 'Were' being the operative word. No more. You are finally going to pay for what you did, and you're going to pay now."

Steve yelled, "No! No!"

Greg walked up to Steve and spun the chamber. He put the muzzle of the gun up against Steve's head when he heard something. It sounded like a woman's voice, but what would a woman be doing in this sleazy part of town, and in this very building in a secluded area?

The voice simply said, "No."

Greg turned to face the door with his gun drawn. He moved quickly and silently toward the door. No one was there. No one had come into this room, and the outer door was still closed as it had been when Adam left.

He heard the voice again. "If you kill him, you are no better than he is. And you *are* better than he is. He ultimately will answer for his sins and his crimes. His time on this earth is limited. He may not pay in this world, but he will pay in the next. I know this. Leave him here and call his family. Your soul will be at peace. His will not."

Greg wasn't sure who was talking to him. But once he heard this voice, he knew he should leave and not kill Steve Goldrick. It was not his place to kill him.

Later in his life, Greg would look back on this moment. He was absolutely sure he had heard a woman's voice speaking to him. He didn't know it was Fannie speaking to him. He didn't know who Fannie was. She had spared Steve Goldrick's life, but she had saved Greg's.

CHAPTER 65

"Where is your sister and the baby? You know, so tell me now and it will be over with. You made a mistake getting involved in the mess to begin with, but now if you help us fix this, it will go better for you and Fatima. It's still not too late to fix this."

This was how the conversation had been going for quite a while between Detective Powers and Vladdina. Vladdina had been lamenting the situation, but not providing any more concrete information.

Detective Powers had tried a variety of ways getting her to talk. She had been the most successful not with bullying and intimidation but with some compassion and reason. Detective Powers thought she ought to continue in that vein for a bit longer before she started playing "the bad cop." She needed Vladdina to focus, and right now Vladdina was wailing. Detective Powers wasn't sure if Vladdina was wailing about what she had done and that she had gotten Fatima involved, or if she was lamenting that she had been caught.

"I'm going to get a cup of coffee. I'll bring you back one, but then we have to get to the bottom of this."

Detective Powers's departure from the interrogation room was motivated not from the need for a caffeine fix but from the fact that she wanted to see if Vladdina calmed down if she left the room, and whether this wailing was an act to gain sympathy or some other ulterior motive. Detective Powers took her time getting the coffee and went to talk to Detective Brogan to tell him what had been going on in the interrogation room. They spoke for a few minutes and then they walked to the one-way window of the interrogation room to watch what Vladdina was doing when she was alone in the room.

As they watched, it appeared that Vladdina calmed down somewhat, even though she was still crying a little bit.

"How much more time you going to give her?" Detective Brogan asked.

"Not much more before I switch tactics to much more aggressive."

As they watched, Vladdina put her head down on the table in front of her. Detective Powers thought this might be a good thing. It was a gesture that Vladdina was tiring both mentally and physically. Detective Powers waited only another minute before going back into the interrogation room. She didn't want Vladdina getting comfortable or taking a nap and getting a new burst of energy.

She made noise as she entered the interrogation room, and Vladdina sat up from the table as if she had been startled out of a nap. Detective Powers handed a cup of coffee across the table to Vladdina and then sat down in the chair across from her.

"Okay, Vladdina, this is it. I want to help you, but you need to tell me the whole truth, and you need to do it now. We're wasting a lot of time, and we still don't know where the baby is. That's the last and certainly the most important piece of this. The rest of this is just the backstory. We need the most important thing, and you know what that is. We need to know where Grace is. If you're not going to tell me, then we'll just charge you and you can go think about this in jail. Detective Brogan has been saying that we should just end this now and he'll take you off to jail. So this is your last chance. I'm the only thing keeping you out of jail right now."

The fear in Vladdina's eyes glowed red hot for the first time. "I know you don't believe me that I don't know where Fatima is, but I don't. I told you that I came to Richmond because she was not answering her phone or my texts to her. I will call her now if you want, and you can hear for yourself that she is not answering her phone."

"Okay, let's do that, but we have to set a few ground rules first. You have to speak to her in English, not Russian. Second, you have to agree in advance what you're going to say to her, and we are going to be monitoring and recording the call. Unless you agree to all this, then you and I are done. Decide now. What's it gonna be?"

"Okay, I agree."

"If you try to double cross us, or you switch to talking to her in Russian, we're going to end the call. Got it?"

A meek yes came from Vladdina.

CHAPTER 66

Abby finally got to her hotel room and sat down heavily in the easy chair in the room and put her feet up on the ottoman. She flicked on the TV with the remote, more for some noise in the room than anything else. Maizie had been more of a handful than she had expected, and Abby was glad she had been there for both Maizie and for Rick. They both seemed to need her, but right now her emotional gas tank was running on fumes.

It had been an endless day starting many hours ago on the trip to LaGuardia to take the plane to Richmond. It now seemed like days ago, rather than just hours ago. There had been so many emotional ups and downs, so much hope and disappointment. Abby wanted to get up to take a shower before she went to bed, but right now she was just too bone tired to move. Maybe in a few minutes she would gather her strength and get up to take a shower.

Abby never realized that she had fallen asleep in the chair. She had slept there all night. As she opened her eyes, she saw daylight streaming through the bottom of the curtains. As she looked at the clock, she was surprised to see it say 7:23 a.m. Her back screamed as she moved to get up out of the chair. Hopefully, a hot shower would help loosen the kinks.

The next question that came to mind was if Maizie and Rick had heard from the Richmond detectives. They probably hadn't heard a thing or Maizie would have called her, even in the middle of the night. It seemed as if they were so close to getting Grace back, yet they couldn't seem to get over this last and most important hurdle.

Just as Abby finished her shower and put on her robe, she heard, "Abby, it's Mom."

Abby spun around toward the direction she thought she heard the voice. In a split second, she realized that once again she wasn't hearing her mother through her ears. It only seemed that way. "Mom, I'm so glad that you are able to talk to me directly again."

"Yes, it was a royal pain for me to have to go through Jason. He's a very nice young man, and I wish I had known him before I died. But as I said to him, he's too nervous. I told him he should take a Valium. You really should talk to him about taking it to calm himself down."

Abby smiled and laughed to herself. It sounded like the old Fannie. Opinionated and in her mind, she was always right. "Go on, Mom. I'm so glad to talk to you myself without any intermediary. And you sound pretty feisty, too."

"Well, this woman, with the baby, Flatulence, or whatever her name is, has the baby."

Even under all this stress, Abby had to laugh. "Mom, flatulence means gassy. Her name is Fatima. We know she has the baby. But what about her?"

"Well, she and the baby are in Springfield. I saw it."

"Are you sure?"

"Yes, I saw a sign that said Springfield."

"Oh my God, that's great. We can tell the police, and they can pick them up! We'll have to call the police, and I have to call Maizie and Rick right now."

Even as Abby was elated, it was as if someone with a giant pin stuck it in the balloon. How were they going to tell the police that they got a tip where Fatima and Grace were? How were they going to tell the police that it was Abby's dead mother who told them where Fatima and Grace were?

"Mom, are they in Springfield, Virginia, or Springfield somewhere else?"

There was a long pause as Fannie considered this. "I don't know. Are there Springfields somewhere else?"

Abby grabbed her phone out of her purse. First, she dialed Rick's phone. He answered on the third ring. It sounded as if she woke him up. He sounded groggy. Then she remembered that Rick said last night that he and Maizie were both going to take a sleeping pill since their body clocks were still on Dubai time and they had been flying for hours.

"Rick, sorry to wake you up, but I just heard from my mother that she thinks Fatima and Grace are in Springfield. Can you come to my room right now?"

"Sure, be right there."

Then Abby called Jason and told him the same thing she had just told Rick.

"Mom, what did the sign say exactly? Did it say, 'Welcome to Springfield, Virginia,' or was it a sign on a store?"

There was a pause and Fannie didn't answer right away.

"Mom, can you think about this and try to describe what you saw?"

Before Fannie could answer, there was a knock on the door, and it was Maizie and Rick. As soon as the door closed, there was a second knock, and it was Jason.

Maizie and Rick each had on T-shirts and sweatpants. Rick looked haggard, and he had very visible stubble on his face. Maizie, who was always well put together and never left the house without perfect hair, makeup, and clothes, had the worst case of bed head that Abby had seen in a very long time. Her hair was literally sticking out in all directions. Jason had on the white robe from the hotel. He also looked beat, and Abby noticed how white his legs were sticking out from the robe.

Abby thought to herself that these were funny things to notice in yet another moment of high stress, yet this was what had registered in her brain.

"Mom says Fatima and Grace are in Springfield. I don't know if that means Springfield, Virginia, or somewhere else. Mom said she saw a sign that said Springfield, but that's all we've got." With that, Abby handed her iPad to Jason, as it was just booting up. "Jason, do you want to see where Springfield, Virginia, is, and if there are other Springfields in neighboring states?"

Jason nodded and his finger swiped across the screen. Everyone in the room waited expectantly for the answer. "Google says there are forty-one states that have a town named Springfield. There is a Springfield in Virginia, Massachusetts, North Carolina, South Carolina, New Jersey, Tennessee, and West Virginia, to name a few."

The pained expression on Jason's face said what each of them was thinking.

"Look, I doubt that she would go to Massachusetts or New Jersey, but that leaves a bunch of neighboring states where she might have gone," Abby said. "Let me ask Mom again what she sees. Mom, I assume you heard what's being said here. There are a number of places named Springfield. Can you try seeing something else to help us know which Springfield it is?"

The four of them waited expectantly for Fannie to answer Abby. Jason piped up, "Abby, I'm really glad that Grandma is talking to you now instead of to me. It's stressful enough waiting for an answer, and I just don't want to be the one hearing it."

Jason's comment broke the ice, and everyone had a small laugh in an extremely tense situation.

Abby waited a few more seconds hoping for an answer from Fannie. Nothing. Jason, Rick and Maizie were all standing. No one could contain their emotions, and they were all standing looking intently at Abby.

Finally she asked again, "Mom, do you see anything you can identify and tell us about?"

After what seemed like an eternity, Fannie answered Abby. "There's a sign that says, 'Austin Peay two miles.' I have no idea what that is."

The three of them looked expectantly at Jason, who started typing furiously on the iPad. His response was, "It's Austin Peay State University. It's in Clarksville, Tennessee." Jason worked the iPad again. "Okay, okay, Clarksville, Tennessee, is right next to Springfield, Tennessee. Let me google how far that is from here." The excitement was rising in his voice, and the excitement in the room was rising exponentially. Jason continued. "It's 639 miles from Richmond to Springfield, Tennessee, and it's nine hours and thirty-five minutes driving time." Jason looked up expectantly from the iPad.

CHAPTER 67

Back at the Richmond police station, they had set up the recording equipment for Vladdina to make the call to Fatima. When they were ready and had rehearsed what she was going to say on the phone, Vladdina made the call, but again the call went to Fatima's voice mail. She left yet another message for Fatima to call her.

Since it was now getting late, Detective Powers arranged for one of the women officers to stay with Vladdina outside one of the rooms. There was a cot and some blankets in the room. It wasn't the best of accommodations and it wasn't a hotel, but Detective Powers had been threatening Vladdina with jail, and she didn't want to put Vladdina in a cell if she was cooperating.

Detective Powers decided to return to the police station early the next morning, so the detectives could huddle and decide what to do next. As she was about to leave her house in the morning, her cell phone rang, and it was Mr. Singleton. He said that they would like to meet with her and that they had some information to give her, and he wanted her to brief them on what had happened with Vladdina. They agreed to meet at the police station in a half hour.

▪▪▪▪▪▪▪▪▪▪▪▪▪▪▪▪▪▪▪▪▪▪▪▪▪

Before Rick called Detective Powers, the four of them felt they ought to discuss what to tell her about how they received the information that Fatima and Grace were in Springfield, Tennessee.

Rick spoke first. He seemed to be energized now that they had some information from Fannie. "I say we tell the detective that we got the information from a psychic. There are police departments around the country that use psychics to help them find missing persons. Tell her we are so desperate that we consulted a psychic. I don't think anyone would fault us for trying anything we can to get Grace back at this stage.

"We've been halfway around the world to try to find her and so we're willing to use any means possible. The detective didn't say on the phone that Vladdina had given up Fatima's whereabouts, so we say we tried an alternate route."

"What do we tell her if she wants to talk to the psychic?" Maizie asked.

"We tell her the psychic only wants to talk to us. No one can force the psychic to talk to anyone," Abby added.

Rick spoke with authority. "Who do we say the psychic talked to? We have to have this story down perfectly. It's far-fetched as it is, so there can't be any holes in the story. Don't forget that this woman is a detective, and she's used to poking holes in people's stories. If she gets a whiff of a lie or an inconsistency, then we're dead in the water."

"Say the psychic talked to me. She did," replied Abby. "I'll tell her what Mom said to me. I can be very clear about what she said and what I heard."

"And why did the psychic talk to you and not to Maizie or me?"

"Because I have used this psychic before, and her information has proven reliable."

Now Jason spoke up. "Even though Grandma says Fatima is in Springfield, we still don't know where exactly she is. What do we want the detective to do with this information?"

"Good point, Jas. I guess we want her to contact the police in Springfield and have them start looking for her or for her car."

Maizie said, "Suppose she doesn't believe us? Suppose she thinks that talking to a psychic is a lot of crap? What do we do then?" Maizie's voice quivered.

Abby answered. "I spoke to Mom. She knows what she saw. I believe her. I have to convince the detective that what I heard is true. I have to be very convincing. I think I can be. If it means getting Grace back, I will be."

Rick said, "Look, Abby, this isn't all on you. If the police won't help us, then we get a private detective to find her in Springfield. It's probably not that big a town, so I would think we get Adam to go there and find her. She won't necessarily stand out. But once she opens her mouth and she has a Russian accent, she will stand out. She's not one of the locals. She'll be noticed."

CHAPTER 68

Detective Powers had the woman officer make sure Vladdina was fed a decent breakfast and let her take a shower. She had arrived at the police station before Rick, Maizie, Abby, and Jason. She had the team who did the recordings on the phone ready, and she wanted Vladdina to make one last call to Fatima before she saw the Singletons. Maybe they would get a break and Fatima would answer the phone. Detective Powers really wanted to give these parents some good news.

Detective Powers prepped Vladdina again. "Don't just tell Fatima to call you. Tell her to go to the nearest police station and turn herself in and give the police the baby. Tell her you're in custody with the Richmond police and that it's over. By turning herself in, she helps you and she helps herself."

Vladdina made the call, but again the call went to voice-mail. She left the message about turning herself in and helping them both.

□□□□□□□□□□□□□□□□□□□□□□□□□

What Vladdina didn't know was that Fatima had listened to all her voice mail messages over the past few days. She was too upset to take the call or call Vladdina back. Fatima wanted to be far away from Richmond, and she wanted some time to think. So far her actions had been motivated by a fear that gripped her like a vise.

She had heard a story on the news a few weeks earlier that this woman had left her baby at a firehouse and that she had walked away. She hadn't been arrested. That was what Fatima wanted. She wanted Grace to be safe, but she also wanted to get away from this horrible situation. She didn't want to go to jail. From her days in Russia, she was very afraid of the police. She didn't want anything to do with them, so Vladdina's message to go to a police station upset Fatima. She definitely wasn't going to walk into some police station and give them a child they had kidnapped. What was Vladdina thinking?

Fatima made up her mind. She would drop Grace off at a firehouse and then she would get in her car and drive away. She didn't know where she would go, but at least Grace would go home to her family. Grace and the family both deserved this.

She bathed Grace and put her in a cute outfit. Fatima's English was not as good as Vladdina's and her written English was worse. She took a pen and ripped off a piece of paper from the pad by the bed. On it she wrote, "Grace Singleton. Parents from NY. They looking for her. Find parents for baby."

She drove to the firehouse she had seen on her way into town. She parked the car by the curb near the firehouse. She took the car seat with Grace in it out of the car. She kissed Grace on the cheek. "You a good little girl. I love you. Find your parents. Have good life." She walked up to the door of the firehouse and kissed Grace again. "You will have a long life. Go home to parents. You all be together and have a happy life, little one."

She put the car seat down on the driveway near the main entrance to the firehouse. She walked down the driveway, got back in her car and drove about a mile until she saw a parking lot. She pulled into the parking lot and dialed 911.

"911, what's your emergency?"

"I see baby in front of firehouse. Tell the fireman."

"The baby is in front of the Springfield firehouse? Did you leave her there?"

"Make sure the fireman get her." With that Fatima hung up.

The 911 operator called the dispatch operator at the firehouse. "Phil, it's Frank at Emergency Services. Just got a call from a woman who says she left a baby outside the firehouse. Then she hung up. Want to have one of the guys check? Can I stay on the line to see if it's true?"

"Sure, I'll have someone check right now. Hold on."

About ninety seconds later, Phil came back on the line.

"Yeah, it's a cute little girl. She looks to be well cared for and well fed. The guys said there's a note that her name is Grace, and her parents are in New York. Might have been a kidnapping or a custody dispute. We'll take her over to the hospital to be checked out. You want to tell your guys at the police station to come to the hospital. Apparently, no sign of the woman."

CHAPTER 69

Detective Powers was frustrated that she didn't have better news for the parents. It had taken a lot of time and effort to get Vladdina to talk. They hadn't really had any success in tracking Fatima's cell phone because she kept it off most of the time. If only Fatima had answered her phone, things might have been very different.

Detective Powers braced herself as she knocked on the door where the family was waiting. She had spoken to them on the phone yesterday, but now meeting them in person was even more difficult. They all looked haggard and stressed out. This last day must have been a killer for them. *If only I had better news for them.* That phrase pinged around in her head on a continuous loop.

After brief introductions and handshakes, they sat down at the table. Detective Powers said, "You said on the phone that you have information for me."

Rick took the lead. "Detective, I'm an attorney in New York. I am not in the habit of doing anything crazy. In fact, it's often my job to clean up the crazy things my clients do. You know that my wife and I just flew in from Dubai following up on a lead on the kidnapping. Then we flew here last night.

"Abby is my mother-in-law, and she consulted a psychic while we were on the way back from Dubai. Abby is a financial planner, so I'm trying to impress on you that you're not dealing with a bunch of lunatics." Rick hesitated to see what reaction he was getting from Detective Powers.

It did not appear he was getting a negative reaction or a skeptical look on her face.

"Go on," she said as she addressed Abby.

Abby explained what she had learned from the psychic, being careful not to say it was her deceased mother. She finished the explanation by saying she would like the detective to call the police departments in Springfield and Clarksville and see if they would canvas the motels in that area as a start to see if they could locate Fatima and Grace. Abby picked up on Rick's earlier theory that a Russian woman with a baby would stand out in a town in Tennessee.

Detective Powers listened intently to the explanation and then sat there quietly for a few moments. Abby felt a knot in her stomach, since she was afraid that the detective would say no.

"I've seen PDs use psychics before. You've certainly explored all the normal channels. I say we try something different.

"We'll make some calls to Springfield and Clarksville. We'll email all the documents we have to them. It's too bad we don't have a picture of this Fatima to give to them. I'll try to see if Vladdina has one on her phone. I need some time, but sit tight. I'll be back as quickly as I can."

Not even ten minutes had gone by when Detective Powers sprinted into the conference room where Maizie, Rick, Abby, and Jason were sitting. "Great news. We called Springfield, and the lieutenant I spoke to said a woman dropped off a baby girl at the fire department about an hour ago, with a note saying the baby was Grace and her parents are in New York."

It took about two beats and then all four of them started screaming, jumping up and down, crying and hugging one another.

CHAPTER 70

They were able to get on a flight from Richmond to Nashville Metropolitan Airport late in the morning. It would certainly be faster than driving over 600 miles from Richmond to Springfield, Tennessee. The airport in Nashville was about thirty miles away from Springfield. No matter how fast the plane got them there, it still was not fast enough to get the four of them there and the last thirty-mile drive seemed agonizing.

Fortunately, the plane was on time, and they had reserved a rental car before they got on the plane. But right now every minute that ticked by was another minute without Grace.

Detective Powers had worked it out with the police in Springfield that the four of them could go straight to the hospital where Grace was being checked and they could see her immediately. Any paperwork that needed to be completed could be completed after they had Grace. Abby felt her heart thumping in her chest, and it only grew more intense when the plane landed.

Surprisingly, very little was said in the car as they drove from the airport to Springfield. Jason drove, since Rick and Maizie declined saying they didn't know what time their body clocks were on. At least Jason had been on the East Coast the whole time. Jason, who normally had a lot to say, was also extremely quiet. Abby declined as well, since she wanted to think about her recent interactions with Fannie.

Rick was doing the navigating on his phone but, except for telling Jason where he was supposed to turn, didn't have anything else to say. Maizie was so excited, and her leg was tapping in the car. Every so often she would say, "I can't believe we are finally going to get her back." Basically, that was the extent of the conversation. Maizie and Rick were sitting in the back seat of the car, and Rick was holding Maizie's hand.

Finally, Abby broke the silence and said, "I've been thinking about this, and we will have Grace back in large part because of Mom. She located Steve, and then she located Fatima for us. I don't understand why, Jason, you were the only one who could hear her, and then both of us could hear her. From what she says, I don't think she gets it either. It just seems to happen, but clearly she wanted to help us, and she did help us big time.

"I wish I knew if she is still going to be able to talk to us now that this nightmare with Grace is over. I thought after she came to say goodbye when we were at the beach house years ago that we weren't going to hear from her again."

Rick was the first to answer. "Maybe she is able to help us when it comes to huge problems in our lives, but not the mundane things."

Then Maizie chimed in. "Why don't you try talking to her now and see if she answers and what she has to say? I would certainly like to talk to her and thank her for what she did. She answered me when I asked her to help us when we were in Dubai, and then I heard her say the word 'Richmond.' Go ahead and talk to her now, Mom."

"Jason, are you okay if I talk to her now? You're not going to drive off the road if you hear her?"

"Go ahead and talk to her. Maybe you'll be the only one who will hear her."

Abby nodded her head yes and started. "Mom, I guess that

I have been designated as the spokesperson. I don't know if you heard this whole conversation in the car, but we wouldn't have found Grace without your help. You found Steve, and then you found Fatima. We all want to thank you for what you did. This could have turned out far worse without your help, so we all wanted to say thank you.

"We also want to know if you will be able to talk to us in the future, now that this ordeal will be over. I have certainly missed talking to you these past few years. It meant so much to me to be able to hear you myself."

Abby stopped and waited, hoping for an answer from Fannie. When there was silence, Maizie jumped in.

"Grandma, I need to thank you myself. My heart has been broken without Grace. I'm sure as a mother and a grandmother, you can understand what I was feeling. I told you when I was speaking to you when I was in Dubai that I'm really sorry I didn't get to know you when you were alive. I think we would have been close."

Fannie smiled and then answered, but it was only Abby who heard her. Abby looked around the car and said, "I hear her. Do you?" The other three in the car shook their heads no.

Fannie said, "I love you all, and I have been given this great gift to talk to you from the other side twice now. So many people who are still alive would love to be able to talk to a loved one on the other side. I don't know why I have been given this gift, but I am so grateful to be able to talk to you and to help.

"It may be that our bonds of love are so strong, and it shows that love can transcend death. The people on Earth don't seem to get that death is just a step along the way to something much greater. I hope that I will be able to continue to talk to you, but I don't know.

"Even if I can't talk to you in the future as I am talking to you now, I want you to know that I am always with you and I try to watch out for you. I see how things are going in your life. We will have to wait to see if I can continue to talk to you going forward.

"But most important of all, know that I always love all of you and I am always with you. Now go find that baby in the hospital. I want to see the reunion."

Abby wiped the tears off her cheek and told Maizie, Rick, and Jason what Fannie had just said.

They were almost at the grounds of the hospital.

CHAPTER 71

A very young police officer from the Springfield Police Department had been sent to the hospital to watch over the baby and to talk to the parents when they arrived at the hospital. His shift was just about over, and he called the desk sergeant to say he would stay until the parents arrived. He had been at the hospital a long time, and he wanted to meet the parents. He didn't want to miss this reunion.

A nurse came in with a bottle for the baby. Officer Shelton looked at her and said he would like to give Grace her bottle. While he had been waiting for the parents, he had grabbed a few children's books in the pediatrics unit and read to her. Grace looked at him as he read her the stories, which he was sure she didn't understand.

The nurse shrugged and put the bottle down on the nightstand. She picked Grace up from the crib and handed her to the young officer. "I hear there is quite a story with this baby. I'm glad I'm going to be here when the parents get her. We often see a lot of suffering in this hospital, but this is going to be one of the great moments we will both remember our entire lives." She handed him the bottle. "Let me know when she's done." With that she turned and left the room.

As Grace was halfway through her bottle, the door to the room opened and four people bounded into the room. For a second, the young woman looked panic stricken because the crib was empty. Then she saw the young officer holding Grace and rocking her.

Maizie yelled one word. "Grace!"

ACKNOWLEDGMENTS

Many thanks to Richard Lavsky for all his help with the computer issues and for helping me with the many times I was "stuck."

Thanks to Maggie Branath for helping me to bring Fannie to life in the first place.

Thanks to Annalinda Ragazzo for jumping into action to help in proofreading the manuscript.

ABOUT THE AUTHOR

Noël F. Caraccio is a full-time practicing attorney in Westchester County, where she has lived her entire life. She has served on numerous not-for-profit boards, including Marian Woods, School of the Holy Child, Westchester County Bar Association Grievance Committee, New York State Bar Association, Bonnie Briar Country Club, and WARC Properties. She is an avid golfer and belongs to Bonnie Briar Country Club, where she won the Women's Club Championship. The coauthor of *Secrets Change Everything*, the prequel to *Secrets and Revenge*, Noël is also the author of *Shattered City* and *Stand in the Box*.

Author photo © Richard Lavsky

SELECTED TITLES FROM SPARKPRESS

SparkPress is an independent boutique publisher delivering high-quality, entertaining, and engaging content that enhances readers' lives, with a special focus on female-driven work. www.go sparkpress.com

The Long-Lost Jules: A Novel, Jane Elizabeth Hughes, $16.95, 978-1-68463-089-9. She thinks he's either a nutcase or an eccentric Oxford professor. He thinks she's the descendant of Henry VIII's last Queen, Katherine Parr. They both harbor deep secrets, but their masks slip as they join forces to investigate the mystery of Queen Katherine's lost baby—endangering their hearts, their carefully constructed walls, and possibly their lives.

Indelible: A Sean McPherson Novel, Book 1, Laurie Buchanan, $16.95, 978-1-68463-071-4. Murder at a writing retreat in the Pacific Northwest, but this one isn't imaginary. Authors only kill with words. Or do they?

Gatekeeper: Book One in the Daemon Collecting Series, Alison Levy, $16.95, 978-1-68463-057-8. Rachel Wilde—sent from another dimension to bring defective daemons in for repair—needs to locate two people: a woman whose ancestors held a destructive daemon at bay and a criminal trying to break dimensional barriers. Helped by a homeless man with unusual powers, she uncovers a rising shadow organization that's changing her world forever.

Watermark: The Broken Bell Series, Elise Schiller, $16.95, 978-1-68463-036-3. When Angel Ferente—a teen with a dysfunctional home life who has been struggling to care for her sisters even as she pursues her goal of attending college on a swimming scholarship—doesn't come home after a party on New Year's Eve, her teammates, her coach's church, and her family search the city for her. The result changes their lives forever.

Firewall: A Novel, Eugenia Lovett West. $16.95, 978-1-68463-010-3. When Emma Streat's rich, socialite godmother is threatened with blackmail, Emma becomes immersed in the dark world of cybercrime—and mounting dangers take her to exclusive places in Europe and contacts with the elite in financial and art collecting circles. Through passion and heartbreak, Emma must fight to save herself and bring a vicious criminal to justice.

Pursuits Unknown: An Amy and Lars Novel, Ellen Clary. $16.95, 978-1-943006-86-1. Search-and-rescue agent Amy and her telepathic dog, Lars, locate a missing scientist who is reported to have an Alzheimer's-like disease—only to discover that someone wants to steal his research for potentially ominous purposes.